Chapter One

The man's heavy black leather boots crunched the pebbles and stones beneath him as he walked across the pebbled beach. The night air was cool and smelled strongly of salt and seaweed. The water that gently lapped at the rocks sounded so calm and relaxing, you would never know the secrets and fears it hid that night.

He walked towards the water's edge then splashed through the gentle tide until he passed an outcrop of rocks and found her.

The mermaid lay still, frozen in the surf, her eyes glassy as she gazed up at the night sky. The water that had once been her home now teasing her as it tried to call her back, lapping tantalisingly over her shimmering turquoise tail.

The man grunted as he scooped his hands under her armpits and began to drag her away over the rocky ground, her cold skin glowing translucent in the moonlight, her green hair plastered to her face and chest like seaweed.

From the water, three pairs of eyes watched.

"We couldn't have done anything," said Ashalia grimly.

"I don't believe you," said Hexanna, the rage in her voice barely disguised.

"We need help," whispered Brinly. "We've tried, we've failed. How many more do we need to lose before we just admit it?"

"And who do you think can help us?" asked Ashalia, turning on her friend with anger, the water sloshing around her. "Who could possibly do anything to stop it?"

"I don't know," admitted Brinly. "But there has to be someone. There just has to be."

⌘

Lilly Prospero gazed out of the window of her dad's car, the traffic on the motorway trundling past and her father's news debate show failing to inspire her mind to anything other than drudgery. Snoring next to her, her head on Lilly's shoulder, was her best friend Saffron Jones.

"Half an hour," said Lilly's mum from the front seat. "We'll be there in time for lunch."

"Cool," Lilly mumbled unenthusiastically.

"Cheer up, love," said Lilly's dad. "It's a holiday!"

"Whatever," muttered Lilly. She was aware that her parents were exchanging looks of desperation, but turned away and gazed out of the window again. She didn't want to go to Whitstable. She didn't want to go anywhere. Just two weeks ago her pet rabbit, and Guardian, Jeffrey had been murdered, a woman intent on murdering thousands of people in the name of power had tried to kill Lilly, and Lilly and Saffron had killed her to save their own lives. And she couldn't tell anybody about it. All she wanted to do was curl up in a ball, eat chocolate, read books and try to process everything she had seen and done. Instead she was on the way to Whitstable for two weeks on a pebbly beach trying to pretend she wasn't an Ultimate Power with the ability to control and manipulate the essence of life itself with a blink of the eye.

The car pulled off the motorway and Saffron snorted a little, a blob of drool dripping onto Lilly's pink hoody. Lilly smiled, she was glad her friend was sleeping. For two weeks now Saffron had been waking in the night screaming and had been absolutely exhausted because of it.

This book is dedicated to Jonathan McKinney,
My best friend, my business partner, my inspiration, and father to my
beloved children,
Without him I wouldn't have the life I have, and the life I love.

"Here we go," said Lilly's mum, as the car pulled up to a hotel which looked like a long row of attractive terraced houses with a long white balcony connecting them. "The Marine Hotel."

"Are we here?" asked Saffron, rubbing her eyes as the car engine noise died. Her long red hair was messy and sticking up at funny angles and her green eyes looked dull compared to their usual sparkle, but she was smiling.

"Can we go down to the beach?" Lilly asked her mum as they grabbed their suitcases.

"Sure," her mum agreed. "We'll check in and take the bags up, then we'll come and get you ready to go and find lunch. Stay in sight of the hotel, okay?"

The girls thanked her and headed over the road and down onto the sand and pebble beach.

"This is lame," grumbled Saffron as she stepped awkwardly on the pebbles, her sandals not offering much protection. "We can't even sunbathe. These stupid little rocks will get in the way!"

"The sea's beautiful though," said Lilly, gazing out at the water as the light danced on the surface in glowing spots of yellow and white.

"I don't like the water," said Saffron, her face darkening.

"I know," said Lilly, slipping an arm through her friend's. Last time Saffron had been in the water she had drowned, only surviving it because of Lilly's power, and at a cost. Her life was now entirely dependent on Lilly's own, tying the two girls together on a level so fundamental that being apart for too long caused Saffron physical pain.

They sat down on some rocks and Lilly closed her eyes as the sun warmed her face, the sound of the ocean offering a soothing background noise. She tried to embrace the calming sensation and let everything she was stressing about wash away. If she was here she might as well try and enjoy it.

"What was that?" asked Saffron suddenly. Lilly opened her eyes and followed Saffron's eyeline.

"What?" asked Lilly, staring.

"Someone's out there."

"Probably a diver or something," said Lilly gently, knowing her friend was afraid. "Don't worry."

"Yeah, I guess," said Saffron, looking anxious, and peering through squinted eyes across the water.

Behind them they heard Lilly's mum call out, "Girls!"

As they stood to go to her, Saffron stopped and stared out to sea one last time, a concerned look on her face.

"Honestly, nobody's in danger, don't worry," Lilly reassured her, putting an arm through Saffron's and giving it a quick squeeze.

"Yeah, you're probably right," Saffron agreed, sounding unconvinced, and together they walked back towards the hotel.

3

"Are you sure she's the one?" asked Brinly, squinting in the sunlight towards the shore.

"Yes," said Oberus, his grey eyes foggy and his green hair thin and patchy.

"But she's just a child!" protested Ashalia. "What could she possibly do?"

The elderly merman turned his wizened face towards Ashalia, a look on his face that made Brinly's spine shudder. "Are you questioning the knowledge of The Ancients?"

"No," said Ashalia frowning. "But how do you expect some human child to do anything to help us?"

"I do not know how, I just know why," he said, turning back to shore and staring blindly at the two girls that walked down the beach towards them.

"Okay then, why?" asked Hexanna, irritation creeping into her voice. Brinly shot her a look, nervous about an Ancient being involved at all, especially if he was upset by the process of helping, but Hexanna pointedly ignored her.

"Because it is her duty," said Oberus, looking at Hexanna with obvious disdain.

"It's a human's duty to help us?" Ashalia asked in disbelief.

"Humans are the whole problem!" cried Hexanna in despair, running her long porcelain white fingers through her short green hair.

"I have given you the tools to help yourselves," said Oberus, huffily. "If you do not take my advice, it is not I who shall suffer. It is not my people being hunted."

Ashalia watched as the Ancient disappeared below the surface and swam out of sight. "What happened to that 'we're all one race' claptrap?" she asked Hexanna.

"You know they only want us to buy into that so we don't cause trouble," Hexanna grumbled. "You know they don't give a damn about us! Wait. Where's Brin?"

The two mermaids looked around in confusion, when suddenly Brinly's head bobbed up above the surface just metres away from where the human children sat on the shore.

"What's she doing?" hissed Ashalia. "They'll see her!"

They dived down, swam through the water and grabbed Brinly by the fin, pulling her roughly below the surface and out of sight.

ॽ

After an afternoon of wandering around Whitstable, checking out the views from the harbour and listening to a folk band play outside The Old Neptune, it was agreed that dinner and bed was in order.

"You girls can choose a pay per view film, but only one, okay?" said Lilly's mum sternly as they got up to their rooms. "And don't go raiding the mini bar!"

"Yes mum," said Lilly as she and Saffron headed into the twin room they were sharing next to her parent's. "Goodnight!"

"I wish we were old enough to go out drinking and stuff," grumbled Saffron, as she gazed glumly out of the window, her chin on her hand. "Look at all those people out there having fun and we're stuck in here."

"I don't want to go out," said Lilly, picking up the remote and flicking on the TV. "What do you want to watch? They're showing The Hunger Games."

Saffron ignored her and kept staring out of the window. It was nearly ten thirty but outside was still fairly light in the orange summer sunset, and the sound of the people moving along the sea front was clear. Lilly kept flicking through channels. She had no desire to be out there with people. She was tired in so many ways and just wanted to rest. Besides, things always seemed to go wrong when she went off on adventures. She had no desire for yet more disasters in her life.

"Lilly, there's someone out there," Saffron said, pushing the window open and craning out to see.

"Of course there is," said Lilly, rolling her eyes and setting up the film ready to view. "It's Saturday night in a tourist town."

"No!" cried Saffron, turning to her with a wild look in her eyes. "In the water!"

"Okay, so someone's taking a swim!" Lilly felt exasperated.

"No, they're too far out. They could be in trouble!" Saffron insisted, staring out of the window then turning to Lilly, a look of excitement on her face. "Come on!"

"What?" demanded Lilly, sitting up as Saffron raced past her. "Where are you going?"

"To see who it is!"

"What?" Lilly asked again, getting off the bed and staring at her friend in bewilderment. "Why?"

"Because we have to!"

"We do not have to do anything!" Lilly insisted angrily.

Saffron turned to her and stared at her intently. "What did we say?"

"When?" Lilly asked guiltily, knowing full well to what her friend referred.

"Last week."

"Dunno," Lilly muttered, looking down and tucking her short brown hair behind her ear then picking nervously at her thumb nail.

"Yes you do!" Saffron said, annoyed. "The way we do good with what we have is to help people. Now I've spotted someone who might need help and you're just going to ignore it?"

"They don't need help!" Lilly protested, fully aware she was going to lose this battle of wills but needing to at least try. "They're taking a swim!"

"At night? Alone?" Saffron asked. "Seriously?"

They stood in silence, staring at one another for a moment then Lilly flung her hands in the air. "Fine. We'll go. But when we see everything is fine we need to get straight back here before my mum finds out we've gone. She'll do her nut if she realises we've disappeared!"

"Deal," said Saffron, grinning.

Grabbing their bags and the door key, the two girls slipped out and hurried through the corridors keeping their steps quiet and their ears pricked. Lilly's heart pounded in her chest. This was such a terrible idea. She rubbed her sweaty hands on her jeans.

"Shh," Saffron whispered theatrically to Lilly, peering round a corner towards the main staircase down to reception. Saffron did not seem to share Lilly's fear and instead seemed to be drunk on excitement.

"Clear?" Lilly whispered, looking around nervously, certain her parents would come walking up the stairs as they headed down, or hotel staff would spot them sneaking out and sound the alert. This was such a bad idea. She really didn't need more trouble in her life!

"Let's go," said Saffron in a hushed voice, looking back at Lilly and nodding confidently.

Together they stepped round the corner and walked straight into a young man with a porter's uniform on, pulling a gold suitcase rack behind him. "Ouch!" he cried, startled and wincing.

Lilly quickly pulled her foot from his boot and felt her cheeks flush. "Oh, sorry, I erm, sorry," she stuttered awkwardly.

"That's okay," he said with a broad, professional smile, then looked them up and down curiously, a smile playing on his lips. "Where are you two going?"

"Listen up… Hogarth," said Saffron, smiling broadly as she peered at the badge on the boy's uniform, and using an odd fake voice that made Lilly pull a face. "We're just popping out for a moment. We won't be long. So just carry on with your suitcase work and we'll be back safe before you know it."

"Right…" he said, cocking his head to the side. "Does yeh mum know you're sneaking out?"

"Yes," Lilly lied then felt her cheeks redden further. "I mean… we're not sneaking. We're just walking. Like normal people. People walk all the time you know!"

Saffron shot her a look and Lilly shrugged guiltily.

He laughed loudly and grinned at them. "Sure you are," he said, winking at Lilly. "Well, keep safe, yeah? And I won't say anything."

"Thanks Hogarth," said Saffron.

"Dougal," he said. "The name's Dougal."

"Bye Hogarth," said Lilly.

Aware that the young man was watching them as they walked away, Lilly and Saffron hurried down the stairs, across the reception hall and out of the front doors into the warm breeze of the evening, without looking back.

ᚱ

"And how do you propose we make contact?" asked Hexanna grumpily.

"I don't know," said Brinly with a sigh, pushing the dark green hairs away from her face, irritated by the way the tendrils clung to her cheeks. "I hate being up here. Hair is not designed to be out of the water!"

"Look, all these humans trotting by and not one of them noticing us," Ashalia said, rolling her eyes. "I hate humans. They're so convinced they're the centre of the universe. They're either assuming we don't exist or they know we do and they want to kill us. They're a horrible species."

"Look," whispered Brinly, peering towards the shore then ducking out of sight, swimming as fast as she could.

"Not again!" exclaimed Hexanna as they dived down after her, chasing her tail as fast as they could.

Coming up to the surface next to Brinly, Ashalia spotted the two human children racing down the beach towards them, engrossed in animated conversation.

"Hide!" Hexanna cried, tugging at Brinly's arm, but Brinly refused to be pulled away, pulling her arm back.

"You want to make contact?" asked Brinly, turning to her friends. "Then now is our chance."

"But how?" whispered Ashalia, nerves betraying her usually confident attitude. "Wait, Brin… we should talk about this more…"

Brinly grinned at them and then turned towards the shore. "HEY!"

ᠵ

"There's nobody out there!" Lilly insisted, nervously looking back at the hotel, convinced she was going to see her mother storming out after them flapping her arms in panic because Hogarth had raised the alarm.

"There is," said Saffron defiantly, staring ahead. "Look! Right there!"

Lilly sighed and turned back to look out to sea but still couldn't see anything. "Come on Saff! You're imagining it!"

"No I'm not!" Saffron insisted. "I know I saw someone! Why don't you believe me?"

"Saff," Lilly put a hand on her friend's elbow and tried to pull her back from the water. "Come on. I know you have nightmares about the water. It's okay to be a bit paranoid."

Saffron spun towards her angrily. "I am *not* paranoid!"

"HEY!" came a voice.

Both girls turned suddenly towards the water, where they could see three faces staring at them, and one long, thin, glistening black arm waving.

They stared in silent confusion then Saffron grinned at her, "See? I told you!" She turned to the women in the water and started approaching the surf calling out, "Are you okay?"

The women started swimming towards them, staying too far out to walk to, but close enough to see. Lilly stared at them, her skin starting to crawl. The women looked wrong somehow. Their faces were too thin, their fingers too long. The one with pale skin looked ghostly white, and the two with dark skin looked like oil. They didn't look normal, they didn't look right.

"Saff," she whispered nervously, pulling at Saffron's arm again. "They're fine. Let's go."

"Is everything all right?" Saffron called to the women, ignoring Lilly and shaking her arm free.

The women stayed in the water, their large eyes staring, unblinking. They seemed to be as nervous of Saffron and Lilly as Lilly felt of them, but that did nothing to ease her anxiety. If anything, it made it worse.

"Saff," Lilly hissed again. Despite the relative warmth of the evening, her whole body felt cold. Her arms prickled and ice cold water seemed to be dripping down her spine. Saffron started walking towards the sea, her face blank as she stepped into the surf. The women stared at her in silence. "Saffron! Stop!"

"Who are you?" Saffron asked.

The women swam closer, well into the shallows, but stayed below the surface. "We are told you can help us," said the one who had called out. Her voice seemed far away and yet close at the same time. Like the sound of the ocean in a shell against your ear.

"We can," Saffron said, stepping further into the water.

Lilly felt paralysed by fear. The women terrified her, the ocean looked threatening and dangerous, and she wanted to run. She tried to call out again to Saffron but her voice wouldn't work. She tried to reach out and grab her but she couldn't move.

"We are being hunted," she said. "By your kind."

"My kind?" asked Saffron.

"The Harvesters," said the pale skinned woman, watching them intently with huge pale blue eyes full of mistrust.

The tide suddenly pulled back, revealing the women's bodies. Lilly screamed.

Chapter Two

"WAIT!" Saffron cried out as the mermaids flung themselves away, diving below the surface and out of sight. "COME BACK!"

The first mermaid's face appeared again, further out, her long green hair swirling behind her in the water like a veil. "Are you going to hurt us?"

"No!" Saffron insisted, stepping further into the water that now lapped around her thighs, apparently completely unaware of the cold.

The other two appeared again from below the surface of the water, their faces revealing the fear they felt.

"I told you, we can't trust humans," said the one with the short hair in a low growl, not taking her eyes off Saffron.

"Why don't you trust humans?" asked Saffron.

"You don't know?" asked the first mermaid, swimming a little closer.

"We didn't even know there were mermaids," said Saffron, looking down, embarrassed. "Wait, Lilly, did you know?"

"No," said Lilly quietly, wishing she could run away but feeling too frightened to move.

"You're scared of us," said the third mermaid, swimming closer, her face tilted as she examined Lilly. "Why? We have never hurt you."

"We've never hurt you either," said Lilly. "But you don't trust us."

The third mermaid laughed a cold and bitter laugh. "You think you've never hurt us?"

"We didn't even know you existed," said Saffron.

"You are the people of The Harvesters," said the first mermaid, her voice calm. "It took until the Beings Protection Laws before you even acknowledged us as having autonomy."

"What?" asked Saffron. "What's a Beings Protection Law?"

"They're mortals," said the short haired mermaid. "Come on, Brinly, mortal humans can't help us. Oberus was wrong."

"We aren't!" Saffron insisted, looking back momentarily at Lilly for support, before turning back to the mermaids. "We're like you."

"Like us?" scorned the pale mermaid.

"Are you of Power?" asked the one they called Brinly.

"Yes," said Saffron earnestly. "We both are."

Lilly felt sick. She wished they were back in their hotel room, watching a film and sneaking cans of coke out of the mini bar. She didn't understand why but the mermaids terrified her and she wanted to get away from them fast. The wind started to pick up, blowing her hair around her face. Saffron's auburn curls flew around her like a lion's mane. The mermaids remained unchanged, their wet hair clinging to them as they hovered in the icy water, not even the lapping of the water around them having an effect on their disquieting stillness.

The third mermaid swam rapidly towards Saffron, her dark eyes flashing purple as the light of the moon bounced off them. "Prove it."

Saffron stepped backwards, startled, and stumbled away from the approaching mermaid. Lilly ran to her and dragged her out of the water. The mermaid laughed.

"Come on, Hexanna," said Brinly, swimming up to her, her voice low. "They're children."

"That one is different," said Hexanna, staring at them where they stood huddled on the beach together.

"I know," said Brinly. "But we need them."

"If you're of Power, prove it," said Hexanna again, then cast a look at Brinly and said begrudgingly, "Please."

Saffron nodded and reached her hand out to Lilly. Lilly looked at Saffron, then at the outstretched hand, then at the waiting mermaids. Her heart hammered. She had not used her power in two weeks. Not since the battle that had killed her Guardian and nearly killed them. She didn't move, she didn't know what to do. She didn't want to use her power. She just wanted to be left alone.

"We said we would help people," said Saffron, staring at Lilly and stretching her arm closer.

"Okay," Lilly said after a moment, then nervously took Saffron's hand.

Suddenly the air was filled with a spiralling cloud of colourful butterflies that poured from Lilly's free hand, swirling through the air, colours of turquoise, yellow and red. Suddenly it changed and Lilly watched as doves now escaped from her hand. Beautiful white birds, flapping frantically as they broke into reality, finding a freedom in a life they had never experienced before.

Lilly pulled her hand from Saffron's and stepped back as the butterflies and doves spiralled away free and into the night, the sound of wings flapping and beaks cooing disappearing into the slowly descending darkness.

"We believe you," said Brinly, watching the magically created creatures disappear overhead.

३

"You're awake," said the man, watching the captive mermaid as her drooping head started to move, her eyes blinking furiously as she struggled to regain focus.

"Where am I?" she asked, her voice weak. "What's going on?"

"You'll be hungry, of course," he said, stating a fact rather than expressing concern for her wellbeing.

"Yes," she whispered.

Mermaids were not accustomed to having any part of themselves out of the water for any great length of time and it always took them time to adjust. She was suspended by a sturdy corset about her waist chained to the edges of the tall, narrow tank. Whilst he had to keep the majority of her submerged to keep the product fresh, he preferred their heads exposed for ease of communication and access, however their mouths always dried up far quicker than any humans. She was a splendid specimen. Her turquoise tail was powerful, her long emerald green hair, that now sat fluffy and dry against her neck before trailing into the water, was thick and strong.

"If you're hungry, I shall get you food."

"Let me go!" she suddenly cried out in a desperate wail, wet tears sliding down her dry cheeks, leaving shiny wet trails on her skin before dropping with a splash. "I shouldn't be here. I have nothing you need! Nothing! Please… Oh please… I need water."

The man went to the back of the room, loaded a small metal tray then returned. Climbing up a small stepping stool in front of the tank, he dropped some pieces of crab meat and grape caulerpa into the water in front of her, then held a metal cup out for her to take. Keeping her fed and healthy was essential until he had obtained everything for which she needed to be kept alive. He prided himself in supplying a high quality product.

She sipped at the water, relief in her eyes, then shoved the food into her mouth.

"Hold still. This was easier when you were unconscious," he said, retrieving a large pair of shears from the tray, then setting it aside.

"What are you doing?" she howled, pulling her head away from him as the metal blades glinted.

"A new order has just come in," he said. "Three coils. If you don't hold still I will get your ear too and then it won't be as fresh."

ʒ

"You are aware of those who can enchant?" asked Brinly, sitting in the surf, watching Lilly and Saffron as they perched on the rocks.

"Yeah," said Lilly. "Make things do things using spells and stuff."

"That's right. And are you aware of the potion masters?"

"No," Lilly said, frowning as she thought. "I don't think so."

"Potion Masters use liquids," Brinly said. "Drinks usually. They make beings, erm, 'do things'."

"What are Harvesters?" asked Saffron.

"Humans, like you," said Hexanna grimly. "Why are you not aware of anything?"

"We're new to it all," said Lilly feeling embarrassed and picking at her thumb nail. "It's only been a few weeks."

"Right," said the third who was named Ashalia sounding exasperated and tossing her hair over her shoulder. "You remember when Brinly mentioned the Beings Protection Laws?"

"Yes," said both girls.

"Well, they weren't passed until 1977," said Ashalia bitterly. "Until then, Mers, Faeries, Jinns, Trolls, everything that wasn't human were classed as UnBeings."

"UnBeings?" asked Saffron.

"Humans, you, were the normal," said Ashalia bitterly. "Anything else was just 'other'. If you weren't human, you were nothing."

"We weren't allowed to be farmed, per se, but that was more to do with keeping reality hidden from the mortals," said Hexanna. "But we could be caught and used. Harvested."

"The Beings Protection Laws classed all that are able to communicate with humans in their own languages as Beings," said Ashalia, a look of disgust on her face. "The total arrogance of it. Until then, it was believed that we couldn't feel like humans, couldn't think like humans. Apparently we couldn't even feel pain."

"Our lore, our traditions, our language…" said Hexanna, tailing off as tears started sliding down the slickness of her skin. "We lost so much just to be accepted by your kind."

"Many of our ways have been lost over time, purely for survival," explained Brinly. "Even though most of us are so accustomed to avoiding humans at all cost, even though we have kept ourselves away from dry land and not interfered in your ways at all, we are still taught the languages of the humans whose landmasses are closest to our homes."

"Your people still see us as halflings," Ashalia continued. At Lilly's side Saffron flinched at the word. "Mongrels."

"Not us," said Lilly, as she slipped a hand into Saffron's own, feeling her tremble. "We wouldn't say those things or do those things."

Ashalia's eyes flashed angrily. "Well forgive us for not rushing to accept that. Your kind have destroyed us, oppressed us, treated us like objects for hundreds of years. And it continues now, despite these claims of equality. Perhaps if you stop killing us, we will stop thinking of you so negatively."

"Sorry," Lilly whispered, her eyes dropping.

"So, are you part human?" asked Saffron nervously. "Are you a mix?"

"We are Beings in our own right," spat Hexanna in disgust. "We are Mer."

"Mer," said Saffron carefully. Lilly felt completely overwhelmed. She looked around as night descended and took a moment to fully comprehend that she was sat on a beach having a conversation with mermaids. Mermaids who, with their peculiar look and oceanic eyes, made her flesh cold and her belly churn. "So, what are The Harvesters?"

"We got off track," said Brinly, running her long, black, pointed fingers through her hair. "Humans have long used parts of us in their enchantments, their potions. Some Mer still choose to have that relationship with rare trusted humans. They donate their hair or fluids for instance."

"Most of us do not," said Hexanna, giving a cold shudder. "Most Beings do not. And never would."

"Before the laws, if we were caught we were Harvested," explained Brinly. "The Harvesters were in charge. It was tricky, but there were many and they had strengths and spells and enchantments. We, and other Beings, would be captured and harvested."

"That's awful," whispered Saffron.

"Yes," agreed Ashalia, glaring at her furiously. "It is."

"And now, it is happening again," said Brinly. "Someone new is Harvesting. We don't know how he is doing it, but he is freezing our kind."

"Freezing?" asked Saffron.

"Paralysing. Locking." Explained Hexanna.

"He controls where we wash ashore, and he collects us," said Ashalia. "Then those that are taken are never returned."

"Last night he took our friend Mabli," said Brinly, her head drooping. "When she is… finished… he will take another. And another, and another. Every few days, another is taken. It's always the same. A Mer suddenly freezes and their body is caught in an eddy, no matter where they are, and they're washed ashore."

"Why don't you just leave?" asked Lilly. "Swim somewhere else, somewhere safe."

"This is our home!" said Ashalia angrily, her eyes flashing with emotion, pain and anger. "We've been treated like vermin for most of our existence by your kind, and now you want us to be forced out of the home we've known and loved our entire lives as well? Just because you can't be trusted not to kill us?"

"Ash, it's okay," said Brinly gently, placing a hand gently on her arm. She turned to Lilly and Saffron again. "Some left. But it's made no difference. Something about the fact we're from here originally seems enough. Wherever they are they are caught. Those who had tried to flee were either taken, or returned home because they soon realised there was no point fleeing anyway."

"That's terrible," said Lilly. However much these strange beings scared her, nobody deserved this treatment.

"What can we do?" asked Saffron.

"Find him," said Brinly, her face full of hope, almost desperation. "And stop him."

Chapter Three

"Isn't this a beautiful town?" asked Lilly's mum brightly as they explored Whitstable town the following morning.

"Yeah," Lilly grunted, shielding a yawn behind her arm and feeling distinctly unenthusiastic.

"Were you two up all night gossiping?" asked Lilly's dad, eyeing them suspiciously. "You've both been completely useless all morning!"

"Yeah," said Saffron, catching Lilly's eye. "We have lots to talk about."

"You're together all the time!" said Lilly's mum with a laugh. "What could have happened between bedtime last night and breakfast this morning to require so much conversation?"

The two girls looked at each other again, but neither answered. Saffron was almost giddy with excitement about the mermaids, she seemed driven and alive in a way Lilly hadn't seen in weeks. Lilly wished she could share her friend's enthusiasm, or even understand it. Instead she just felt flat and uncomfortable.

"What's that?" Saffron asked, suddenly pointing to a poster in a small, dirty shop window on the other side of the road, and darting across to look at it.

"What?" asked Lilly, hurrying after her.

"Mermaid festival," Saffron whispered, putting a hand against the smeared glass where the faded poster was stuck inside.

"You girls like mermaids?" asked a voice from the shop door, making them jump.

"Erm, not really, no," said Lilly, turning to look at the old woman who had stepped out of the shop door.

"I do," enthused Saffron.

The old woman stared at them intently for a moment then looked up as Lilly's mum and dad crossed the road towards them. "Your daughters are beautiful," she said.

"Oh, thank you," said Lilly's mum smiling. "They're pretty fabulous young women."

The woman smiled warmly. "Have you taken them to Mermaid's Cove?"

"No," said Lilly's mum curiously. "I don't remember seeing anything about it in the flyer from the hotel."

"Oh, it hasn't been called Mermaid's Cove for a long time," said the woman, turning back to the two girls. "Many years now. It's down near the East Quay. A beautiful stretch of coast."

"Thanks! We'll check it out," said Lilly's mum, putting her arms around Lilly and Saffron. "Sounds like a good opportunity for the afternoon, right girls?"

"Sure," said Lilly hesitantly, nervously looking at the old woman then looking away again. Something about the way she was watching them made Lilly's already churning insides seem to squirm even more.

Lilly's parents began chattering and heading away from the shop with Lilly and Saffron following behind. Lilly glanced back over her shoulder and saw the old woman standing in the shop doorway still watching them. She held her gaze for a moment then looked away again, feeling sick. She was not enjoying her holiday at all so far.

"Why didn't you tell her I'm not your daughter?" Saffron asked Lilly's mum after a moment.

"Because I'm happy for her to think you are," said Lilly's mum, putting her arm round Saffron's shoulders and squeezing. "I can correct people if you prefer."

"No!" Saffron said quickly. "No, it's fine. I like it."

They went to turn a corner to go down a side road and when Lilly glanced back the woman was still watching.

ς

"What's going on, Grandma?" asked Coral, approaching her grandmother with Sylvie the tabby cat walking purposely ahead of her.

"She's here."

Coral stepped out of the shop and stared down the street where her grandmother was looking. "Where?"

"Gone. But she'll be back. And we'll be ready." said Coral's grandmother with a stern look on her face. "Sylvie, follow them. Keep low. Tell me if you see anything."

"Of course," nodded the tabby, then slunk out of the shop and, keeping to the shadows, hurried off down the street.

"What are you doing?" Coral asked, watching as her grandmother disappeared through the tiny, dark shop crammed with antiques and knickknacks, then stepped round the till and through the small door into the back room.

"Come, child," she called. Coral hurried after her, stepping carefully passed the piled up furniture, and into the back room. "Call the others."

"Yes, Grandma," said Coral with a dutiful sigh, watching as her grandmother started pulling ancient texts off the shelves and gathering peculiar ingredients in thick glass jars. She sat on one of the plush chairs that lined the walls, closed her eyes, and felt her body fall away beneath her and she appeared at her grandmother's side, wondering if she would ever see even a slightly startled look on the old woman's lined face.

"What are you waiting for? Go!" said her grandmother crossly.

Coral nodded obediently and then vanished.

३

"Mermaid's Cove?" repeated the man they'd stopped to ask as he sat outside a coffee shop reading a newspaper. "I've lived here a few years now but never heard of it!"

"Oh, she said it's not been called that in a while," said Lilly's mum. "Near the East Quay?"

"The East Quay is that way," he said, sounding confused and gesturing down a street to their left. "Near The Lobster Shack. Couple of minutes' walk."

"Thanks," said Lilly's mum, and they headed down the road he had indicated.

As they approached the beach they saw the wooden groynes stretching out into the water. Some children in smart clothes were playing round the picnic benches and deck chairs that ran across the terrace by the restaurant that looked out onto the water. A crowd of people in formal wear stood having a drink in the sunshine and a bride in a long white lace dress stepped out and called to one of the children.

"Beautiful," said Lilly's mum smiling, then looked out at the water. "So, this is Mermaid's Cove? I was somehow expecting something a bit more… dramatic."

"Why would she send us here? It looks like the rest of the beach," said Lilly's dad grumpily.

"It doesn't," said Saffron breathily, stepping onto the sand and stones and walking towards the water. A warm summer breeze caught her tumbling curls and blew them around her. "It's different."

"What's with her?" asked Lilly's dad.

"I don't know," said Lilly, her heart pounding. It was like she was under the same thrall she'd been captured by when they had spoken to the mermaids the night before, not feeling the cold of the water and almost seeming hypnotised by them. "I'll find out."

Running down the beach, Lilly caught up to Saffron and took hold of her hand.

"Lilly, can you feel it?" Saffron asked, gazing out at the water with a troubled look on her face.

"Feel what?" Lilly asked, looking around. Three of the children had kicked off their shoes and were picking their way across the beach on the other side of the groynes. The air was warm with a soft breeze, the sea was gently lapping in front of them and overhead some seagulls swooped. The quay was quiet and unremarkable. As her father had said, no different from the rest of the beach.

"This place is different," she said, her voice faint.

"Different from what?"

"Everywhere," Saffron said, turning to her, her green eyes swimming with tears. "It feels like... like..."

"What?"

"Fear."

"Are you okay, Saff?" Lilly asked.

"No," said Saffron, her face starting to crumple. "No, I'm not. I'm really not okay."

"Oh, Saffron," Lilly whispered, pulling her friend into a hug as the warm air swirled around them.

"I died, Lilly!" Saffron sobbed into her shoulder. "I died. I died in the water and now they are dying in the water and nobody is helping them! We have to do something, Lilly. I can't bear it! It's so wrong, it's so awful. Please, please can we do something. Please can we help them. We need to! We just have to do something for them!"

"We will!" Lilly swore, taking Saffron's face in her hands, her friend's pain tormenting her with the guilt she already felt about that day. "We will help them, Saffron. We will help them."

"You promise me?" Saffron asked, looking at Lilly desperately.

"Yes," Lilly said. "I promise. I'm in. We'll help them."

"Thank you, Lilly," Saffron wept, flinging her arms back around Lilly's neck. "Thank you so much."

ʒ

Sam Wilkes sat outside the Lobster Shack watching the girls on the beach. He held his phone in his hands and blended in with the wedding guests that moved around him. The red head held his attention and he stared at her. The pain in her eyes stole his focus.

He liked Mermaid Cove and often came here to think and plan, tending to prefer the peculiar isolated loneliness of the bay to interacting with other people. Today was the first time he had seen anyone outwardly respond to the area the way he inwardly felt when he was there. The way he knew anyone should feel when in such a place.

ʒ

"Grandma needs you," said Coral as she appeared in front of Maud, the coven Seer, as she sat at her kitchen table.

"Good grief, child!" protested the old woman, sloshing tea over her front. "I do wish you wouldn't do that!"

"It's faster than phoning," said Coral, shrugging.

"Yes, well, be that as it may. It is most intrusive."

"If you were better at your job I'd never be able to surprise you," said Coral snidely.

"You are getting far too uppity, young lady," scolded Maud, mopping the tea off the table cloth with a tissue she pulled from her sleeve and eyeing Coral's translucent form crossly.

"Everyone else is on their way," said Coral, ignoring the woman's protestations. She resented her role. She was quite capable of being part of the actual coven, not just an errand runner for her grandma and her friends, but nobody would acknowledge it. "You're the last."

"Of course I am," Maud grumbled. "You always leave me 'til last."

"That's because I look forward to coming to you the least," muttered Coral. "Head for the shop."

"Insolent, you are, young lady."

Coral rolled her eyes then vanished from the room, reappearing in an instant back in her grandma's backroom and landing in her own body. She breathed hard for a moment, regained control of her flesh and stood. "They're on their way."

"Good," replied her grandmother, again no note of surprise at the unannounced reanimation of her granddaughter's body. "Now mind the shop for me whilst I work."

"Yes, grandma," muttered Coral, grumpily. She stepped out of the back room where her grandmother was casting assorted powders and liquids into a steel dish, the smell of incense potent in the air, and sat on the counter in the little shop, watching the world pass by behind the grubby glass windows.

ᛉ

"Please," the mermaid in the tank wept. "I'll volunteer. I'll give you anything I've got. Just let me go."

He ignored her pitiful cries. He had heard them before. Sitting at his desk he tapped away on his computer, whilst carefully packaging hair, skin cells, scales and saliva with neat silver labels on plain black packaging.

"I'm thirsty," the mermaid said miserably. "Please can I have more water. My mouth is so dry. My skin hurts."

The man stood and turned on her, watching as she recoiled. "You ridiculous half breed," he muttered, before picking up the cup of water at his side and approaching her with it.

"I'm not a half breed," said the mermaid audaciously. "My name is Mabli and I am Mer."

"Well, Mabli," sneered the man. "You're a half breed. If you want this water it would do you well to pipe down."

Mabli looked at him hard, a ferocious glint in her blue eyes that gave him a moment's hesitation he was careful to hide. Holding out the cup, she took it and swigged the liquid into her mouth, rolling it around for several moments, her eyes closed in bliss, before swallowing it down.

"Mer are not half breeds," she said coldly. "Our ancestry dates back before the time of the humans. You think because you've spread like a parasite over this planet, leaving fire and death in your wake, that you own it. We just choose to not leave marks over this world like you do."

"Thanks for the history lesson," he said, rolling his eyes disdainfully and taking the empty cup from her. "But this parasite has customers. And a product that is getting increasingly irritating."

Mabli went to protest but closed her mouth. The man turned away and went back to his computer and logged onto the black market community. Several messages waited in his inbox. He smiled coldly and began opening them.

३

"Dad, can I use your laptop?" asked Lilly over dinner in the hotel dining room, nervously pushing spaghetti around her plate.

"Why?" he asked suspiciously, a piece of steak hovering halfway to his mouth.

"Me and Saff just want to look up some local history and stuff," said Lilly. "I promise, no Facebook."

"Fine," he agreed begrudgingly. "But I want it back in the morning."

"Thanks dad," said Lilly, accepting the computer from him, then nodding to Saffron. The two bid goodnight and hurried from the dining room and up the stairs towards their bedroom. They heard Lilly's mum call after them about their unfinished meals but ignored her, slipping into their bedroom before anyone could stop them.

"Right," said Saffron as she shut the door. "Let's do it."

"I don't even know what to search," muttered Lilly, feeling exasperated. "Do I just search "Buy Mermaid Parts" or is that ridiculous?"

"I don't know," said Saffron. "Try it I guess!"

Lilly tapped on the keyboard. "Okay, it's a bunch of sites selling fancy dress and ornaments and stuff."

"Useless," grumbled Saffron, wandering over to the window and peering out at the water. "They're not out there."

"They're probably busy," said Lilly, feeling relieved. She didn't relish the idea of another night on a windy beach talking to the mermaids. "Okay, how about magic mermaid potions?"

Saffron pulled a face. "I bet it throws up kid's toys."

"No!" said Lilly, triumphant as the search results came up. "There are websites about spells and magic and stuff! And some freaky looking YouTube videos... I won't watch those."

"Let's see," said Saffron, landing on the bed beside Lilly and turning the laptop towards her. "Click that one, look, it says 'become a mermaid.'"

"Why do you want to see how to become a mermaid?" Lilly asked suspiciously, looking at her sideways.

"I don't," said Saffron with a shrug. "I'm just curious. I didn't know it's something you can become."

"This is nonsense," said Lilly. "If it doesn't work, wait a full month and try again? And all this 'blessed be' stuff. I've never heard anybody say that in reality."

"It sounds good though," said Saffron. "But you're right, this is nonsense."

"What else do we search?" Lilly asked.

"I don't know, do we even know if he's going to be doing this online?" asked Saffron. "I mean, maybe they have some secret magical market place. Diagon Alley style."

"Everything's online," said Lilly. "And Adamantine is loaded with tech. Really high grade tech. We're magical not Victorian."

"True, true," agreed Saffron.

"Maybe we search for magical people in the area?" Lilly thought aloud. "I mean, if we find out where they hang out, we could go talk to them and find out what they know. Right?"

"Yeah, sounds like a plan," agreed Saffron, wandering back to the window and gazing out at the ocean. "I wonder if they know."

"Who know what?"

"The other people. The magical people." Saffron said, her voice quiet and dreamy. "I wonder if they know about the mermaids."

"They must do," said Lilly frowning. "At least that they exist. Not that they need help."

"I hope so," she said. "What if they do know and just won't help? I mean, someone's buying this stuff right?"

"Yeah," said Lilly, tapping into the computer. "But they won't be nice people. We'll only talk to nice people. If they seem dodgy we can just walk away and find another way of doing it."

"Promise?"

Lilly looked up at her friend who was now gazing at her, her face pleading and earnest. "I promise."

Chapter Four

"Good job your mum agreed to us having some time alone," whispered Saffron as they hurried through Whitstable high street the next morning. "I never thought she would."

"I know," agreed Lilly. "She's been so over protective recently."

"It's just along here," said Saffron. "I remember. It was at that corner near the hairdressers."

"What do we say?" Lilly asked, her mind racing. Finding the base of a coven had been hard enough, but actually approaching them was something else.

"I don't know, hello I guess," said Saffron. "Look, there. There's the mermaid festival poster!"

The two girls hurried up to the grubby little antiques shop then hesitated. Taking a deep breath, Lilly pushed open the door and stepped inside.

"Can I help you?" asked a voice from the back of the shop. It was dark and dingy, stacked with furniture and ornaments, lamps and frames. Lilly peered into the gloom and spotted a young girl with thick black curls sitting on the counter at the back with a bored expression on her face.

"Hey, erm, yes actually," Lilly said as she stepped carefully towards the girl. Looking at her she looked completely unremarkable and not in the least bit magical. Her dark curls were held back by a thin white zigzag band and she was wearing a long sleeved white t-shirt and jeans on her plump frame. "I think."

The girl looked at them and cocked her head curiously. "What are you looking for?"

"Mermaids," said Saffron. "Or people who know about them anyway."

"The old mermaid festival poster?" the girl asked. "It doesn't happen here anymore. Are you tourists?"

"Sort of," said Lilly throwing a panicked look at Saffron. "Erm, I'm not sure you can help really. Erm…"

"Real mermaids," said Saffron, rolling her eyes at Lilly then turning to the girl again. "We need to know if anyone round here is selling bits of real mermaids."

The girl stiffened then slid from the counter. "You need to leave."

"What?" asked Lilly. "Why?"

"Because I'm not having any part of that," she said coldly and pointed a finger at the door, eyes full of disgust as she looked them up and down. "Get out. Now."

"No!" said Lilly, holding her hands up. "We don't want to *buy* bits of mermaids!"

"What?" asked the girl, her eyebrows knitting together. "What do you want then?"

"To find the person who is selling," said Saffron. "So we can stop him."

The girl's eyes shifted nervously and she turned her head, her eyes flicking to the back door then hastily around the floor in front of her. She stepped forward her voice lowering. "Are you the one?"

"The one what?" asked Saffron.

"The one we've been waiting for," she said, looking them up and down.

"I, erm…" Lilly said, feeling flustered.

"You say you want to stop him?" asked the girl, her eyes narrowing.

"We want to try," said Lilly.

"Meet me at Tea And Times in ten minutes," said the girl watching them as they hesitated nervously. "I'm serious. Get out."

Lilly and Saffron backed away and stepped back out into the street, hurriedly closing the door behind them.

"Well, that was odd," said Saffron, looking at Lilly with a confused face.

"Do we meet her?" asked Lilly.

"Damn right we do!" said Saffron, a wild grin springing to her face. "This is pretty exciting. Come on, let's go find the place."

३

"We request an audience with Oberus," said Ashalia, dropping her dark eyes downwards respectfully at the archway to the dwelling of the Ancients. The frail looking oil skinned Ancient eyed the three with suspicion, but moved aside and allowed them to swim past.

The Ancients gave Brinly the creeps. Their devotion to purity and the old ways was, in some ways, admirable, but it gave their dwindling numbers a dogmatic fanaticism which viewed Mer as a subspecies, and treated them as such. Humans were seen as rodents, spreading disease and violence across the planet like a plague.

As the three moved through the drifting seaweeds of the ocean floor, past caves and rocks where the Ancients drifted around whispering, she felt their hollow eyes following her. When she met a pair of eyes they quickly moved away, not in shame but in disgust. In some ways they resembled the Mer, but their tails were longer, their scales moving over their whole bodies not giving way to skin, and their features were flatter. Their magic was potent and supremely powerful, providing a shield from the surface world that prevented land dwellers from being able to discover their existence. The Mer had only been granted the knowledge of them, and the ability to find them, by the Ancients own graces. Brinly knew that should it come down to it the Ancients would sever all communication with the Mer to protect themselves in an instant, rather than help save their fellow ocean dwellers.

"There," muttered Hexanna, spotting the Ancient coiled on a rock, slates on his lap and surrounded by faces that watched him.

"Oberus," called Ashalia, swimming forward.

"You have returned again," snarled Oberus, looking at them disdainfully. "Did you choose to go against my advice?"

"No," said Brinly. "We spoke to the humans as you advised."

"Humans?" came a cry from behind Oberus, as an Ancient sat up and looked outraged, her eyes flashing. "Why do you come to our realm to talk of Humans, Mermaid?"

"They sought our advice, I cast stones," said Oberus by way of explanation to the Ancient behind him. She glared again at the mermaids then swam away. Oberus watched her go then turned back to Brinly. "Why have you returned?"

"We hoped you might have more." said Ashalia. "We want to save our friend. Mabli was taken. The children we're relying on are so young, we want to help them. Is there any way we can get her back?"

"Do I look like a fortune teller to you, child?" growled Oberus. Behind him, the Ancients muttered disapprovingly and he turned on them. "Be silent. I chose to advise; I am secure in that decision."

"Maybe you could come to the surface with us again," suggested Hexanna. "Talk to…"

"The surface?" came a roar from behind Oberus as a large, powerful looking Ancient whose silver scales gleamed like armour across his body swam towards them from behind a tall, pointed rock. "Oberus, explain yourself!"

Brinly watched him, huddling close to Ashalia and Hexanna in terror, as he ignored them completely and rounded on Oberus.

"Apologies sir, I had wanted to help," said Oberus, lowering his head in a bow before looking up at the warrior Ancient with a nervous look on his wizened face. "Lord Bray, the Harvesters are back."

"And what concern of that is ours?" demanded Lord Bray, his voice deep and powerful. "Do you think we are not aware? We are always aware of threats to our waters."

"I am sorry, Lord Bray," said Oberus. "I should have realised."

"You," roared Lord Bray, turning on the three mermaids. "What makes you think we should be in servitude to you? Why would you summons one of us to the surface?"

"We didn't summons him," protested Ashalia hotly. "We asked for help."

"We do not help your kind," said Lord Bray, pointing his spear at them. "Oberus acted rashly."

"He might have saved our lives! The lives of all our people!" cried Brinly, angry that the Ancient was being treated so poorly for doing something good, furious at the lack of regard Lord Bray was showing for their right to exist. "Oberus pointed us to the human who can stop The Harvester!"

"The Harvester has no knowledge of us. It is not our concern."

"But…" cried Ashalia, outrage on her face.

"LEAVE US!" boomed Lord Bray, fury radiating from his powerful body, his spear held aloft.

Startled and afraid, the three mermaids tumbled through the water and then darted hastily past faces of anger and judgment, and out of the arch into the open water, leaving the realm of the Ancients far behind them.

They swam fast, Brinly felt her eyes prickle and her heart race. She despised the attitude of the humans towards her people, but in some ways the Ancients were even worse. They were more closely related to her than the humans yet chose to treat her as dirt purely because she resembled the humans more closely than their pure line did. She knew that their ignorance rooted in an assumed superiority, which she resented. She expected such things from the humans, but ocean dwellers should be better than that.

They didn't stop swimming until they were far away from the realm of the Ancients then, too tired to do anything more, they rested on the ocean floor in some reeds and closed their eyes. Mabli's face flashed in Brinly's mind as she began to fall asleep.

"I'll save you," she whispered to the vision. "I promise I will save you."

३

Mabli's eyes regained focus again as the bright lights perforated through the darkness that had swamped her. She tried to remember what had happened, then remembered she had passed out in pain as the Harvester had scraped hundreds of cells from her tail. Looking down she saw the patchy wreckage that had once gleamed so majestically, now rough with raw flesh exposed to the water in pulpy messes. She felt like she needed to cry, but her eyes and face were too dry to relinquish any moisture.

Looking up she saw him packaging locks of her thick blue hair into a black, plastic container. Holding a hand up to her head she felt the uneven chopped chaos that was her hair now. Where once it had flowed down her back and swirled in the water around her, it now felt tufty and rough. She let out a moan of despair. Her skin cracked as she moved her face, the unnatural dryness seemed to leave her face feeling rigid and sore. Her eyes hurt. Her lids stuck grittily to them.

"You're awake," commented the man turning around. "You may have preferred to stay asleep. I need more blood."

"Please," Mabli begged, watching him pick up the syringe and fix a needle into it. "Please, I have nothing left. I am so weak."

"Oh you have plenty left," said the man dismissively. "But don't worry, soon your pain will be over."

Mabli shuddered. She felt so weak, so broken. She missed the ocean, the freedom to move and live like she was supposed to. She missed her family, her friends. She missed natural light and fresh air and salty water. "Please just let me go," she whimpered. "I don't deserve this. I have a family; they'll be so frightened. Please just let me go to them."

The Harvester set the syringe down and turned to look at her. His brown eyes looked thoughtful and deep for a moment, almost soft. She wondered if she had somehow got through to him.

A door at the back of the room opened and though it was shadowy back there, Mabli could tell it was someone smaller and younger than the Harvester.

"HELP!" she screamed out. "Please! He's kidnapped me!"

The young person's head turned towards her, shadows masking the face and age of whoever it was, but she was certain they made eye contact. She went to call out again but the Harvester held a hand up at her aggressively and she fell silent in automatic fear, then cursed herself silently.

"The packages are out in the hall," the Harvester snapped. "Get going. I'll need your help later with the tail."

The young person grunted an acknowledgement of the instructions then stepped back out through the door closing it again.

"Oh please," Mabli wept. From somewhere inside her, her body managed to produce tears. They stung her sharply as the drops hovered in her eyes before slowly breaking free, leaving a peculiar sensation of slug trails down her cheeks. She had never felt her tears on her skin until the Harvester.

"Oh, don't waste those," said the man, picking up a glass vial and hurrying over and collecting the two drops from her face. "I thought we'd drained you of those."

"Why?" Mabli begged him. "Why are you doing this to me?"

He chuckled. Pushing a stopper into the glass vial he pulled out a pen and wrote on the label then set it on the desk by his computer, and picked up the syringe he had prepared. "Because it's my duty to serve humanity and your kind exist for this purpose."

He approached her with the needle and she felt the sharp sting of the metal violating her skin as she hung limply in her restraints, helpless and too weak to argue anymore.

३

Sitting nervously at a small corner table in the little café, Tea and Times, Saffron and Lilly sipped on lattes and waited for the mysterious girl from the antiques shop to arrive.

"She can't be the person we were looking for," Lilly whispered. "If that's where the coven meet why would she send us here?"

"And what did she mean 'the one'?" Saffron whispered with a slight grumble. "You're always 'the one' for something, you are."

Lilly shrugged awkwardly. "I guess so."

"Hey there," came a voice.

The two girls looked up, surprised, and saw Dougal Hogarth standing over their table smiling at them, a cup of coffee in his hand. "Hogarth?" asked Saffron in surprise.

"Glad to see you survived your adventure last night," he said. "I'd have been riddled with guilt had ya not."

"Oh, yeah," agreed Lilly. "We're fine."

"I was just sitting over there," he said, nodding back towards a corner table. "When I saw you come in. Thought maybe I could join ya?"

The door opened and the curly haired girl walked in, her dark eyes flashing as she spotted them and headed over.

"No," said Saffron hastily. "But thanks. But we're meeting a friend."

"Okay, no problem," he said stepping back to allow the curly haired girl past. She glared at him as she sat down. "I'll see you girls around then."

"So, who are you?" asked the girl, as Hogarth returned to his table.

"Lilly," said Lilly. "And this is Saffron."

The girl looked them up and down suspiciously. "And you're looking for someone selling mermaid parts?"

"Yeah," said Saffron. "But again, not for us. To stop it happening."

"Are you sure that's what you want to do?" she asked, leaning in, her eyes narrowing as she stared at them.

Lilly frowned crossly. "Of course that's what we want to do! Why wouldn't we?"

The girl's eyes softened momentarily. "People don't," she said sadly, then stood up quickly. "Look, if you don't know about this world then I made a mistake, you're not who I thought you were. Nobody mortal stands a chance."

"We have power," said Lilly quietly, glancing nervously around. The café wasn't busy but a couple of tables were occupied and Lilly was aware of Hogarth glancing in their direction every so often, a confused look on his face. The last thing they needed was more attention.

The girl sat back down. "What power?"

"I'm, erm, I'm…" Lilly hesitated. She was embarrassed. She couldn't describe her power without sounding like she was bragging, but she couldn't demonstrate here like she did for the mermaids. The girl was looking at her with an eyebrow raised and her arms folded. She realised this was their only lead so far and if she didn't explain then she could lose it and they'd be stuck. A sharp elbow in the ribs from Saffron confirmed it for her. "I'm The Ultimate Power."

"The what now?" the girl asked.

"I control life and death," said Lilly, her cheeks reddening as she picked at her thumb nail. "I give life and take life. Easily."

Lilly expected a reaction of some sort. She expected her to be impressed if she was honest. Everyone had always treated her like she was something special. "And what can you do?" the girl asked, looking away from Lilly as if she'd just said she works at The Co-Op.

"I'm an Enhancer," said Saffron. "I boost other people's power."

"And how do you expect to do anything about The Harvester?" she asked. "Are you sure you'll even be able to contact the Mer?"

Lilly went to speak, to give the girl a mouthful about how little she knew, when Saffron interrupted her. "Hang on," she said crossly. "You're interrogating us like we're suspects of something. We don't even know your name. We don't even know if you're the person we were looking for! We came to you remember? You wouldn't even know about us if we hadn't!"

"Yes I would," said the girl, her voice losing its hard edge. "Maud Saw it."

"Maud?" asked Lilly, frowning with confusion. "Who's Maud?"

"The coven Seer," said the girl. "She said the girl with the ability to connect to the Mer and fight the Harvester was coming, and that she'd come to us looking for them."

"So it is your coven then," said Lilly.

The girl hesitated then said in an embarrassed voice, "Actually no. It's my grandmother's coven. I'm not a member."

"Seriously?" spat Saffron, standing up and looking outraged. "For God's sake. You've been acting all superior over us and it's not even anything to do with you! Come on Lilly, let's go look for Grandma."

Lilly stood and followed Saffron to the door, but the girl behind them stood and called out to them. "Wait! Please. Let me explain."

Saffron turned and looked her up and down with a withering look so full of disgust that it reminded Lilly of when they had first met and Saffron had despised her immediately. She was instantly grateful not to be on the receiving end of those looks anymore. "Don't bother."

The two girls walked out of the shop with Hogarth and the girl staring after them. They turned to walk down the street back towards the antiques shop, but the girl followed them out and came hurrying down the path after them.

"Please," she said, all ferocity lost and a genuine look of worry coming over her face. "If you do manage to make contact with the Mer you'll be in danger. Please don't go to my grandma. I have somewhere you'll be safe until we can figure out how to stop him."

"What do you mean by danger?" asked Lilly. "You're going to have to give us all the information here. We can't do anything with riddles."

The girl sighed and nodded. "I'm sorry, okay? I just don't trust many people. I thought my grandmother was looking for you to help the Mer and I was relieved someone was going to do something about this. But it's a lie. Look, we can't talk about this here. Can we go somewhere safe?"

Lilly and Saffron caught each other's eyes then hesitantly Lilly said, "Yeah, fine. Where?"

"My friend Sam lives near here. He's safe. We can trust him."

"Wait, what's your name?" Saffron asked her.

"Coral," she said shyly. "Coral Friday."

"Lead the way, Coral," said Lilly.

Chapter Five

"It's been three days," said Ashalia, gazing up at the light that glimmered through the water. "It won't be long now."

"Oh Mabli," wept Hexanna, putting her face in her hands. "We can't give up."

"Lilly and Saffron will help us," insisted Brinly. "We're not alone anymore!"

"We are *always* alone!" said Ashalia angrily, turning on her. "You saw how Lilly was looking at us. She was scared of us!"

"It's only because she doesn't understand," said Brinly, sadly. "We look different from her. She just doesn't understand and it scares her. It doesn't mean she'd betray us."

"I'm too young to die," sobbed Hexanna, a fear coming over her face that Brinly suspected had been threatening to take over her for a long time. She looked petrified. "I can't die this way. I can't!"

"I know," said Brinly gently, putting a dark hand against her friend's pale skin. "But we need to focus on saving Mabli. We can save her now. We have to believe in them. They're our only hope."

ʔ

"Sam?" called Coral as she knocked on the door of the little attic flat over a pink painted oyster restaurant.

The door opened and a young man peered out from behind it, his large brown eyes looked nervous and his hair was wet. "Oh, Coral," he said, a note of relief in his voice. "It's you. Who are your friends?"

"Lilly and Saffron," she said, her voice low. "We need to come in."

He looked around anxiously then held the door open and the three girls stepped inside. The room was tiny with bare wooden floors, a little kitchenette on one side and a sofa bed pulled out with a messy duvet on by the window. A little TV was crammed in the corner and a laptop sat open on the bed. A door to the left hung open and steam was in the air. Turning, Lilly saw Sam still had a blue towel round his waist and was rubbing at his wet hair with a green one.

"I'm Saffron," said Saffron, a little too eagerly Lilly felt.

"Sam," he said, his eyes lingering on her for a moment longer than Lilly felt was necessary. "I'll just pop and get dressed. Coral, fold the bed back up would you? There's beer in the fridge. Oh, and some coke and stuff."

As Sam grabbed a pair of jeans and a grey t-shirt from a wicker chair by the bathroom and disappeared inside, closing the door behind him, Saffron turned to Coral with her green eyes wide. "Wow," she said quietly.

"Erm," said Coral, shifting uncomfortably on the spot and tucking her dark curls behind her ear before going over to Sam's bed and tidying it up, shoving the bed back into the sofa base.

"What Saffron means to say," Lilly interjected quickly whilst shooting a silencing glare at her friend, "is that your boyfriend seems lovely."

"Oh, yeah," said Saffron nodding enthusiastically. "Totes."

"He's not my boyfriend," said Coral quietly as she repositioned cushions on the sofa and sat down in the corner of it, gazing out of the little, low window onto the street below.

Saffron stuck her tongue out at Lilly then grinned smugly.

Sam opened the door again and stepped out, his unkempt hair rubbed roughly dry and sticking up at funny angles and his feet bare below the ripped cuffs of his jeans. "Okay, so, what's going on then?"

He went over to the fridge and pulled a beer out, popping the top off on a device screwed to the side of his kitchen cupboard and ignoring the metal cap as it landed on the counter top with a ting.

"You know Maud talked about the girl? The one?" Coral asked him as he lowed himself into the old chair that creaked beneath him.

"Sure. So, she's the one then?" he asked nodding his head at Saffron.

"Me?" asked Saffron, her face flushing. "Oh no, not me. I'm not any one. I'm Saffron. Lilly's the one. She's always the one. If there's a one to be found you can be sure it's Lilly here!"

"I'm Lilly," said Lilly, holding up a hand in an awkward wave.

"I see," said Sam. "So, Lilly. You reckon you can make contact with the Mer, do you?"

"Actually we already have," said Lilly, not certain if she was betraying the mermaids by telling them or not. "We've spoken to them."

Coral turned her face in shock to Lilly, "You spoke to the Mer? How did you manage to summon them?"

"Summon?" asked Saffron with a confused frown. "We didn't. They came to us."

"Seriously?" asked Sam, his mouth open wide. "Well, Lilly, you really are the one!"

"You need to tell us what you know," said Lilly. "Everything. We promised we'd help and you're our only lead."

"Their friend Mabli was taken a couple of days ago," Saffron went on. "We said we'd try and save her but we don't know where to start."

"Mabli?" asked Sam, his head cocking to the side.

"Yeah, she was the last one to go," said Saffron. "Apparently they're being frozen, like paralysed, in the water and washing up on the shore. Then the Harvester somehow knows where they'll be and collects them."

"And they asked you for help?" asked Sam. "They're scared?"

"Terrified," said Lilly.

"My grandmother's coven wants to stop him too," said Coral.

"But didn't you say we can't trust them?" asked Saffron. "That we'd be in danger?"

"Oh you're in danger all right," said Sam seriously, leaning forward on his knees, his hands clasped under his chin. "If the Harvester finds out you're in communication with them he could use you. There are powerful magics they can work with mermaid parts, especially illegal mermaid parts, and humans with an existing connection are incredibly valuable and rare. If he knew you had that connection, he would come for you and he would use you."

"But what for?" asked Lilly. "He's already capturing the mermaids and they can't stop him. How would the connection help him?"

"The spells to capture mermaids are very, very hard to work," explained Sam. "The Harvesters were highly trained and incredibly technically advanced people back when they were around. To be the apprentice of a Harvester was one of the most sought after and respected roles a young person of Power could take. Even then there weren't many because of how complex the magic was that was needed. They were usually potion masters, occasionally Speakers although there aren't many Speakers around. If he had someone with your connection he would be able to perform a stronger spell to lure more mermaids in at once, to Harvest a whole school of Mer, rather than just one at a time."

"Wow," said Saffron, entranced.

Lilly rolled her eyes. She had historically shocking taste in boys and wasn't going to let the obvious intelligence and knowledge of this good looking young man lure her into trusting him automatically. Saffron, however, appeared to share none of Lilly's trepidation.

"I get that his Harvester guy is a bad one," said Lilly. "But what about your grandma, Coral? Didn't you say she wants to stop him?"

Dragging her eyes away from Saffron and Sam, Coral turned to Lilly. "They do," she said. "But it's not that simple. Do you know there are Mer that choose to donate to humans?"

"Yeah, the mermaids said that," said Lilly nodding. "They seemed kind of sniffy about it."

"Understandably," said Coral. "It's pretty controversial. But they work on a quid pro quo basis. The Mer donate things such as hair, saliva and semen, and the humans in turn offer things such as enchanted objects or potions back."

"Okay," said Saffron. "I'm still not following."

"My grandmother needs a Mer to agree to a deal like that," said Coral. "She and her coven have been around a long time, long before Harvesting was made illegal. It wasn't a well loved business for quite a while before it was outlawed. Those who did it and used the services of the Harvesters thought it was totally amazing and honourable work, but for a lot of people in our community it was seen as dirty work."

"Highly skilled professionals were suddenly looked at like poachers," said Sam.

"Understandably," said Saffron. Sam nodded.

"Thing is, my grandmother's coven used to be pretty powerful," Coral went on. "They were well known for their work. Respected. My grandmother used Mer parts in a lot of her potions. Most of the produce they were using is gone and their stocks of the bits that are left are running really low. I've heard them, time and time again, complaining about how they need hair from a pixie or a tooth from a Mer, stuff like that. If they can get you on side they won't need to get in on black market trading, which is dangerous and difficult to become involved in at the best of times."

"So they want to become Harvesters?" asked Lilly.

"No, not exactly," said Coral. "But they want to start replenishing their stocks. Maybe get the glory days back, fix whatever pickle they're in that seems to be stressing them out so much. I mean they were always a bunch of cranky old bitches, but honestly they're getting worse. Whilst the Harvester is at work the Mer are going to be on heightened levels of caution, avoiding the humans at all costs. If he is stopped, and they can use someone with a connection to whom they owe a debt of gratitude to, hopefully they can start having things they need donated."

Lilly shuddered. "So they want to use me to manipulate the Mer into agreeing to it? Out of gratitude for saving their lives?"

"Pretty much," said Coral. "But it's gross. If they want to do it then fine, that's their business. But trying to force them to feel indebted to do it because you want to use bits of their body?" She shook her head, her eyes dropping. "Nobody has the right to anybody else's body. Nobody."

"Coral, you okay?" asked Sam, standing up and approaching her, his hand resting gently on her shoulder.

Coral sniffed, a single tear sliding down her dark brown cheek. "I'm okay," she said and wiped the tear away. Catching Lilly and Saffron's confused but troubled looks she said, "My mum. She was taken. Too soon. That's why I'm with my grandma now. She was a campaigner for the Beings Protection Laws, my mum. She was a good woman."

"So we need to find him, right?" said Lilly. "Find the Harvester and stop him before he kills Mabli and takes someone else."

"But how?" asked Saffron.

"I don't know," said Coral sadly.

"And how would you even stop him?" asked Sam. "He's powerful and strong and you're... well you're just a girl."

"You're damn right Lilly's a girl," said Saffron confidently, grinning at him proudly. "Lilly's power can stop anyone!"

Sam shot her an impressed look and Lilly smiled wanly. She really didn't want to have to use her power against anyone ever again, even someone who mercilessly killed innocent people like the Harvester. Could she really go into battle planning to kill? Her insides turned to ice as she recalled the feeling of ending lives, stopping people breathing in a second with nothing more than a thought.

"I'll do some research," said Sam. "See if I can find where he's selling from and track it back to his server."

"You can do that?" asked Coral.

"Of course," said Sam, nodding his head at the laptop that lay on the floor where Coral had left it. "There was no point before. We couldn't have stopped him. Knowing he was doing it was never going to be enough to put an end to it!"

"Okay," said Lilly. "You do that and we'll come back tomorrow."

"You can't go anywhere!" insisted Coral. "They'll find you!"

"We can't stay!" insisted Lilly. "We're on holiday with my parents!"

"And anyway, Lilly will keep us safe," said Saffron.

"We'll see you tomorrow," Lilly promised, realising for the first time how Saffron had absolute faith in her ability to protect her. How vulnerable that made her if Lilly were to fail.

Coral and Sam begrudgingly agreed to their leaving, on the understanding they returned the following day and were extremely careful in the meantime. Lilly's gut was in turmoil. How did she manage to get herself into these situations? All she had wanted was to get through the holiday and have some rest, avoid drama. Yet the first thing she did was land smack in the middle of the biggest drama she could imagine. And, despite her promises to herself, she kept dragging Saffron along with her. They walked in silence, Lilly barely noticing their surroundings, her mind too caught up in how to stop anything happening to Saffron in what looked to be yet another dangerous road to start them down, all because of her stupid power.

Chapter Six

As they walked down to the beach that night, sneaking out after Lilly's parents had gone to their room and managing to avoid Hogarth or any other suspicious hotel staff, Lilly watched as Saffron chatted animatedly next to her. Her green eyes sparkled with life and excitement, her hands gesticulating animatedly. She hadn't seen such joy and energy in her friend since before her death in the river that seemed to have sucked the energy from her. Since then everything about her had seemed weakened and dulled. Until the night they had first met the mermaids.

"But wouldn't it just be the most amazing life?" Saffron gushed as they crossed the road and stepped onto the beach.

"Not really," said Lilly, shrugging. She didn't see the appeal of the mermaids at all and couldn't understand Saffron's overwhelming vitality for their existence, however grateful she was to see her friend back to normal.

"They're just so free!" Saffron insisted, holding her arms out. "They can just live and be in the water, nobody demanding of them or wanting from them, just free to explore and swim the oceans."

"They're being hunted," said Lilly quietly. "They're trapped. They could be killed any minute."

"So could we," said Saffron, her voice lowering. "At least they're free until that happens."

Lilly tried to think of something to say but couldn't. She watched her friend walking through the late evening twilight and felt a cold chill run up her spine.

As they reached the shore, Lilly spotted three pairs of eyes emerge from the water and watch them, before ducking back under and reappearing closer as the mermaids' poked their heads and shoulders out of the water.

"Have you found him?" asked Brinly, the whites of her eyes glowing against the oil slick darkness of her slippery skin.

"Not quite," said Lilly. "But we're close. We found someone who can track him."

"Who?" asked Hexanna brusquely. "What have you told them? What do they know? Are they human?"

"A girl called Coral who can astral project and her friend Sam," said Saffron. "We've not told them much except that we needed help. We didn't know how to find him."

"Can you trust these people?" asked Ashalia.

"Definitely," insisted Saffron. "Coral is passionately against harvesting. She would never do anything that let it happen."

"And the boy?" asked Hexanna suspiciously.

"Coral trusts him," said Saffron. "And he's the one who's going to find the Harvester for us."

Brinly nodded thoughtfully. "We trust you," she said after a moment. "If you trust them then that is good enough for us."

"Can you tell us about this guy?" asked Lilly, turning the subject to business. She didn't want to go in blind and wanted to avoid using her power to kill him if at all possible. The more she knew, the more chance they had of rescuing Mabli and stopping him without anything having awful having to happen. "What have you seen? I want to know what we're dealing with as much as possible."

"He's tall," said Brinly, her face thoughtful. "And big. Really strong looking. He drags them away like they barely weigh anything."

"Humans are hard to age," said Hexanna. "You all look the same. Older than you but not elderly."

"So grown up and big?" asked Saffron.

Ashalia nodded. "Yes," she said. "And his eyes are cold. There's no warmth there. He doesn't see us as Beings in any way, there's no remorse or regret. Nothing. We're objects to be used and that's all to him."

"Sam said he will have a power," said Lilly. "Something he can use to make the spell that freezes you. Do you see him do anything?"

"No," said Brinly, her eyes dropping and her voice straining. "We don't know it's going to happen until it does. We get no warning. Every few days one of our kind just freezes. We never see him do anything to cause it to happen, but he's there to collect within minutes."

"Okay," said Lilly, turning to Saffron and feeling incredibly nervous. "Can we do this?"

"Of course we can," said Saffron with a confident smile. "You're the most badass person around, and with me backing you up nothing can stop you. Nothing in the world."

ʒ

Lilly's mum and dad weren't happy about their announcement that they wanted another day alone, but after a brief conversation in which Lilly pointed out that it was their holiday too, and they were after all growing up and needed to be trusted as such, a disgruntled agreement was reached as long as they swore they'd be back at the hotel in time for dinner.

Knocking on the door to Sam's little flat over the oyster bar, Lilly looked at Saffron anxiously. She wished Saffron showed half the nerves in her face that Lilly could feel boiling away in her gut, but instead her friend grinned back at her, high on the adrenaline rush of it all.

"Yo," said Sam, pulling the door open and letting him in. Lilly was relieved to see the boy was dressed this time, though from the look on

Saffron's face she could tell that that feeling wasn't shared. "Coral should be here in a minute, she's just getting away from the old biddies."

"Did you find him?" asked Lilly.

"Yeah, no problem," said Sam. "He's working out of a warehouse round the back of the Lobster Shack."

"Is that the place by Mermaid Cove?" asked Saffron.

"The very one," said Sam. "So, what's the plan?"

"My idea was that Lilly create a poisonous snake or a tiger or something and get it to attack him," said Saffron, to which Sam raised his eyebrows in surprise.

"But I pointed out," Lilly interjected, rolling her eyes, "that then there would be a poisonous snake or a tiger loose in the world that shouldn't be here and would probably be killed or captured and trapped. Which isn't fair."

"So we decided Lilly should just kill him herself instead," said Saffron.

"Kill him?" asked Sam blanching. "As in, just kill him?"

"That is *not* the plan!" Lilly said, glaring at Saffron. "I don't plan on killing him. I can use my power in a weaker way and just knock people out."

"Well she's done it once," said Saffron. "And it was by accident."

"There is that," said Lilly blushing. "But I think I can do it. And I am going to try. And Saffron's my enhancer; she can help me control it. I'm definitely getting better at controlling what I do with my power and if I can knock him out then we can free Mabli and then call the police on him!"

"The police?" asked Sam with an eyebrow raised. "For mermaid abduction?"

"Okay, well, is there a magical police?" asked Lilly, feeling frustrated with herself for not thinking of that.

A knock came at the door and Sam crossed the tiny attic space and pulled it open. "Hey," he said as Coral stepped in smiling at him.

"Hi," she said in a voice so earnest and devoted that Lilly felt the girl's unrequited love pouring from every cell of her being.

"Hey Coral," said Saffron.

"Oh, hi!" said Coral, obviously caught unawares by their presence. She looked disappointed and Lilly felt guilty. She had obviously hoped for some time alone with Sam before they set out on their mission.

"We were just talking about what to do with The Harvester when Lilly knocks him out," he explained as he fetched her a bottle of cola out of the fridge and tossed it to her.

"*If* I can knock him out," said Lilly, an icy chill running down her spine as she imagined what was coming. "If I can't and he just dies... well... then I guess we'll have to figure out how to get rid of the body."

"Can you definitely kill him?" asked Coral.

"Yes," said Lilly with a small nod. "That's my power. I can kill him."

"Okay," she said. "Shiny. If you can knock him out, I'll astral project to The Commission. I don't know if they'll do anything but we have to try. He has to be stopped."

"And if he dies?" asked Sam, a freaked out look on his face. "What then?"

"Then... we cross that bridge when we get to it," said Coral shrugging. "I'll steal some Dissolution from my grandma or something. I, for one, won't mourn the death of such a monster."

"Yeah," said Sam anxiously. "Okay."

"Let's go," said Saffron.

ʒ

The Harvester put his phone down thoughtfully.

"Right," he said, turning his face to Mabli. "The time has come."

"What?" she asked, her voice weak and hoarse. Her whole body hurt, her eyes stung, her arms were too weak to move and her head lolled to the side as a painful fuzz ricocheted around inside her brain.

"I had hoped to get some last produce from you, but spells need casting and a tail needs removing," he said. "And time is up."

"Am I going to die?" Mabli whispered, trying to focus her dry and tired eyes on the man sat at the desk in front of her prison tank.

"Yes," he said.

"Thank you," Mabli said, relief flooding her body. "Thank you."

ʔ

"Are you sure about this?" Coral whispered as they approached The Lobster Shack. "It doesn't look like there's anywhere suspicious around here. Look at all these people, why would he do it near tourists?"

"What are you expecting?" asked Sam. "A neon sign? A Bat-Cave?"

"I dunno," said Coral shrugging. "Just something more... suspicious I guess."

Lilly looked around. The late morning sun was high and hot, a light puffy cloud drifted overhead in the breeze. The air smelled salty from the water and fishy from the restaurant close by. Around them teenagers wandered by smoking and kissing and laughing. Families ate ice creams and couples approached the restaurant with hungry looks on their faces. It was entirely non suspicious.

"I think it's awful," said Saffron darkly. "Everything about this place is just so filled with pain."

"Really?" asked Coral, looking around. "I don't see it."

Sam put a hand gently on Saffron's back and looked into her eyes. "I feel it too," he said kindly. "This is the place."

Coral's face fell and Lilly wanted to give her a hug. She had felt the pain of competing for a boy's attention with Saffron before and knew it never went well. You always came away feeling unworthy.

"Are you ready, Lilly?" Saffron asked her. "I've got your back, but you can do this. I know you can do this."

Lilly nodded nervously. "I think so," she said honestly. She'd never failed before. She'd made more lives than she was happy to admit, souls that now existed where they shouldn't and were entirely dependent on her own survival, but she had taken even more than she could cope with. She had never failed to create or take a life when she set out to do it, and her power was only growing. If someone needed to die she knew, in her heart, that she was the one person who could be counted on to do it. But that wasn't the issue. Whether she should take it was the problem. Whether she could live with herself seeing another pair of eyes suddenly grey over as death took hold of their bodies on her own command.

"Then let's go," said Coral.

Stepping round the back of The Lobster Shack and down a path, they came to a small warehouse set back from the waterfront. Lilly felt her skin start to go cold. She was fifteen years old and about to face an adult murderer. Next to her, Saffron slipped a hand into hers and Lilly squeezed it. It wasn't reassurance, though it provided the sensation of that, it was to ensure their powers could work together immediately if they were needed.

"Ah!" came a cry from behind them.

Turning, Lilly saw Sam tumble roughly to the ground, his leg twisted awkwardly beneath him.

"Sam!" cried out Coral, rushing to his side. "What happened?"

"I don't know!" he howled, clutching at his leg. "I just went over. It was like someone pushed me!"

Lilly spun around, trying to sense if an invisible person was lurking, waiting to attack. "Is someone there?" she called out quietly, not wanting to alert The Harvester to their presence if she could avoid it.

The air was silent, other than the cars and noises of the seafront of restaurant.

"Can you get up?" Coral asked Sam, crouching at his side.

He tried but cried out again, falling back to the ground. "No!" he said. "I can't!"

"Did the Harvester do it?" Coral asked, turning her face up to Lilly and Saffron, panic in her eyes. "Has he set up traps? Is there someone here?"

"I don't know," said Lilly quietly. "I can't hear anyone."

"Do we leave him or go back?" asked Saffron.

"Leave me," said Sam, wincing and trying to lift his leg, but failing with a heavy groan. "I'll try and join you if I can get up."

"Are you sure?" asked Coral.

"Yes," said Sam emphatically. "It'll be fine."

"Okay," Lilly agreed, nodding to Saffron. She didn't need Sam, though backup was always useful, all she needed was herself and Saffron. "Wish us luck."

Coral hesitated but stood up and joined Lilly and Saffron at the door of the warehouse. Together they faced the door and braced themselves for whatever was waiting within.

"Good luck," said Sam as Lilly pushed open the door and they stepped inside.

Chapter Seven

Inside the warehouse was gloomy and dark. They were in a small entrance hall with no light beyond what came in through a dirty corrugated panel of clear plastic above the door that had swung to with a quiet clunk behind them. The peeling door to their left had a "toilet" sign on, the one to their right had a sign saying "janitor".

"I guess we go through there then," said Lilly, pointing to the unmarked door ahead of them. Her heart was pounding in her chest and she could hear the other two breathing hard and rapidly. She gently squeezed Saffron's hand and looked at her nervously. "Ready?"

"No," admitted Saffron, with a half smile. "But let's go anyway!"

"Coral?" asked Lilly, looking at the newest girl in their party.

"I'm ready," she whispered, her voice barely audible and her eyes wide. Lilly knew this must be the first time she had faced a danger of this type, the first time she had stormed a citadel to free an innocent.

Lilly nodded the most confident nod she could muster, turned to the door and pushed it open.

Inside they found a room the size of Lilly's primary school assembly hall with high ceilings and no natural light. The centre was brightly lit by three bright, fluorescent pendulum lights hanging over what looked like a tall, narrow aquarium. To their right was a large desk with a computer and a stack of papers and folders, a mug of coffee and a knife. There were shelves covered in jars and boxes and vials. To her left she saw something that made her blood run cold. There was a metal table with a drain and a pipe running down to a glass jar which was half full of a thick, dark red liquid. The table had thick leather straps attached to it with sharp steel buckles.

"Oh my god," whispered Saffron, dropping Lilly's hand and stepping forward. "Look in that tank."

Lilly approached the aquarium and saw a heavy leather corset harnessed to the sides by solid metal chains suspended in the water.

"She's gone," said Coral, her voice hollow. "That's where he kept her."

"Where is he?" asked Lilly, looking around.

The sides and back of the room were gloomy. She couldn't see beyond the tank and she couldn't hear anyone move.

"What's back there?" asked Saffron, stepping round the horrifying mermaid cage that stood looming like a watery coffin in the centre of the room. "There's a cauldron look. And books."

Lilly followed her and saw what she was looking at. Then she saw something else.

Behind her, Coral screamed.

The severed head of Mabli the mermaid, her hair cut in tufts and chunks, lay in a metal tray on a set of scales. A collection of teeth sat in another at its side, glistening like shiny white pearls.

"Where's her body?" whispered Saffron, her voice faint. "Where's the rest of her?"

Behind them, Coral let out a yelp of panic and Lilly spun around. A large man stood holding her tightly against his chest, a curved knife held against the girl's throat. Lilly reached out and grabbed Saffron's hand, this time purely for the reassurance. Coral looked terrified, visibly trembling as she gripped the man's hand, the vicious silver blade so hard against her throat that her dark skin was beginning to ooze a trickle of blood across the shining surface of the knife.

"You made a mistake in coming here," he said with a matter of fact tone to his voice that suggested it was not a threat, just an observation.

"Drop the knife," said Saffron, her voice angry and threatening. Lilly knew she was trying to intimidate the man that loomed before them, though she doubted it would have any effect on him. "And we might let you live."

The Harvester chuckled. "No," he said simply, amusement showing on his face. Lilly knew he saw them as little girls. And right at that moment she felt like one.

Tears started to slowly slide down Coral's cheeks as the blood on the knife thickened, dark red running down the blade and dripping onto the floor.

"Do you know who she is?" demanded Saffron, standing forward and brandishing her finger at Lilly, fire in her eyes. "Do you know what she can do to you?"

"Yes," he said calmly. "Yes I do. And I think, Lilly, you should come over here and trade places with your friend."

"No," said Lilly, holding up her hand. She focussed, she concentrated. This had gone on long enough and she knew she could stop it. She wouldn't let him intimidate her anymore. She could do it. She could knock him out without killing him if she thought about it hard. She didn't want to be responsible for another death, she didn't want more blood on her hands, but the sight of Mabli's severed head and ripped out teeth, the way he held the knife to Coral's throat as he must have done to Mabli, made her stop caring as much. She would try and knock him out, but she wouldn't worry too much if she went in too hard. She flicked her hand at him and said firmly, "Drop."

In front of her the man cocked his head to the side and smiled. "I admire your confidence, young lady."

Lilly's heart slammed in her chest. He hadn't even faltered. Next to her Saffron slipped her hand into Lilly's. Lilly held up her hand again and, with a little more force this time, and the strength of Saffron's enhancing power warming through her body, said again, "Drop!"

"Help me," whimpered Coral, shaking with fear as the man remained standing, the knife still tightly against her throat, his strong, firm arm wrapped tightly around her, preventing her from moving.

"Lilly," whispered Saffron next to her, gripping her hand tightly, fear coming out of her in waves.

Lilly looked at her friend then turned back to the Harvester. She couldn't let Saffron down. "DIE!" she shouted at the Harvester, throwing everything she had into the command.

The knife dropped to the floor with a clatter and the man stumbled backwards. Coral fell forwards and Saffron rushed to catch her, pulling her upright and hurrying her back behind Lilly.

"Thank you," Coral wept. "Thank you."

"I haven't done it yet," Lilly whispered, watching as the Harvester stood up before her, his previously placid and oddly amused face now showing signs of anger.

"What?" Saffron cried out. "Do it again!"

"DIE!" Lilly shouted, blasting at him with furious power.

Again the man stumbled backwards, this time falling to the ground behind him. But, after taking a moment to regain his composure, he once again stood.

"You silly little girl," he said darkly, his eyes flashing.

"No!" Lilly shouted in horror. Why wasn't it working? She was giving it everything. She had killed with far less effort than this. She had taken the life of someone so filled with vitriolic power that she had been certain she would die herself.

"You don't actually think you can kill me, do you?" he asked, laughing coldly.

"We need to get out of here," whispered Coral, her hand to her neck as blood crept through her fingers.

"You're going nowhere," said the man through gritted teeth. "You girls are far too much trouble."

Next to them, Coral suddenly froze and her body dropped to the floor.

"What did you do?" Saffron screamed, falling on her knees to the girl's body which lay still and limp on the ground.

Lilly looked in horror at the Harvester but was surprised to see an equal measure of confusion on the man's face. He had no idea what had happened to Coral either.

ʔ

Outside, the apparition of Coral appeared where they had left Sam on the ground.

"Sam?" she called out, looking around. She couldn't leave her body for too long, not injured and not somewhere she couldn't be sure it was safe. Leaving her body left it completely vulnerable and at the mercy of those around her, but she had to do something and Sam was their only hope. "Sam are you okay?"

She couldn't see him anywhere. Panicking, she ran around looking for any sign of him, terrified that whatever had pushed him down and hurt his leg had come back and finished the job whilst they'd been inside. She ran to the road and peered around the edge, careful to avoid being seen, but still nothing. The boy was nowhere to be found.

ʔ

In fear, Lilly helped Saffron drag Coral's motionless body across the floor of the warehouse whilst shouting "DIE!" at the Harvester and firing every bit of hatred she felt in her body at him every time he tried to follow them.

Each time she hit him with the powerful command he stumbled, and each stumble seemed to be harder to recover from. Fury was now etched across his face, as well as pain, but he still did not stop. Nothing she did, no matter how much energy and hate and anger she pushed into the commands she was throwing at him, nothing stopped him. Nothing could kill him.

"I can't do it," she sobbed to Saffron, physically exhausted from the effort. "I don't know why. I'm trying, I'm trying so hard, but I can't stop him."

"I know," Saffron said in quiet acceptance, her face pale and her hands shaking. "We need to run but we can't leave Coral! What's happened to her?"

"I don't know!"

Coral suddenly sat up. "Sam's gone," she said.

Lilly and Saffron fell backwards hard in shock. "What?" Lilly asked, thoroughly confused.

"He's taken Sam," she said. "I went outside and he's gone. He wouldn't leave us. The Harvester's taken him."

"We need to get out of here," Saffron hissed, watching the Harvester pushing himself up to sitting again. "We can't kill him."

Coral turned and they watched as the man started to stand, his face contorted with venomous rage. He looked in pain, he looked weaker than he had before, but he did not look dead or even hurt in any significant way.

"How?" asked Coral.

"I'll stand over him, I'll just keep hitting him with it whilst you run. I'll follow when I can." Lilly instructed them. "Don't wait for me. I'll meet

you outside Tea & Times. I'll get him as much as I can and try to make
sure he doesn't follow me. But… if I can't… if he…"

"Lilly," said Saffron, her eyes wide with fear. "If he wins… if he kills
you… If you die, I die."

"DIE!" Lilly shouted at the Harvester as he dragged himself to his feet.
She turned back to Saffron as the man crashed to the floor again. "I know.
I promise I'll try. I don't know what else to do! I have to do something!"

"Okay," said Saffron, then flung her arms around Lilly's neck. "But
please don't die. Please come back."

"I promise I will try," Lilly whispered as she held her tight for a
moment then turned back to the man who was again back on his feet,
clutching his knife before him with a wild look in his eyes. "Go!" she
shouted to Coral and Saffron, then ran at the man with her hands out,
shouting "DIE! DIE! DIE!" as loud as she could, and feeling waves of
energy and heat blasting out from her skin in a brutal and almost
overwhelming power.

ᚱ

Saffron and Coral ran out into the scrappy bit of land in front of the
warehouse, behind The Lobster Shack, where they had left Sam.

"I astral projected here," Coral said as they ran. "He's not here. I
couldn't find him anywhere. He's done something to him!"

"We need to keep going," Saffron insisted. "What's the quickest way to
Tea And Times?"

"But Sam!" Coral cried, stopping and grabbing Saffron on the arm.
"We can't leave him!"

"He's not here to leave!" insisted Saffron. "And we can't do anything
for him if we're dead!"

"He wouldn't leave me!" Coral insisted. "We need to look for him! We can't just leave him!"

"We will die if we stay here!" begged Saffron, taking Coral's dark hand in her own pale one. "We can find Sam later! He's probably hiding somewhere! But if we don't go the Harvester will come and finish the job and then we can't help Sam *or* the mermaids!"

Coral hesitated, looking around anxiously, then with tears in her eyes she nodded her agreement.

"This way," said Coral, leading the way down the road away from Mermaid Cove.

Saffron suddenly stumbled, clutching at her stomach and falling to her knees. "Wait!" she called out.

"What's happened?" Coral asked, hurrying back and kneeling on the pavement beside Saffron.

"Lilly's hurt," Saffron sobbed. The pain in her gut was agonising. It felt like she had been stabbed in the side and her whole body ached as a burning spear like pain shot through her. "I can't move."

"We need to keep going," Coral urged her, looking around anxiously. Saffron was aware that people were giving them funny looks as they passed by but she couldn't move, she could barely breathe the pain was so intense. "Come on, if he catches up to us…"

"If he kills Lilly it doesn't matter anyway!" Saffron said through gritted teeth, clutching the pain in her side as her head swam. "I can't survive without her."

"I know you guys are close and all…" Coral started to say.

"No, I literally can't," said Saffron, looking up at her, her body screaming inside. "I will die. I'm only alive as long as she is."

"Oh god," said Coral, frowning nervously. "Okay, but we still need to move. People are looking and we can't have questions. We need to go."

Coral slipped an arm under Saffron's shoulders and helped her to her feet as Saffron cried out in pain. Together they stumbled down the road and up a street to the Tea And Times café where they had first spoken. Every few seconds Saffron stopped to sob out in agony, the feeling of wretched pain eating through her body so much she was constantly certain she would pass out before they got there.

"Here," said Coral as they finally made it to the front of the little café. She carefully lowered the sobbing Saffron onto a bench, and sat beside her, supporting her as carefully as possible. "Lilly will be here soon, I'm certain of it."

"I can't breathe," Saffron wept. Her body felt icy cold. "She's dying."

"What do I do?" asked Coral in a panic.

"Find Lilly," Saffron begged her. "Save Lilly."

Coral hesitated then nodded and ran. She raced as fast as she could through the streets and back towards the Lobster Shack. If Lilly was there she would find her.

Chapter Eight

"Grandma!" Coral called out as she appeared ghostlike in her grandmother's shop. "Grandma, are you here?"

"Coral?" the old woman's voice came out from the back room.

Coral ran through past the counter and found her grandmother sitting cross legged on the floor reading an ancient book. "Grandma, I need a potion," she said. "My friend has been stabbed."

"Take her to the hospital," said her grandma, looking up at her momentarily before returning to the book.

"The knife might have been enchanted or laced with a potion," said Coral. "I need a cleansing potion and I need to find Dorothy to come and heal her when she's been cleansed."

"You know my stocks are running low, Coral," said her grandma, pushing herself to her feet with a pained look. "If she's been stabbed with an enchanted blade she's probably already dead."

"She would be if she wasn't the Ultimate Power!" cried Coral, as her grandmother's eyes widened. "Two lives depend on this, Grandma! And if you're looking for the one who can help stop the Harvester, help you connect with the Mer, then you'd better meet me round the back of the Lobster Shack in the next few minutes or that is never going to happen!"

"Coral, you tell me what's going on right now…" started her grandma.

"Just come and find us, Grandma!" Coral cried, exasperated.

Her grandmother fixed her with a piercing look, her dark eyes full of suspicion, but then she nodded. "I will find you."

Vanishing from her grandmother, Coral reappeared in the living room of an old house overlooking the sea front. "Dorothy!" she called out. "It's Coral!"

"Oh, hello dear," said a kindly faced woman with smiling eyes and a very colourful scarf draped elegantly over her shoulders. "What can I do you for today? Is Opal up to something exciting today?"

"I need you to heal my friend," she said. Of all the women in her grandmother's coven, Dorothy was the only one she truly cared for. "She's been stabbed. Grandma's meeting me there with a cleansing potion just in case, but she'll need healing fast. Can you come?"

"Of course, dear!" said Dorothy, picking up a patchwork handbag from the chair by the front door. "Where am I going?"

"The land at the back of the Lobster Shack," said Coral. "Down by Mermaid Cove."

"I'll fire up the old Range Rover and be there in a jiffy," she said with a serious nod.

"Thank you," said Coral with gratitude. "Thank you so much."

Coral flashed back into her own body where it lay beside the bleeding Lilly and sat upright. "Lilly," she whispered gently, stroking Lilly's hear off her clammy face. "Help is coming."

"Saffron?" Lilly whispered.

"No, it's Coral," she said, gently. "But Saffron's safe. She's okay. Lilly, where's the Harvester?"

Lilly lifted a trembling arm and pointed towards the warehouse. "In there," she said in a breathy and distant voice. Coral looked at the warehouse anxiously, expecting the man to come crashing out of the doors any second. "Unconscious."

"But then how did he stab you?" Coral asked, confused.

But Lilly's head lolled to the side and her eyes closed before she could reply. Coral wanted to shake her or something, anything to bring her round, but without knowing the extent of her injuries from the deep gash in her gut, she was too scared to move her.

Behind her she heard footsteps and she turned to see her grandmother coming towards her carrying a glass jar with a crystal clear liquid in it. "Is Dorothy on her way?" she asked, kneeling over Lilly's body, her old knees scraping on the rough stonework, though her face betrayed no sign of discomfort.

"Yes," Coral said. "The Harvester is still in there. We need to get her moved fast before he wakes up."

"The Harvester?" asked her grandma, as she gently pulled Lilly's t-shirt up to reveal the angry and bloody slash mark in her gut. "Have you been working behind my back, Coral?"

Coral didn't answer, not sure what to say. Her grandmother began gently pouring the liquid that oozed out of the jar like syrup, but as clear as perfect water, onto the wound. Coral expected a hiss or something to show it was working, but instead the syrup soaked into the skin and vanished as quickly as it landed.

"That will cleanse any curses or potions out of the wound," she said. "Not knowing what we were dealing with I had to use my strongest cleanser, Coral. I hope you're aware of how precious this substance is and how hard it is to make, especially given the current climate."

"Thank you, Grandma," said Coral, slipping a hand into Lilly's. "She's still alive but she's weak. I hope Dorothy can help her."

"Dorothy is the best Healer this area is ever likely to see," said her grandmother sternly. "You'd do well not to doubt her."

They heard the sound of an engine and wheels began crunching over the stones. Dorothy Grace stepped from the large vehicle and hurried across towards them, her floral skirts flying behind her. "Oh the poor darling," she said, lowering herself down beside Lilly. "Is she cleansed?"

"With the Inoculance," said Coral's grandma, moving in closer to Dorothy so Coral was pushed out of the way. She rolled her eyes and stepped back, now wasn't the time to fight for her place.

"Perfect," said Dorothy quietly, and she placed her middle fingers lightly either side of Lilly's wound and began to hum.

Soon the only sound Coral could really hear was the gentle sound that Dorothy was humming. It seemed to fill the air, drowning out passing traffic and the noises from the restaurant and seafront, yet remain so quiet she couldn't quite hear every note. She thought of Saffron alone on the bench outside Tea And Times. Was she unconscious too? Was she dead? Would anyone find her? A young girl alone and unconscious on a bench in the middle of a town was incredibly vulnerable to passing evil doers, but Coral knew she had to save Lilly in order to save Saffron, so she stayed put.

"There you go dear," said Dorothy after what could have been thirty seconds or an hour, snapping Coral out of a daydream state she had been lost in, too entranced by the sound to comprehend the passage of time. "Try sitting up now, if you can."

Coral watched as Lilly's eyes regained focus and she pushed herself awkwardly to a sitting position. "What happened? Who are you?"

"My name's Dorothy Grace," said Dorothy gently, an arm around Lilly's shoulders in case she fell back again. "I'm a Healer. And this is my friend Opal Friday, she cleansed your wound with a powerful potion, you'll not be plagued by any residual curse."

Lilly looked at them both in confusion but said, "Thank you," with earnest gratitude. "Where's Saffron?"

"We need to get to her," said Coral, stepping in front of her. "She's on a bench outside Tea And Times where you said to meet. I had to save you because she was dying too. I had to leave her."

"You left her?" asked Lilly in horror, trying to force herself to stand up. "Alone?"

"I had to!" Coral insisted, guiltily. "If you died she would die anyway! If I stayed she didn't stand a chance."

"I know," Lilly said, nodding with a painful wince. "You're right. But we need to get to her right now."

The three of them helped Lilly to her feet and over into Dorothy's car.

"Tea And Times, on high street near Iceland?" asked Dorothy, as she slid behind the driver's wheel, Coral's grandmother slipping into the passenger seat whilst Coral and Lilly climbed into the back.

"That's it," said Coral.

"Let's go," said Dorothy, turning on the engine and seeming quite chipper about the adventure she had suddenly found herself on.

᛭

The journey from the warehouse to the Tea And Times was just a couple of minutes in the car but Lilly felt her body healing and recovering to the point of near normality by the time they got there. Where Dorothy's fingers had sat on her abdomen was filled with a lingering warmth that seemed to radiate outwards through her whole body.

A small crowd was standing round the bench out front and Coral gasped, "That's where I left her."

Looking down at her front Lilly quickly zipped up her hoody to cover the ripped vest and blood stain, all that was really left as evidence of her attack. The last thing they needed right now was more attention.

Dorothy pulled the car up on the pavement squarely over double yellow lines, then all four jumped out and hurried over to where Saffron was lying on the bench looking sick and weak, slumped on the side of the bench, but alive.

"Saffron!" Lilly cried, pushing her way through the crowd

"Is this your friend?" a man asked as Lilly sat down beside Saffron and wrapped her arms around her.

"Yes," said Lilly, nodding and feeling tears trickle down her cheeks. "Saff, are you okay?"

"She drunk?" asked a woman in Adidas tracksuit bottoms and a Juicy vest.

"She's not drunk," snarled Lilly. "She just felt poorly.

"Let her through, you bloody vultures!" shouted Coral's grandmother, clapping her hands in a shooing motion at the watching audience. "The girl is sick and we need to get her to a doctor!"

"Come on, Lil," said Coral, glaring at everyone around them. "I'll help you get her to the car."

"Hang on," said the man, his voice concerned. "Honey," he said to Saffron. "Are you sure you know these people? I still think we should call your parents for you."

Saffron looked up at him with vacant eyes. "Yeah," she said weakly. "Lilly?"

"I'm here, Saff," Lilly said gently, stroking the damp auburn curls away from Saffron's sweaty and deathly pale face. "I've got you."

"Drugs!" said the Juicy vest woman. "She's doped up, look at her! Younger and younger, these days you know. She's barely old enough to smoke, this one!"

"Move!" growled Lilly as she and Coral took Saffron on either side and carefully pulled her to her feet.

Together they lead her through the watching people and, with a degree of dragging and shoving, managed to get her into the back of Dorothy's Range Rover. She sat between Lilly and Coral, her head flopping over onto Lilly's shoulder as Dorothy pulled the car away from the curb and back out into the afternoon traffic.

"We'll get her back to the shop," said Coral's grandma. "Then you can tell us what the hell has been going on."

३

The Harvester looked angrily at the computer. His head hurt and his body ached, but he had survived the unsurvivable. The Entity Elixir had done its job well, despite needing his halfwit apprentice to step in at the last minute. As much as he didn't appreciate the meddling, he recognised that he'd have been in trouble if the boy hadn't done what he did. However, as successful as the elixir was, he was now left in a frustrating, and potentially harmful, situation.

The message on screen from Iago Banc read, "When will the tail be delivered? I do not appreciate waiting."

The Harvester rubbed at his temples, frustrated and stressed. The Entity Elixir was one of the most difficult to create potions, and whilst there were various methods of achieving it, all involved incredibly rare and hard to obtain ingredients and all were time consuming and complex. Bane was, he suspected, wanting to use the tail to create the elixir himself and had been promised delivery of the latest mermaid tail harvested that day. Not coming through filled the Harvester with a sick feeling in his gut, not because it was professionally inept, but because Bane was a Bone Breaker who worked hunting dragons. He was not the kind of man you wanted as your enemy.

"Soon," he typed. "There has been a slight hold up but the tail will be delivered tomorrow."

He hit send then roared in rage. He would need to capture and Harvest a Mer by tomorrow. The production of the potion to capture the Mer almost as difficult and time consuming as the Entity Elixir, and there would be a great deal of money lost in freshly cut merchandise if the Mer was to be killed immediately. Yet there was no choice.

Lilly Prospero needed to be stopped. He only had so much Elixir available to him, and he couldn't afford to chance her getting the better of him again. However much the Elixir protected him from a magically induced death, if he were to be weakened by the girl's immense power again there was nothing to stop her from slitting his throat. It was pure luck she had been stopped this time. No, the girl had to go. And she was too strong to be taken out without planning, without weakening her defences. But it could be done. And he knew just how to do it.

Chapter Nine

Carefully, Lilly and Coral helped Saffron through the tiny antiques shop and into the dimly lit coven room tucked behind it, and lay her down on a burgundy and gold patterned chaise beside a heavily laden bookshelf at the back. The room smelled of incense and spices and Lilly found herself wanting to sneeze, but she held it in in case it was offensive.

Dorothy knelt beside Saffron and tenderly placed her middle fingers on Saffron's temples. Her skin was sallow and glistening with sweat and Lilly found herself trembling with fear for her friend. "I can't heal her," she said after a moment, a confused look on her face.

"What's going on?" asked Coral's grandmother, turning a serious face on Lilly. "You were stabbed, you survived when you probably shouldn't have done long enough for us to heal you, and you returned to normal in record time. Your friend here, however, is destroyed with no sign of harm and Dorothy cannot heal her. Tell me, child," she said, an aggressive tone to her voice. "What curse did you use?"

"Curse?" Lilly stammered, looking nervously at Coral who shifted foot to foot anxiously. "I haven't used a curse."

"Then why is she bearing your ailment instead of you?" she demanded, her dark eyes still young and powerful inside the gentle folds of the dark, mottled skin around them.

"Opal," said Dorothy in a gentle voice. "Go easy on the girl."

"It's not a curse, I swear," insisted Lilly. "I don't have that power. It's complicated…"

"If you don't explain it to us, I won't know what I can give her to ease the pain," said Coral's grandmother sternly.

"I'm a life giver," explained Lilly. "She died and I brought her back to life, but to do it I had to put my own life essence into her."

"So if you die, she dies," said Dorothy with an understanding nod.

"Yes," said Lilly nervously. "But I'm not dead!"

"But you would have been," said Coral's grandmother. "Your power is strong enough to carry you through some serious levels of harm, that much is obvious, but Saffron here is not as strong as you. She will most likely survive this, if that is how she has survived this long, but her body isn't designed to handle this level of trauma in the way yours is."

"Can you do anything for her?" asked Coral.

"I can't heal her," said Dorothy. "But I can ease a little of her discomfort. Most of the pain is artificial. It's her body reacting to things that aren't happening and there's no way to heal that."

"I can make a soothing remedy," said Coral's grandmother, walking to a set of shelves at the side of the room and pulling jars and boxes down. "But again it won't be a fix. It'll simply be a disguise. A sedative really, something to stop her mind from reacting so strongly which should give her body a chance to recover from the stress."

"Thank you," said Lilly. "Anything that can help her."

Coral's grandmother placed the jars and boxes down beside the cauldron in the centre of the room and began carefully tipping and sprinkling. She did not measure anything but seemed very exact in her actions. The whole time she chuntered quietly to herself, a frown of deep concentration on her face. "Root of ginseng, and some dried amla," she said, dropping some powders in. "A touch of goji can't hurt," she whispered as she tipped in some berry looking things. "Roseroot will give her some strength and skullcap should reduce the stress." Lilly watched in fascination as the small cauldron began to release a fragrant smoke. "And some belladonna," she whispered, holding a small jar up and tapping just a tiny dusting of powder in.

Dorothy sat with a hand gently on Saffron's temple, a soothing and gentle hum drifting from her. It was even fainter than before, but it was there and just the sound of it felt comforting.

"Lilly?" Saffron whispered, her eyes flickering open a little as she looked around.

"I'm here," Lilly assured her, taking her hand gently. "We're getting you something that can help."

"It hurts," she said breathily. "What happened?"

"I was stabbed," Lilly explained, stroking her friend's face gently and feeling incredibly guilty. "And your body thinks it was stabbed too. Someone snuck up on me whilst I was blasting the Harvester. But you're fine, I promise. You're going to be just fine. We're with people who can help."

"Rest now," said Dorothy softly. "Opal's going to bring you cup of hot tea and I'd like you to drink down as much of it as you can, all right dear?"

Coral's grandmother approached with a white china teacup decorated with pink flowers and green leaves in her hand. The 'tea' inside was a funny green colour but smelled delicious. Saffron reached out and took the cup, sniffing, then took a sip.

"Drink it all up," instructed Coral's grandma, her voice less soothing than Dorothy's, but still not as harsh in tone as Lilly had heard from her previously.

Obediently, Saffron drank some more then, as she came to the end of the cup, her eyelids started to sink heavily.

"She will need to sleep now," explained Dorothy, taking her hand away. "A good few hours."

"But... but..." protested Lilly anxiously. "But I promised my mum and dad we'd be back at the hotel in time for dinner!"

Coral looked at her watch. "It's half two now," she said. "Will she wake up in time?"

"No," said Coral's grandma in a matter of fact tone of voice. "She'll probably sleep until morning now."

"Morning!" gasped Lilly. "What am I going to do? What will my mum say? She'll kill me!"

"Well, unless she does a better job than the Harvester she won't have much luck," said Dorothy. "Give her a call and tell her you're staying with a friend. You can stay here, we'll look after you."

"A friend?" asked Lilly, shaking her head. "We don't have any friends here! She won't believe me!"

"Well you don't have much choice," said Coral's grandmother crossly. "If you had done the sensible thing and come to us first," her eyes flashed momentarily at Coral, "then perhaps this could have been avoided. However, until then, you're going to have to stick it out if you want your friend to live."

"Crap," Lilly muttered under her breath.

She pulled her phone out and stepped outside the shop to make the call and saw three missed calls and eight texts from her mum waiting for her already. The excitement and drama of the morning had totally distracted her from her phone and she knew she was about to be in for a serious telling off.

Gritting her teeth, she pressed to phone her mum. It didn't even make a full ring out before her mother's manic voice answered. "Lilly?" she demanded. "Lilly, where are you? What's happened? Are you okay? Lilly?"

"I'm here mum," said Lilly guiltily. It wasn't her mum's fault and she knew she'd be worried. "Sorry. We got distracted."

"All day?" Lilly's mum demanded. "Where have you been?"

"We have just been out with some friends," Lilly said vaguely, desperately hoping her mother wouldn't expect more, though knowing the chances were small.

"Friends?" came her mum's voice. "What friends? How could you ignore your mother for people you who don't even know! Where are you? Where's Saffron? She's not answering either!"

"She's with our friend Coral," Lilly said nervously. "We're probably going to stay with Coral tonight… we thought we'd do some, erm, late night fishing…" She slapped herself in the forehead with her left hand and rolled her eyes. Fishing. As if she and Saffron were going to go late night fishing. As if her mum would agree to late night fishing. Idiot.

"You are bloody well not doing any such thing, Lilly Elizabeth Prospero!" screeched her mum. Lilly cowered despite being nowhere near her. Lilly's mum rarely lost her temper, always seemed to find the calm and logical in even the most stressful of situations. But when she lost her top, she really lost her top. "Robert! She thinks she's going late night fishing with some girl she's just met! Lilly you are doing no such thing! You get yourself and Saffron back to this hotel right now!"

"No mum, I'm sorry," Lilly said nervously. "Even if we don't fish we're still staying at Coral's. It's important mum. I can't explain why."

"Where are you?" her mum howled. "Tell me where you are and we'll come and get you!"

"No," said Lilly, a tear creeping out of her eye. She seemed to have been hurting and betraying her mother more and more since she discovered her powers. The stronger she got the more she hurt the person who had loved her and stuck by her from the day she had been adopted. She hated herself for it, but Coral's grandmother was right; she didn't have a choice. "I'll see you tomorrow, mum."

She hung up the phone, wiped her eyes and stuck the phone back in her pocket. She hated herself, both for lying to her mum and for letting

Saffron get hurt. She had promised herself time and time again it wouldn't happen anymore. And yet, first sign of danger, she was right back there.

"Hey," came a voice from behind her.

Lilly jumped out of her skin and turned around to see Dougal Hogarth standing nearby, eating his way through a bag of Skittles. "Hogarth?" she asked, baffled. "What are you doing here?"

He held up the bag of sweets. "Eating," he said. "What are you doing? You okay?"

Wiping the back of her wrist across her eyes, Lilly nodded. "Yeah, I'm fine."

"Sure?"

"No," she admitted with a sigh. "I just hate making my mum mad. But I'm all right."

"What's ye name then?" he asked, cocking his head to the side. "Seeing as we are bumping into each other all the time. We might as well get to know one another, right?"

"Lilly," she said, looking at the floor shyly. "Lilly Prospero. But I have to go."

"Are you sure you're okay?" Hogarth asked her, stepping forward with a worried look on his face. "I swear I won't tell your mum. But you look like you could use a friend. Do you want to come and get a cup of coffee with me?"

Lilly sniffed and nodded. "I would," she said, her voice cracking. "I really would. But I have to go, I'm sorry Hogarth."

"Anything I can do?" he asked, stepping towards her with a worried look on his face, his eyes focussed intently on her own.

"Yeah actually," said Lilly, picking nervously at her thumb nail. "If you see my parents at the hotel, they're Alice and Robert Prospero, can you just let them know we're safe? Say you've seen us, and that we're okay."

"Sure," he said with a nod. "I can do that."

"Thanks Hogarth," she said, sniffing wetly and pushing open the shop door. "Bye."

"Right, first things first," said Coral's grandmother as Lilly reappeared shoving her phone in her pocket. "Tell me everything you know."

"First thing's first, we need to find Sam!" protested Coral. "The Harvester took him!"

"Then he's dead," said Coral's grandmother dismissively.

"First things first, we need a cup of tea," said Dorothy. "Tea, then talking."

ꝛ

Coral's grandmother and Dorothy busied themselves discussing secretive things quietly in the corner, peering at books and potions. Lilly heard a few words she recognised, "Mer" and "Harvester", but generally they kept their voices too low to hear. Every so often Dorothy came over to Saffron and gently placed her hands on Saffron's head, a low hum emitting from her briefly, then she'd return to her work.

Lilly sat with Coral at Saffron's side. A tabby cat had slunk in through the back door and leapt up to perch on the chair closest to the chaise, watching them with a haughty look that reminded Lilly of Priscilla, her own cat that she had left at home under the careful care of her grandmother. She wondered if this was a witch's familiar. She talked to Coral about things that she and Saffron had been through together, how they had grown from enemies to friends to even closer, how Lilly had come to depend on Saffron just as much as Saffron literally depended on her.

"I've never had a friend like that," said Coral, her eyes sad. "There's magic kids around, obviously, but we're not mates or anything. I've never really had a chance to get to know anyone because I'm always here, helping my grandma. Well, anyone other than Sam…" she stuttered as her eyes filled with tears and she hurriedly wiped them away with the back of her sleeve. "And now Sam is…"

"I'm so sorry, Coral," said Lilly, putting an arm around the girl's shoulders.

"He was all I had, really," she said, sniffing as tears ran down her cheeks. "He's the only person who's ever really stuck with me. I've always been too busy with the shop and helping Grandma and I just… I've never… he was all I had."

Lilly wished she could offer words of comfort or anything that would make Coral feel less wretched, but what could she do? What could possibly be said to make her feel any better? She hardly knew her and she couldn't imagine the pain she was in. Throughout it all, whatever had happened, Saffron had been her constant. To not have that in a world so full of confusion and complexity must be incredibly lonely, she thought.

The bell on the door of the shop tinkled as the door opened.

"Coral?" came a voice.

"Sam?" Coral called out, her head snapping up and her eyes wide as she flung herself to her feet and charged across the room and out into the shop. Lilly followed her in surprise, watching as Coral suddenly burst into tears at the sight of Sam and rushed over to him. She flung her arms around his neck and sobbed into his shoulder. "Sam! I thought you were dead! Where were you? What happened? Are you hurt?"

"I'm okay," he said, wincing at the impact of the weeping girl, but staying upright and not complaining. He put his arms around her and rested his chin tenderly on her shoulder. "Sore but alive, which is more than I had expected."

"Where have you been, young man?" demanded Coral's grandmother, appearing at Lilly's side and eyeing the boy with cold suspicion.

"Grandma," scolded Coral, turning away from Sam to glare over her shoulder. "Let's get him inside, he's hurt."

"It's okay," said Sam gently, putting a hand on Coral's arm and walking with a limp and a strained face towards the back room. "I know it's crazy I'm alive. If the Harvester had got his hands on me himself, I'm pretty sure I wouldn't be. I really could do with sitting down though."

Coral slipped an arm through his and everyone stepped aside to allow him through. He carefully lowered himself onto a chair and awkwardly tried to position his leg without pain flashing across his face.

"Who did get you then?" asked Lilly.

"I don't know, I never saw them," he said with a shrug, before wincing again. "He dragged me away and smacked me in the back of the head and left me in a ditch."

"Must have been the same person who stabbed you inside, Lil," said Coral, nodding earnestly and gazing adoringly at Sam. "He's obviously got an assistant."

"An apprentice," said Dorothy, approaching them. "The Harvesters always trained an apprentice and it would appear this one has continued that tradition. Would you like a cup of tea, Sam dear?"

"Oh, thank you," said Sam, smiling.

"Can you heal him, Dorothy?" asked Coral. "His leg and head are hurt."

Dorothy eyed him curiously. "Would you like me to do that?"

"No, no," said Sam, holding up his hands. "I'm fine, honestly. Nothing a little rest and some determination can't fix. I've never really been keen on magical cure-alls... I like to let my body get strong enough to cope on its own, you know?"

"I see," she said, nodding sagely. "I shall get to making that tea then."

Chapter Ten

"They said they'd go today, right?" whispered Ashalia, gazing out towards the coastline.

"Yes," said Brinly nervously. All three had been tense waiting for news and longing for their friend's safe return. But as the hours went by, and there was no sign of Mabli or the two humans, the more anxious they became.

"They've failed," sobbed Hexanna. She had been taking it particularly hard, Brinly observed as she slipped an arm around her friend's shoulders. Hexanna was usually so strong, so ferocious, but Brinly had always known it was masking a vulnerability that had now broken free. "He'll come back for someone else now."

"We don't know that," Brinly reassured her. "We can't know."

"The Ancients could stop him," said Ashalia angrily. "If they wanted to. If they wanted to they could destroy the whole country with the power they have stashed away being spent on protection and isolation charms."

"Sometimes I think the only reason they don't is because they want to stay unknown," said Brinly. "It's the same everywhere. They are more concerned with remaining hidden and keeping themselves 'pure' than anything else in the world, but with their revulsion of the humans, and their disregard for us, sometimes I think they really would begin wiping everyone out if they decided it was worth bothering with."

"So, here's what we know," said Dorothy before taking a sip on a delicate china cup of Earl Grey, then pointing at the blackboard they had been working on. "The Harvester is freezing or paralysing his victims. They are then washed ashore at a place of his choosing."

"Which, if he's a potions master as you suspect by the paraphernalia in his workshop," Coral's grandmother continued, "means he must be casting a potion into the water to freeze the Mer as well as potion that controls the flow of water to bring the frozen body to shore. Otherwise they'd be strong enough to fight it."

"So, in theory," Dorothy went on, "if we can find out where he's likely to cast from next we could get there first and stop him when he tries."

"How would we find out?" asked Sam. "There's no way of knowing."

"Maud might be able to find something," said Coral's grandmother. "If not, it's not the end of the world. He keeps them around for a few days before finally," she ran her finger across her throat, "so if we can't do preventative measures we can at least move in after and stop him then."

"Except," Dorothy went on, "he is almost immune to Lilly's powers, magically one assumes, and working with some unknown invisible apprentice."

"He wasn't invisible when he attacked me," Lilly said, nervous to be interrupting the women's flow.

"You saw him?" asked Coral in surprise.

Lilly nodded, as around the room faces gawped at her. "Yeah, I did."

"You didn't mention this before!" stated Coral's grandmother, eyebrows raised.

"I forgot," said Lilly, picking at her thumbnail. "It was so fast and so much has been going on. But I saw him."

"What did you see?" asked Sam.

"Not a lot," Lilly admitted. "I was standing over the Harvester hitting him with everything I had, and I was weak and dizzy and losing strength, then I heard a noise so I looked up and I saw someone behind me reflected in the mermaid tank."

"Who?" Sam asked.

"I don't know," admitted Lilly, blushing. "It was hard to see, then when he stabbed me it took everything I had to get away. I think that's why I could only knock him out a little with the power I had left."

"Young or old?" Coral's grandmother asked, leaning forward and giving Lilly a look she recognised from her teachers when she failed to understand a maths problem. "Black, white, Asian? Tall or short? Fat or thin?"

"The more we know about him the more chance we have of finding him," explained Dorothy gently when Lilly started to look flustered. "Take your time. If we can find him then we should be able to take him out, leaving the Harvester more vulnerable. The Harvester is obviously the strength in the partnership, but this annoying little sidekick could cause problems if left unattended, and he did manage to hurt you."

Sam shuffled in his chair, wincing as he moved his leg. Coral put a hand on his arm and smiled reassuringly.

"Young," said Lilly, frowning and concentrating hard. She tried to picture everything she had been doing but the memory was hazy and hard to grasp. The stabbing pain and subsequent foggy agony, followed by blackness, was all she could seem to focus on properly. She remembered the way the Harvester had kept fighting, kept pushing himself up. She remembered how weak she had found herself growing the more she hit him with and the angrier she got. She remembered him falling back finally, his head slamming onto the corner of the tank and his fight stopping as he passed out before her. Then, as he stopped, how she'd stood up, finally able to breathe properly, and had seen the movement behind her. A reflection. Somebody. Young, male, tall. Dark hair. He'd been there for just a moment when she felt it; the stabbing, searing, agonising pain of the knife cutting into her as he reached round and pulled her close against his body and slammed the knife into her gut. "I hit him hard with my power," she went on, trying to focus. "But I didn't look, I didn't think to. I just blasted him with what I had left then got out. I couldn't walk, I don't even know how I crawled out. The pain was so… overwhelming."

On the chaise Saffron stirred. The deep sleep she was in giving way to a dream or stirring in her brain. The cat gently stepped onto the cushion beside her and sat down, her tail flicking.

"And that's what Saffron's feeling now?" asked Sam, his voice heavy with sadness.

"Yes," said Coral's grandmother in a matter of fact voice, barely looking at the boy. "So, what did he look like?"

"Young, taller than me, white and with brown hair," said Lilly. "But the ripples in the water, the reflection was messy and it was so fast then nothing. I can't remember anymore."

"So a tall, young white man with brown hair in Whitstable," grumbled Coral's grandmother. "That narrows it down."

"Hey Grandma," protested Coral. "She's trying, okay?"

"We need to gather the coven, Coral," said her grandmother. "Go about it, then we can start trying to figure out how to stop him."

ʒ

"A coven is six people with power," Coral explained to Lilly as they sat waiting whilst Sam sat silently at their side, listening with fascination.

"And they do magic?" Lilly asked, whispering, embarrassed about being so uneducated.

"Yes," Coral said. "You know how Saffron enhances your power? Well the coven is sort of like that. They are all connected to one another and their powers are heightened when they're together."

Lilly was taken aback when a stern faced woman arrived three minutes later and pointed at her with a bony finger the moment she stepped through the door. "You," she said abruptly, looking at Lilly. "I know you. And the girl on the couch!" she exclaimed. "Opal, you found her."

"Not without hindrance," Opal said, raising her eyebrows and nodding at Coral who shifted awkwardly. "But yes, the situation was fortunately rectified before too much damage could be done and we are back on the proper course."

"Foolish girl," said the woman, glaring at Coral. Then she turned to Lilly and held out a hand. "Maud Fennyman, I have Seen you and your friend coming to us."

"Lilly Prospero," said Lilly, trying to replicate the woman's formal tone. "And Saffron Jones is my friend. She was hurt."

"I see," said Maud, once again shooting an angry look at Coral. "I trust Dorothy was able to help?"

"Oh yes," Lilly said earnestly. "Thank you."

"Dorothy's power is quite spectacular," came another voice as a tiny Asian woman with a cane and a sharp look in her eyes appeared in the room. "I see you were right again, Maud."

"Of course," said Maud, in a way which Lilly took to be intended with pride, but came across almost defensively. "Mi, this is Lilly Prospero and that," she pointed to the unconscious Saffron with her hair cascading across the burgundy chaise, "is Saffron Jones."

"A pleasure to meet you," she said, holding out a hand that looked weak, but when Lilly took it was surprised to feel the firm confidence of her grip. "Is your friend recovering?"

"Yes, thank you," nodded Lilly nervously, feeling more and more self-conscious as the room filled with experienced and inquisitive women.

"And what is your power, young lady?" Mi asked her as she accepted a cup of tea from Dorothy, then leaned on her cane so she could hold the saucer and sip from the cup. "Are you perhaps a Seer? Or a Firestarter? Maybe a teleporter?"

"I'm the Ultimate Power," Lilly said, blushing and picking at her thumb nail.

"Ah, I have heard of you," said Mi, peering at her with interest in her keen eyes. "Fascinating. You've had some bother recently, yes?"

"Erm, yes," sad Lilly. This was the first time anyone here had reacted to her in the way she had grown accustomed to, and now she was unsettled by it.

"I, myself, am a Reader," she said. "We are rare, certainly, but not as rare as one such as yourself."

"What's a Reader?" Lilly asked.

"Something akin to a translator," Mi explained, then took a sip on the tea as she sat down in a chair, settling herself carefully with the support of her cane. "Any text, any language. I can Read it."

"Cool," said Lilly.

"It has certainly proven useful in our work," agreed Mi, smiling with satisfaction. "And I hope it will prove useful again soon, now that you're here."

Lilly wanted to ask what she was referring to but felt too shy, insecure of how inexperienced she appeared beside these well versed women of Power.

"Who are we waiting for?" asked Coral's grandmother who had been peering at the bookshelves.

"Iris," said Dorothy who had returned to Saffron and was again resting her hands against Saffron's pasty skin.

"Oh, she's always late," grumbled Coral's grandmother.

"Well we can't get started until she's here," said Mi standing back up and crossing the room before carefully lowering herself onto a seat near Saffron's chaise and pulling a book down from the shelf at her side. "So we may as well give her the time she needs."

"I thought you said six?" Lilly muttered under her breath to Coral. "Your grandmother, Dorothy, Maud, Mi and the one they're waiting for only makes five…"

"A round of applause for the girl who can count," came a spitting voice Lilly didn't recognise. She looked around in shock, wondering if the last coven member had been invisible and witnessing everything the entire time.

"Sylvie, she didn't know," said Coral, looking down.

Lilly looked and saw the tabby cat looking back at her. "Well, it's very arrogant to assume," the cat said, sticking her tail up and stalking away from them with her nose in the air.

"I'm sorry!" Lilly called out anxiously after the cat. "I should have thought! I'm not arrogant I swear! My rabbit was a Guardian, I know there are talking animals!"

"It's okay," said Coral quietly as the cat jumped onto a chair beside Mi and glared across the room at them. "She's always been bad tempered since I was a little girl, but she's getting angrier the older she gets."

"Well now that's taken care of, we just need to sit tight until Iris arrives," said Coral's grandmother.

"Can't we just make a start without Iris?" Coral asked. "The Harvester's going to be at it again soon and we don't want another mermaid lost!"

"Do you want to tell Iris that it was your idea to exclude her?" asked Sylvie, her long brown and black mottled tail flicking and her yellow eyes narrowing. "Tell her you find her time keeping unsatisfactory?"

Coral shook her head mutely, a nervous look on her face.

Silence descended. Sam put his arm gently around Coral's shoulders and she leaned into him, a look of calm settling over her face. Mi sat quietly reading the book she'd pulled from the shelf at an impressive speed, her eyes whizzing around fast in her face as she scanned the lines. Coral's grandmother shifted through jars and boxes, her face creased in concentration. Sylvie and Maud sat in the corner, whispering a secretive conversation between themselves and Dorothy sat still and quiet with Saffron, her earnest eyes full of concern.

In a room full of people Lilly didn't know if she could trust, and a situation she didn't feel fully sure she should be in and with the one person she felt completely safe in the company of unconscious, Dorothy felt like a centre of calm and she felt drawn to her side.

Standing up quietly, Lilly slipped away from Coral and Sam and joined Dorothy. The gentle faced woman was stroking Saffron's cheek tenderly and Lilly felt incredibly grateful to her. But could she trust her? She had trusted people enough in her life to know that the majority will betray you, sometimes in the most violent and cruel ways. Would this be the same?

"How is she?" she whispered.

"She's holding on, love," said Dorothy, looking up with a sad smile and putting a soft hand on Lilly's. Lilly felt soft, warmth from her skin that crept from her hand and up her arm, filling her chest with a gentle and soothing heat. She gasped. It was intense. "That's the Healers touch, my dear. I can't turn it off. But why should I want to is my figuring?"

Lilly held her hand to her chest, the warmth from the old woman's touch slowly fading, but leaving her with a lingering sense of peace.

"Right," came a bark from the doorway. "Let's get this show on the road!"

Lilly snapped out of her serene moment to see a small but fierce looking woman approaching. She was old, certainly, but moved like a young woman. Her hair was shaved short and dyed purple, her nose was pierced and she wore jeans and a black vest. Her arms looked strong beneath leathery, tanned skin and her movements were light and swift, but deliberate. Faded tattoos in plain black ink were visible on her shoulders, back and wrists.

"Hello, Iris," said Dorothy, smiling up.

"Coral, who's the man?" Iris demanded, rounding on Coral who sat bolt upright, knocking Sam's arm from her shoulders.

"Erm, Sam," Coral said, looking frantically from Iris to Sam and back again. "He's my friend."

"Hi," said Sam, waving then dropping his hand awkwardly, glancing at Coral for support.

"Out," Iris growled, pointing at the doorway with a straight arm and an angry face. "We don't permit men in here. This is a safe space."

"Sam *is* safe!" protested Coral angrily.

"When this is your decision to make, Coral, you'll be informed," said Iris, not lowering her hand from the dismissing point.

"Grandma!" Coral wailed.

"Listen to Iris," said Coral's grandmother, not looking up from the spice pot she was sniffing.

"It's fine," Sam said quietly. "I'll go, I need to go and lie down anyway. Text me later, okay?"

"Yeah, okay," said Coral sniffily.

"Bye Lilly," said Sam. "I'm glad you're okay."

"You too," said Lilly, waving as Sam left.

"Coral, go and lock the shop door," instructed her grandmother as the women moved to gather into a circle. "Then we shall begin."

Chapter Eleven

Arriving for work in his uniform, Dougal Hogarth spotted a woman and a man sitting at a table in the hotel lobby and talking intently, both holding their phones and the woman frantically typing out a text.

"If Lilly doesn't come home tonight we'll just have to phone the police," insisted the man.

"Excuse me," Dougal said, approaching them.

They jumped and turned. The woman looked at him with a gaunt face and smeared mascara round her eyes from where tears had escaped. "Yes?" she asked.

"Are you Lilly Prospero's mum?" he asked.

"Yes," she said, sliding down from the chair and stepping towards him, her hands out towards him with frantic desperation. "Do you know Lilly?"

"Oh, no ma'am, not really," he admitted. "But I have spoken to her and her friend before."

"Do you know where she is?" asked Lilly's dad, standing up and approaching him.

"Not exactly," he confessed. "But I saw her. She was very upset, ye know? She was upset because she'd disappointed you, not because she was hurt or anything."

"She's all right?" Lilly's mum asked, panic and relief mixed together on her face. "What was she doing?"

"Oh yes," he insisted. "She asked me to tell ye that she's fine, nothing's the matter and not to worry. They were just standing and having a chat, ye know? Totally fine as it seemed!"

"Where was she?" Lilly's dad asked, putting a hand heavily on Hogarth's shoulder, intensity in his eyes.

"Oh, just sitting on a bench on the high street," lied Dougal. "She and her friend there. She recognised my hotel uniform and asked me to pass on the message should I see ye. I said no bother at all."

"Were they with anyone else?" Lilly's mum asked, pulling out her phone and checking the screen. "Anyone you might have recognised maybe? Could you describe them? Are you local? Maybe you knew them?"

"No," said Dougal apologetically. "Not as I saw. But there's loads of kids round here and they all pal around with the tourists as much as each other. I worried me ma staying out with mates many a time growing up, I can assure you."

"Just palling around?" Lilly's mum cried, running her hands through her hair as Lilly's dad put an arm around her shoulders. "She wouldn't just pal around! She's a good girl! She's just a child!"

"She is a good girl, Alice," said Lilly's dad gently, his voice reassuring and kind. "She won't be doing anything wrong, you know that. And what were she and Saffron just saying about how they're grown up enough to do things on their own now?"

"I know!" Lilly's mum cried. "But she was wrong! She's out there with strangers and not even bothering to contact us!"

"Mr Hogarth, was there anything else you could get from her?" asked Lilly's dad.

"No, sir," said Hogarth, shaking his head. He felt quite bad about lying to them, they seemed so worried, but he wasn't about to change it. "But honestly, this is a great area. The kids are good kids and your girls seem like sensible young ladies. I'd be sure they'll be home in no time."

"Well, thank you Mr Hogarth," said Lilly's dad, putting a hand on his shoulder. "Thank you for taking the time to tell us. We're not happy about it, of course, but you've given us at least a degree of reassurance."

"Glad I could help," he said, smiling. And he meant it, but for his own reasons, not theirs.

ϡ

The five women, and one cat, sat on the floor together, circling the cauldron in the middle of the room. Lilly moved to stand beside Coral.

"They're going to connect now," Coral whispered to Lilly, who watched in fascination.

All six women raised their hands to those on either side, then simultaneously push their hands together. The room seemed to vibrate, an energy rushed around them and the women of the coven breathed deeply.

After a moment, Coral's grandmother said, "And now we are ready."

"What's the plan then?" demanded Iris. "Now Maud's girls have shown up, I assume we're going to war with this bastard?"

"Yes," said Coral's grandmother. "Effectively."

"Excellent," grinned Iris, rubbing her hands together with glee on her face. "So we know where he is and how to do it?"

"Not exactly," confessed Dorothy. "Lilly here is the Ultimate Power and she wasn't able to kill him. Weaken him, certainly, but not kill him."

"What could he be using to prevent that?" asked Mi. "Opal, are there potions that could combat a power such as Lilly's?"

"There are," said Coral's grandmother with a thoughtful nod. "But they are incredibly difficult to make, even for me. And most call for illegal ingredients. The wings of a pixie, a unicorn's horn, or, in our Harvester's case, the tail of a Mer."

"Sick," Coral muttered to Lilly.

"You wouldn't say that if the potion created were to save your life," said Coral's grandmother, turning on her with anger. "Indeed, Lilly here was saved by the Inoculance, a potion that uses Mer plasma. Would you prefer she had died?"

"Oh, I erm, no," said Coral awkwardly, her eyes shifting guiltily to Lilly.

"Speak not of what you understand so little then child," growled Coral's grandmother. "It's fine for you to hold those of us that use such products with contempt, but then you must be willing to turn down the help they can provide when it is offered, even when it is essential for your own survival. There are people who depend on these potions and they are dying because you are telling them their lives are not worth saving when you spout your ignorant propaganda."

Lilly felt sick. Would she have accepted the use of a potion that was made from mermaid blood had she known? When she had set herself to the task of preventing that blood from being acquired? When those it was taken from had pleaded her for help and expressed fear and disgust about how it is obtained in the first place? She picked at her thumb nail anxiously and realised that yes she would. In that moment when she was lying in the dirt outside the warehouse, terrified that those inside it would come out and finish the job at any moment, horrified by the fact she might die there in the dirt from her injuries even if they didn't, she would have accepted it without hesitation. She wasn't ready to die, but did that mean condemning other Beings to death to prevent it from happening? If that was true, what made her so different from the Harvester? She looked across at Coral nervously and saw a look of troubled anxiety on the girl's face that suggested her inner monologue was hammering away at her in an equally confusing and painful manner.

"Would this potion," Iris went on, seemingly oblivious to the tension that had settled on the room, "be protection against all death, or just a magical death?"

"Just a magical death," said Coral's grandmother. "There are legends, that I am sure you're aware of, for things one can create to prevent all deaths. They are, however, legends that are, as of yet, unproven. We can be fairly certain that he could be killed by mortal means. If we can weaken him to that point."

"So I can still rip his head off, even if I can't force choke him?" Iris asked.

"If we can get you close enough, have at it," agreed Coral's grandmother.

३

The Harvester carefully measured spoons filled with a valerian solution and tipped them into the simmering cauldron. This was the easy part of the freezing potion, but keeping the temperature completely correct, stirring it for the right amount of time, and casting it at the correct moment was the part that brought him out in a cold sweat. He picked up a tub of ground Schizandra and sprinkled just enough in to give his victim the strength to endure the physical trauma of being paralysed and washed ashore. He had forgotten that in the beginning and kicked himself when he realised why his catches were all dying from stress before they landed on the beach. Most annoying. A total waste of a good product. Of course, the tails and various other body parts had still made the endeavour worth his while, but so much more can be Harvested from a live Mer before the ultimate cut.

He pulled out his phone and quickly typed a message as he lowered the temperature of the burner below the freezing potion. "Updates?"

A few minutes later a reply came back. "Lilly with coven. Enhancer disabled. She's upset and vulnerable. Looks weakened."

"Good." He typed in reply. "Be ready at 9. We cast at 10."

"I'll be there."

ߺ

"Okay, what did you see?" demanded Iris, a stern look on her angular face as she leaned in towards Maud who sat at a table, her elbows up, and her eyes closed in a concentrating frown. Lilly felt herself respecting and fearing Iris in equal measure.

Maud opened her eyes and glared at Iris. "I can't be certain," she said, closing her eyes again in a frown.

"Of course not," growled Iris, slamming her fist on the table.

"Iris," said Mi, approaching her slowly and putting a hand on her tattooed arm. "Gentle now."

"Maud's Seeing hasn't been as strong recently," explained Coral in a hushed whisper to Lilly. "She used to be one of the best but she's losing her touch."

"That can happen?" Lilly asked.

Coral nodded. "Yeah, not to everyone but some people's powers weaken as their body does. Maud has cancer."

"Dorothy can't heal her?" Lilly asked, her eyes wide.

"No," said Coral. "She can lessen the pain but not everything has a magical fix. Or at least not an easy to do one."

Iris slammed a fist on the wall and stalked off. She landed heavily on a chair beside Dorothy who went to place a hand on her arm, but Iris flinched away glaring at her. "I'm quite attached to my anger, thank you."

"Ten o'clock!" Maud suddenly declared. "I heard the bells chime ten o'clock."

Coral's grandmother clapped her hands. "Lilly, now we need to sort out your job."

"My job?"

"You're the one we've been waiting for, correct?" she asked. "The one who can stop him."

"Erm, yes, I think so," said Lilly nervously.

"Then this will only work in your hands," she said firmly. "Coral neglected to take into account exactly how in depth our research and work has become to stop this awful man, and in turn didn't appreciate that you will need more than just your strength if you're to defeat him. We didn't know what power you had, but we knew you'd be strong. We knew he'd have counter measures in place. Maud has been extraordinary, given the circumstances, considering how much we've been able to prepare and research."

"Sorry," Coral muttered again, shuffling her feet.

"It's okay," said Lilly. "I get it."

"The potion I am going to create is powerful," Coral's grandmother went on. "And Mi will need to read the spell aloud whilst you work."

"What do I do?" asked Lilly nervously. She was never certain she had the strength to do what was needed, and had already been proven correct in that concern once against the Harvester. She wasn't eager to fail again.

"You will need to drink the potion right before you attack," Coral's grandmother explained. "Drink it then hit him hard."

"Saffron enhances me," Lilly said. "If that was going to work then it would have already worked!"

"It doesn't enhance you," Coral's grandmother explained, her dark eyes locked onto Lilly's without blinking. Lilly could sense just how strong this woman had been. "It changes you. The potion and the spell work together to adapt your power to a specifically targeted and focussed energy. Whatever he is doing and whatever his protection is, if you, and only you, take this potion you will be able to cut through his defences."

"But how?" asked Lilly anxiously.

"He is connected to the Mer on a deep and dark level," said Mi, standing up and approaching Lilly, her cane wobbling slightly with each step. "That connection is how he is able to do the wicked, wicked things he does. Your connection, the reason you are here right now and able to do something, is for the power of good. Good triumphs over evil. You must know that?" she said with a wink.

"I'll take out his little side kick first," said Iris. "And if it looks like he's weakened enough by your attack then I will gladly step in and take the final hit."

"We move out at nine," said Coral's grandmother. "Let's get to work."

ૃ

As Dougal Hogarth stepped out of the Dog And Doublet that evening, he lit a cigarette and casually blew a wisp of silvery smoke into the cool evening air. It was unusually dark for the season; the clouds were heavy above and a cool breeze was blowing in from the ocean and making the usually skimpily clad tourists pull their jackets around their shoulders and hurry from bar to bar with a sense of urgency. A drop of rain fell heavily onto his nose as he sucked on the cigarette and he glared up at the sky.

"Coming in?" asked an old friend, approaching from pub and spotting Dougal.

"Maybe," said Dougal, shrugging. In truth he had no intention of socialising that evening.

"Not ID'ing too readily tonight?" his friend asked.

"Nah," said Dougal. They were both a good few months shy of turning eighteen, but the pub was known for being lax on its age restrictions.

"Cool man," said his friend with a nod. "Might see you in there."

Across the road, Dougal Hogarth watched as Lilly Prospero, surrounded by a gaggle of elderly women, stepped out of the old antiques shop and began walking with a determined stride down the road. Raising his eyebrows, he flicked the cigarette into a bin, pulled his jacket up around his neck, and quietly followed them.

Chapter Twelve

"What are you doing?" whispered Lilly as she and Coral hid in the bus shelter, waiting to be called on. The glass vial with the carefully and meticulously constructed potion dangled around her neck on a cord.

"Texting Sam," said Coral, not looking up from where her thumbs were frantically moving over the screen of her phone.

"But Iris said not to do anything," hissed Lilly anxiously. She was too scared of the situation to even consider disobeying. The sky had darkened and the wind had picked up. Rain was beginning to lash across the road in front of them and the sea looked rough. Somewhere out there were mermaids, watching and waiting, terrified of being the next victim. Somewhere the Harvester was preparing to commit murder and she knew that her magic couldn't stop him. It was ominous and terrifying and, despite Iris's sharp tone and angry nature, Lilly found great comfort in the woman's competent air and had no desire to go against her will.

"I've not heard from him," she replied. "I'm worried."

Lilly nodded, she understood. She was worried about Saffron and would be texting her in a heartbeat, despite orders, if there was any chance she'd have been able to reply. Dorothy had assured her before they left that Saffron's sleep state was deep and comfortable, and that she was safe in the shop with Sylvie at her side. Lilly felt intensely guilty about leaving her but saw no other option.

"Who's that?" Coral suddenly whispered, looking up from her phone and pointing to where someone stood on the side of the road, peering down towards the waterfront. A young man, brown hair, average build.

"Oh my god," whispered Lilly. "Do you think that's him?"

"I don't know!" Coral whispered back. "What do we do?"

The man turned to the side and Lilly gasped. "Oh my god, it's Hogarth!" she hissed, pressing herself back into the shadows of the bus shelter. "Hogarth works for the Harvester! That's why he's always been lurking around! Oh my god, why didn't I see it?"

"Who's Hogarth?" asked Coral under her breath.

"He's some guy who works at the hotel," Lilly explained. "But he caught us the first night we went down to the beach. And he was there in the coffee shop when we first spoke to you. And he was outside the shop earlier. He's been following me!"

"Scumbag," Coral growled. "Where's he going?"

They watched as Hogarth hurried down to the beach and headed across the sand. "He must be going to cast the potion," Lilly whispered.

"Come on," said Coral. "We can stop him!"

"Us?" Lilly asked, panicked. "We can't! Iris said she'd do it!"

"Do you see Iris anywhere?" Coral asked. "This is our chance, Lilly! They think I'm useless, they think I can't do anything. We can prove them wrong right now! Stop this before it goes any further! Save those mermaids and leave the Harvester without his backup! That's what you want, right?"

"Erm," Lilly hesitated, craning to watch Hogarth disappearing behind some rocks on the shoreline.

"Isn't it?" insisted Coral, a pleading and desperate look in her eyes.

"Yes," Lilly said after a moment. "Let's go."

੩

"Is that Lilly?" Hexanna whispered, peering out across beach from the relative safety of the water.

"I don't know," said Brinly, peering to where her friend was looking. There was certainly someone approaching but why would Lilly be approaching alone? It wasn't Saffron, her mane of red hair was unmistakable, and it wasn't the Harvester because he was large and imposing.

"It must be," whispered Ashalia. "There must be news."

"Whoever it is, it's not moving like Lilly, I think it's a male," said Brinly. Beside her, Hexanna and Ashalia sank lower in the water, an instinctive fear of human males pushing them lower. Brinly stayed at the surface, peering out. "It could be that boy they told us about. The one who's working to help us."

"Brin," whispered Ashalia. "Don't you dare go over there."

"There could be news!" protested Brinly, turning to her friends. "Something could have happened to them. They could need our help."

"Brin, please," begged Hexanna. Her already pale skin looked ghostly white as fear took hold. "Please. We can't risk it! We can't trust them, you know that! Oberus told us who can help us, who wants to help us, and there was nothing about any men!"

"We cannot see all humans the same way!" insisted Brinly. "They make that mistake. They see us as one thing, not individuals with our own wants and needs. We're better than that. We have to try."

With that, she ducked under the surface and swam towards the shore, well aware she was doing so alone. Her friends would not follow this time.

ꝛ

Iris spotted the Harvester. He was standing back from the beach, hidden by the shadow of a building, but staring out to the ocean with a ferocious look on his face. There was no mistaking that he was the one they were looking for. But his assistant wasn't there. He must be moving in to cast the potions for his master.

Lowering herself against the rocks, she crab crawled her way in the dark determined to stop him herself. Despite supporting her coven's theory, she couldn't put the pressure of taking a man's life on a little girl. For her it was another man on the list of dangerous and evil men that needed removing, but for a child it was the start of a slippery slope. If she could stop a child falling down that path she knew she had to. No, she could do this. That man would go down and she would do it alone, just like she always had before.

Lilly and Coral stayed close together as they hurried after Hogarth.

"Can you kill him?" Coral whispered under her breath.

"I don't know," admitted Lilly, for a number of reasons. If Hogarth was protected by the same magic as the Harvester she couldn't stop him anyway. If he wasn't, could she kill someone who had only ever been nice to her? Someone who she actually quite liked? Of course, he hadn't only been nice to her, he had stabbed her in the gut and left her for dead in the dirt. Only she hadn't been dead. He could have finished her off with ease had he chosen to, she was weakened to a point of being incapable of fighting back. He could have sliced her throat or stabbed her in the heart. He showed her a degree of mercy by giving her a fighting chance for survival; could she end his life without offering the same? Could she really carry the weight of a premeditated murder? The deaths she had already caused continued to haunt her, and she had fully intended to kill the Harvester in the warehouse, but that had been self-defence. At that moment Hogarth was setting out to do no harm to her; could she really just sneak up and kill him? Just shoot him in the back, guilty without trial?

"You might have to," Coral insisted, cutting through the internal monologue that was ricocheting round in Lilly's brain, clouding her head with conflict and panic.

ζ

The Harvester watched down towards the seafront where his apprentice was casting the potions that would freeze their next Mer acquisition and bring it to shore at the right point. Hopeless though he often proved to be, The Harvester found himself developing a paternal pride towards the boy which he had always felt lacking. Finally, he seemed to be caring enough about their work to be really thinking. It was a mark of respect for their great heritage which had always been lacking. He nodded his approval as he saw the boy step back. The potion had been cast. It wouldn't be long now.

ζ

Iris moved round the back of a rock, her muscles twitching in anticipation. She could do this. Take him down so they could move forward with their work, and no need for the child to dirty her hands. The thrill of the hunt ran hot in her blood. It was what she was born for. It was what she breathed for. Her power may allow her to suck the oxygen from a man's body, but she was rarely dependent on that. She found more satisfaction in the physical strength she had built and maintained to ensure that even in the face of a magical power that could defeat her own, she would never again be the vulnerable and defenceless child she had once been.

ₐ

"Where's she going?" whispered Dorothy, watching as Iris reappeared, her wiry frame pressed closely to the rocks.

"She's spotted him," said Mi, observing their friend closely. "Look how she's hunting."

"But I thought the apprentice would be down at the shore," said Dorothy, feeling a deep sense of anxiety in her gut.

"Have you Seen anything, Maud?" asked Opal, putting a hand on her arm. Dorothy could hear the tone of Opal's voice softening from that which she usually used and felt grateful. However hard Opal worked to help their friends, the hours of research she had put into what potions she could create, the black market offerings she had sought, her bedside manner had always been painful to witness.

"No," said Maud, scowling and looking away abruptly. She was taking her weakening powers badly and lashing out at those around her, especially those she saw as strong.

Iris disappeared in the distance again. Dorothy sighed. The waiting was hard but at least the two girls were safe. They didn't need to witness this. When Iris brought the apprentice's body to them they could dispose of it quickly with Opal's Dissolution, then The Harvester would be far more vulnerable and Lilly and Mi could take him down. With him out of the way, their work could finally be completed and she could stop feeling like the failure she had been for the last sixteen years. Finally, the Healing she had longed to do could be achieved. Looking out towards the ocean, the moonlight dancing over the ripples of the waves, she wondered who was out there watching them, and who would be the one to save them.

ₐ

"Hello?" called Hogarth, peering out into the water.

"What's he doing?" whispered Lilly, confused. "Has he cast the potion already?"

"I don't know!" Coral hissed, squinting through the dim light. "Just blast him or something. Quickly!"

"He's not done anything yet!" insisted Lilly, hesitating but raising her hands ready. "If he does I will, but… but what if we're wrong?"

"Then do the half blast thing," suggested Coral. "Like you wanted to do on the Harvester. Knock him out."

Lilly dropped her hands. "He's not doing anything… it feels wrong to just attack unprovoked like this!"

"Hello?" Hogarth called out again.

Suddenly Lilly saw Brinly's head popup from the water. Her oil slick skin glistening, her eyes glowing white against the darkness. "Are you friends with Lilly and Saffron?" called the mermaid.

From the shadows up the beach, Lilly wanted to run forwards, wave her arms and stop Brinly coming any closer but she froze. The fear she felt around the Mer seemed to be holding her back, an icy chill running down her spine and acting as an anchor.

Hogarth stepped back, "Yes," he said, his head flicking nervously from side to side, before looking back towards the mermaid that was slowly swimming towards him, her shoulders now exposed. Her movements were creepy. She wasn't swimming with her arms, so appeared to be totally still and hovering through the water like a ghost. Lilly understood Hogarth's anxious appearance, it was one she herself shared.

"Oh my god," whispered Coral. She was transfixed. "That's a real mermaid isn't it."

"Yes, that's Brinly," whispered Lilly. "We need to get her away before something happens."

"Where are they?" Brinly called out to Hogarth, her chest now exposed, the water pulling back and forth and revealing the shells and seaweed that adorned Brinly's body.

Lilly shook off her fear and stepped out of the shadows. Brinly saw her and went to call out when she suddenly froze, her body locking rigid with her mouth still open in a silent cry. She sunk like a lead weight below the surface.

Hogarth stumbled backwards up the beach as Lilly ran forward.

"What did you do?" she shouted at him in rage, then ran straight past him and out into the water to try and catch Brinly's body before the magic current took her. She splashed around, feeling under the surface as the ice cold water bit into her flesh. There was nothing, she had already gone. "Brinly! Brinly!"

"Lilly!" called out Coral. "Stop him!"

Lilly turned and saw Hogarth scrambling away from her, turning to run up the beach. "Stop!" she shouted, holding her hands up. "You murderer!"

"Do it!" shouted Coral, trying to block Hogarth's path but looking terrified.

Lilly sent power at him and in a second his feet stopped running whilst his body kept propelling forwards and he landed face down in the sand with a painful thunk.

Chapter Thirteen

"Iris!" Maud suddenly cried, gripping Dorothy's hand. "He's got her!"

"What?" asked Opal, turning to stare at her. "What did you See?"

"Iris and the Harvester," she said, her eyes dizzying around inside her head. "He stabbed her."

"I'm going," said Dorothy, leaping to her feet and hurrying away in the direction she had seen Iris go before. She wasn't going to let Iris die. She would save her, then when they had stopped the Harvester she would save Maud and Sylvie. Nothing was going to get in her way now. Not now she was so close.

ᚱ

"Grandma!" Coral called out as she and Lilly dragged Hogarth's limp body up the beach. "Grandma, help!"

Lilly saw from the top of the beach the faces of Coral's grandmother, Maud and Mi turn towards them in surprise. "What have you girls been doing?" demanded Coral's grandma, hurrying forwards and helping Coral grip Hogarth's arm as they pulled him. "Who's that? Why didn't you stay put?"

"We caught him!" explained Coral, panting as they arrived where Maud and Mi waited and watched, and dropping Hogarth's arm onto the ground. "Well, Lilly did. But I helped!"

"That's the apprentice?" asked Maud, peering down at the boy who now lay in the sand at her feet.

"Yes," said Lilly, carefully putting his other arm down. "His name's Hogarth, he's been following me, and we saw him go down to the water. One of the mermaids was there and she froze and got caught in the current before I could get to her."

"Is he dead?" asked Mi, leaning over her cane to carefully inspect Hogarth's slack face.

"No," said Lilly. "But he's very unconscious."

"Well done," said Coral's grandma, nodding appreciatively to Lilly. "But we have a bit of a situation at hand right now. The Harvester found Iris before she found your friend Hogarth here. Dorothy's gone to save her so we are going to have to find the Harvester without Iris's assistance. We need to go now before he disappears with his latest victim."

"Lilly and I will get this under control," said Mi, giving Lilly a confident smile that made Lilly really want to prove that she could do this. "Opal, you and Coral stay with Maud and this Hogarth person."

"Is your potion ready?" asked Coral's grandmother.

Lilly pulled it out from under her top and showed her the glass vial. "Ready."

"Remember, as soon as you're ready to hit him, drink the potion then Mi will start reading," instructed Coral's grandmother. "Timing is essential and this could be our only chance."

Lilly nodded, her heart banging and her head pounding. "I can do it," she promised.

Together, she and Mi then turned and set off in the direction Iris and Maud had both gone.

ʒ

"Iris!" gasped Dorothy, rushing towards her friend where she lay in the sand against a rocky outcrop. "I'm here, my darling, I'm here."

She carefully crouched down beside her friend and put her hands tenderly on the oozing bloody wound that was torn into her side. She hummed quietly, feeling the healing warmth spread through her arms and fingertips, then surge into the woman's body. Behind her she heard a crunch as a heavy foot landed on some pebbles, and turned in panic.

"The healer," said the man's voice as he loomed large over her. "Well we can't have that, can we."

At her side, Iris started to cough, Dorothy's hands still against her as her touch began to repair the wound that was threatening to end her life.

"Don't come any closer," said Dorothy, sternly. She was no fighter, but she knew her team wouldn't be far behind her. They were never far from one another when danger was around. "You'll regret it if you hurt me."

"Oh, I have no intention of hurting you," he said with an empty laugh that made Dorothy's usually warm skin chill with an unnaturally clammy cold. "But he does."

"What?" asked Dorothy, then felt hands around her throat and a sharp blade against her throat.

ヲ

"Keep quiet," whispered Mi, as she carefully tried to stop her cane from making too much noise, and tried to keep her feet from shuffling too audibly, lifting them with care.

"I'm trying," Lilly assured her, slipping a supportive arm under Mi's own to offer the woman additional support as the sand moved beneath their feet.

Lilly felt like her skin was prickling all over, her ears hearing every sound from the water to the wind, the cars far up on the road to the crackle of a faulty street light further ahead. Then they heard the voices.

"That was Dorothy," hissed Mi, rooting around in her handbag that hung at her side and pulling out a book with a red fabric marker hanging inside. "He's here. Are you ready?"

"I'm ready," Lilly promised, her other hand gripping the glass vial with her thumb poised to flick out the cap when they found him.

ᚱ

"Load her up," the Harvester instructed, his foot kicking at the mermaid's body that was lying on the ground next to him, sand and dirt crusted in her hair and scales. "I'll get rid of these."

"No problem," said Sam, stepping round the bodies of the women. He looked down momentarily at Dorothy's eyes, glassy and dull, and felt a pang in his heart. She had been so kind to him and was always so kind to Coral. He suspected if he had been looking her in the eye he would never have been able to kill her. "I'll see you at the truck."

Putting his hands under the mermaid's armpits, he began to drag her with far less ease than the Harvester himself had pulled her from the water, but slowly she moved through the sand and up away to the road. He wondered if he would ever stop finding these creatures with their long fingers, weird faces and strange skin creepy. He suspected not, but he felt the same about spiders and eels. Some animals were just not nice to be around.

ᚱ

"There!" whispered Lilly, spotting the man's silhouette. "Are you ready?"

"For this?" replied Mi, fixing her with a piercing gaze. "Absolutely."

They approached the man and Lilly quickly flicked the cap out of the potion and drank it down in a shot. It was thick like syrup with a vague fizz and tasted of peppermint and shoe polish. She grimaced but made sure it was all down, then held her hands up.

At her side, Mi began reading in a language Lilly had never heard. Her eyes flicked to the symbols in the book but they were just shapes and squiggles, nothing even vaguely familiar. She was impressed.

"Lilly," said the Harvester with a cruel laugh. "Your healer is dead, your fighter is dead. You already know you're not strong enough."

Lilly ignored his taunt and blasted him. "Die!" she shouted, hitting him with everything she had.

The Harvester stumbled on the spot but stayed up and laughed again. "A little girl and an old woman with a book," he said, staggering slightly and looking dazed. "Against me."

He began to move forward. Lilly felt her body start to shake. At her side Mi's voice got louder as her chanting speech became more fervent, a note of panic in her voice.

"Die!" Lilly cried, but it came out like a pleading begging sound that made her hate herself. "Die!"

"Give up, Lilly," he said. He looked tired, the fight for keeping upright was obviously hard but he managed and he kept moving. His body shook with the effort but his eyes held a look of such steely determination that Lilly knew he was right. She couldn't stop him. It wasn't going to work. She wasn't the One, she was going to die here on the beach with strangers, whilst Saffron died alone in the shop, and nothing would stop it.

"It's not going to work," Lilly sobbed, her arms shaking with the effort, her eyes streaming with tears of despair.

"Have you nothing else?" begged Mi, stopping her reading and turning to Lilly, putting a frail hand on her arm and looking at her with pleading eyes. "Anything?"

Lilly thought about it as the Harvester kept moving towards her, his body leaning into the invisible wall of pain and resistance that Lilly was throwing between them, strong enough to slow him down but definitely not stop him. She could make life but couldn't see what good it would do. But as taking life wasn't doing any good either, perhaps that was the only option she had. But she had never made a life without drawing before, unless Saffron was there to enhance her. And what life would she make anyway? What could possibly stop him?

"I don't know!" Lilly whispered, frantically searching her brain for an answer.

"He's weak," said Mi, quietly. If we can distract him then we can at least get away. It won't solve anything but we can regroup and figure this out again. Dead we can do nothing."

Lilly nodded and forced herself to think. She would have to do it alone without drawing the animal first, without Saffron, and whilst this murderous man tried to reach her. Her heart banged and she held her hands high. She could do it. She fought through the pain and the tiredness that consumed her body and focussed hard on the Harvester's cruel face. He went to laugh but stumbled on a rock in front of him and fell to his knees.

Lilly took the moment and thought hard, put every bit of energy she had left, and slowly, but surely, a large, bushy black Newfoundland dog began to take shape before them. Lilly could hardly breathe from the effort, her mind was clouding over, but sure enough the dog was coming into existence.

"Help us," Lilly begged the creature as she fell to her knees, just as The Harvester was pulling himself up from his own.

"I'll get him!" said the dog, bounding up and down on his paws then racing face first at the surprised Harvester, who fell back with the weight of the enormous dog landing on his chest.

"That was spectacular," gasped Mi, reaching down to Lilly as her cane wobbled from the effort. "But we need to go, right now."

"We can't leave him," whimpered Lilly, staggering to her feet.

"We can't kill him!" said Mi. "Come on, we'll find a way. But for now we must leave."

"Not him!" protested Lilly. "My dog!"

"He'll find us," Mi reassured her. "Come on, let's go!"

Weak and tired, they ran from the scene. Passing by the fallen bodies of Iris and Dorothy, Mi let out a sob of agony but kept going. Lilly felt her head spin but pushed forward.

Lilly spotted Coral and called out to her, her voice weak and tired. "We need to leave," she wept. "Now!"

"What happened?" asked Coral's grandmother, hurrying forwards and taking over from Mi to help support Lilly. Lilly fell against the old woman's body, her legs nearly giving way beneath her.

"It didn't work," said Mi, hobbling forward on her stick with urgency. "He's slowed down but alive. We need to get out of here before he regains his strength."

"Iris and Dorothy?" she asked.

"Dead," said Mi bitterly.

Coral let out a gasp and covered her mouth in shock.

"Coral, are you able to carry the boy?" asked her grandmother, turning to her.

"On my own?" asked Coral in disbelief, looking at Hogarth's body. "No!"

"Then wake him up and make him walk," she replied. "But make sure he knows we can all kill him, and if he tries to escape we will."

"Please," begged Lilly, fear oozing out of everything she had. "We have to leave."

Coral hesitated then stood over Hogarth's body and slapped him ferociously across the face. No response. She tried again and a vague grunt came from the boy's mouth. "Wake up, you douchebag," she snarled at him, then smacked him again.

Hogarth's eyes flickered open and he looked around in panic. "What's going on?" he muttered, lifting a hand and rubbing his head.

"Get up," instructed Coral. "You're coming with us. If you try anything, we'll kill you."

Hogarth pushed himself to his feet and looked at Lilly in surprise. "Lilly? What's happening?" He was weak on is feet, visibly wobbling.

"Let's go," said Coral's grandma. "Maud, if you See anything at all yell. We can't afford to lose anyone else."

As quickly as they could, the peculiar party made its way from the beach. Coral and Maud either side of Hogarth, frog marching him with venom on their faces, with Mi and Coral's grandmother supporting Lilly ahead. The only sound they heard that disturbed the normality of the evening around them was the occasionally booming bark noise that emanated from the beach behind them. Lilly desperately hoped the dog would be all right. If another life she was responsible for died in her name she could never forgive herself. Death seemed to surround her, follow her, and delight in teasing her with its power.

Chapter Fourteen

Lilly watched in sombre silence with Coral sat at her side, tears rolling down her face, as Coral's grandmother knelt in a circle with Maud, Mi and Sylvie the cat.

"We will never forget you, brave warriors," said Coral's grandmother, her voice breaking and her lip quivering. Mi's chest heaved in agonised silent sobs as she spoke, Maud stared ahead into the distance as though she could neither see nor hear the people around her, and Sylvie's fur was dampened by droplets of sadness that cascaded from her yellow eyes. "You are our sisters, our friends, our loves. This isn't the end for you, someday we shall meet again. Until then you live on through us, through our power and our work. We will complete what this mission set out to do. You have not given yourselves for nothing, lives will be saved because of your sacrifice."

Maud suddenly collapsed in a heap on the floor, gut wrenching sobs heaving her body. "Oh darling, Maud," whispered Mi, stroking her hair. "It's not your fault."

"It is," wept Maud, her usually neat grey hair messy, her tweed skirt rucked up and her face broken in pain. "If it wasn't for me, none of this would have happened. We'd never have taken him on."

"May I remind you," said Sylvie, her voice clear and proud from such a small body. "That this whole thing started because of me. Because of this wretched curse."

Lilly frowned. A curse? She was confused. She thought this had happened because they wanted to stop the Harvester and get a connection with the Mer to acquire donations of hair and saliva. What wasn't she being told? She glanced over to where Saffron lay sleeping soundly on the chaise, her red hair a tangle around her head and her face so pale. Without Dorothy's healing touch would she feel unnecessary pain? For what cause had she been hurt? If stopping the Harvester wasn't the purpose, if saving the lives of the innocent mermaids wasn't why they were there, what was it? She glanced at Coral and saw confusion mirrored on her own face.

"Ladies," said Coral's grandmother. Though her voice was quiet, the room fell immediately silent to accommodate it. "Nobody here is to blame but the perpetrator of these hideous crimes themselves. Nobody. Sylvie, you did not ask for this curse. Maud, you did not ask for the cancer. The Harvester and his cowardly apprentice who currently lies in our closet sobbing like a child committed these crimes against Iris and Dorothy, and they committed them against the Mer people. It was not you, and it was not I."

"Opal is right," said Mi as Maud sat up and allowed her hand to be taken in Mi's. "No matter what you said or did, no matter where you were or what you were doing, neither of you is accountable for this man's crimes. He is to blame for these deaths, not us. He chose this path, we did not force him down it."

Silently Maud nodded, a look of gratitude on a face Lilly remembered as so severe. Sylvie curled her tail around her body and narrowed her eyes.

"Erm…" Lilly said, raising her hand like she was back in school and then blushing about it. "I've a couple of questions…"

Coral's grandmother turned to her, fixing her with a piercing stare. "Yes?"

"Well, erm," she said then gulped. The four women stared at her and she began to feel uneasy. Did they in fact blame her? Had she somehow done her job wrongly? Had Mi blamed her? "It's just…"

"Spit it out," instructed Sylvie. "We have too much at stake here and too much to get done."

"What curse?" Lilly asked quickly. "What are we trying to stop the Harvester for really? And why didn't it work? It made no difference having Mi read and me drink the potion. And will Saffron be okay now Dorothy is… erm… gone?"

Coral's grandmother stood carefully to her feet, her body seeming to creak with the effort of standing but her face full of determination not to let it stop her. "You have arrived at the end of a sixteen year quest, Lilly Prospero," she said, her voice dark. "And we had hoped you were what would finally win our battle. The special girl with the unique connection to the Mer who would harness that to defeat he who threatens them, and provide us with the opportunity to save our sisters."

"What sixteen year quest?" asked Coral. "Why don't I know anything about this? It's been going on my whole life!"

"Perhaps this can wait," suggested Mi. "We have a prisoner to interrogate and a girl to wake up. For now, just know we are running out of ideas and have a dangerous man to stop, who most firmly has us on his radar."

"No," said Lilly, shaking her head and crossing her arms, trying to appear more confident than she really was. "I can't be lied to anymore. I will not help you anymore unless you tell me the truth. What's going on?"

"I'm not convinced you can help us anyway, child," growled Coral's grandmother. "As you say, it didn't work."

Sylvie stood, her head dropping and her tail flicking slightly at the tip. "They deserve to know," she said, her yellow eyes looking to the floor. "If we are going to do this without Iris and Dorothy at our sides, we will need all the help we can get. Or their deaths are for nothing and I am lost."

"Very well," agreed Coral's grandmother. "Sit down, girls. We will tell you everything, but then we deal with the boy in the closet and try to reformulate a plan."

Lilly and Coral sat together and watched as the three women and cat looked at each other anxiously. Lilly had the feeling that a weight was being carried that needed unburdening, though doing so was a challenge in itself.

"I was cursed," Sylvie said after a moment. "Not long before you were born, Coral. As you know, your mother was in love with a man who..." she hesitated, looking up to Coral's grandmother.

"Your father was a cruel man and he treated your mother like dirt," Coral's grandmother went on, bitterly. "He was strong and respected in the community, so your mother felt she had nowhere to go. Nobody would believe her. He sat on a board at The Commission and was involved in the passing of laws."

"I didn't know that," whispered Coral, looking at her feet. "I didn't know anything about him."

"When you were born, your mother started to stand up to him," Coral's grandmother went on. "To protect you. When she realised she couldn't, she finally came to me." Suddenly her face fell and tears began to fill her eyes. "My darling Pearl. She was as head strong and obstinate as you are my dear, despite her fear of your father. It took her a very long time to admit to me that marrying him was a mistake. She couldn't tell me what he was doing and so suffered at his hand to preserve her pride. I could have helped her! And maybe things would be different now... but I just didn't know."

"I offered to watch him," explained Sylvie. "Whilst The Commission would never step in on a domestic charge, there are people who will. But for someone as revered as Alfonso Rattray, nobody would do a thing without evidence."

"Sylvie wasn't always a cat," said Coral's grandmother. "She was a woman, like us, but a shape shifter."

"I shifted into the body of a cat to watch," Sylvie went on. "I am comfortable in this form, confident. I knew I could control the body with ease, and cats wandering through gardens and sitting on windowsills never attract attention. But… one day he saw your mother speak to me. He had shaken you, then attacked her, and she begged me to go for help…" her ears flattened to her head and Lilly felt herself gulp. At her side Coral began to shake, her fingers frantically knitting together. "He was a Speaker. Do you know what one of those is?"

"Yes," said Lilly, remembering her encounters with Tereska the Speaker just a couple of weeks earlier.

"He cursed me," Sylvie went on. "I was trapped as a cat. As an UnBeing I would never be given the respect of being heard as a witness in your mother's defence. He could have killed me but I think he enjoyed watching the realisation on your mother's face… right before… I ran. I ran here to gather Opal and Iris to come to her aid but by the time we got there your mother was already…"

At Lilly's side Coral broke down into tears, her head dropping into her hands as her shoulders heaved. Lilly gently put an arm around her.

"Iris killed him," Coral's grandmother went on. "We removed the evidence of both deaths with the Dissolution and reported that you had been left to my charge. There were questions, but I think his colleagues were aware of his lack of interest in fatherhood. After a time, it was decided he had simply decided he didn't care for parenthood anymore and had taken your mother to start over without you. His choice to leave was respected, your mother's to accompany him less so, and the questions stopped. I raised you from that moment."

"How could you never tell me this?" wept Coral.

"I wanted to protect you," said her grandmother, holding her chin up. "You should not be exposed to the dangers of this world. My darling Pearl died to protect you. I will keep you safe under my care for as long as I am alive!"

"But why the Harvester?" Lilly pressed. "I don't understand what this has to do with me, with this fight."

"There is an antidote," Sylvie explained. "It's complex to make, and requires black market produce. We tried for years to acquire some but, unfortunately, as a group of elderly women, and one cat, we do not hold quite the same respect as we used to. Getting hold of black market products is hard and competitive, and often requires a display of strength and loyalty, assurance that you will not turn the seller in and are truly who you say you are. We tried to make contact with the Mer ourselves, but few are willing to donate, and most avoid humans like the plague. Especially considering what we wanted to ask for."

"When this new Harvester appeared on the scene our chances of contacting the Mer fell even further," Coral's grandmother went on. "Already suspicious of humans, this would drive them further from us even if we were able to find a way to magically communicate with them. We attempted to buy from him directly, but were met with the same barriers. We are women, we are old. He ignored every effort we made."

"So what could would killing him do?" asked Lilly. "And what is it you need?"

"Debt," said Coral quietly at her side. "You want to put the Mer into debt to you, so they donate what you want. And Lilly and her connection to them is how you can make that happen. Right?"

"Yes," replied her grandmother. "We need blood and scales. We need flesh."

"Flesh?" asked Lilly, screwing her face up in disgust.

"Yes," agreed Sylvie. "And, if the old texts are right, flesh could kill off Maud's cancer. Mer do not get cancers. Something in their tissue prevents the degradation of cells that allows cancer to take hold."

"I will not ask them to do that!" insisted Lilly, standing up. "I will fight the Harvester, I will help you in any way I can, but I am not going to get one of those mermaids to chop out a chunk of flesh! That's sick! Just stay as a cat! What right do you have to a human body more than they have to their own bodies! Why do you think you're worth more? They were right! We are a horrible, privileged, self-serving species! We are not worth more than them just because they're different from us! I won't do it!"

"Sit down, child," snarled Sylvie. "This is not about craving a human body, however much I do. I am a cat. I have been a cat for sixteen years and I do not have long left. This body is aging fast, it is weak and it is frail. I will soon die if I do not get the antidote. This isn't about a human form in exchange for flesh, it's about my entire life. What makes you think that my life is worth so little?"

"But you're old anyway," said Lilly quietly, picking at her thumb. "I mean I understand you don't want to die, but is it really worth mutilating an innocent mermaid just for a couple of extra years?"

"I have grandchildren you know," Sylvie said, sitting down and staring hard at Lilly, her tail coiled round her, flicking slightly. "I have never held them. I have never even met them. My son doesn't know what happened to me. I vanished. I cannot be a mother, a grandmother, when I am like this. I cannot give them cuddles when they're sad, I cannot wipe their tears, I cannot give them support when they're struggling. I am a cat and I will not let my family see me in my shame. For a couple of extra years of life, perhaps it is not worth it. For the chance to be the woman I once was for one last time, to be with my family for however long I get, to hold them, to stroke the hair on my granddaughter's head, to tell my grandson his paintings are miraculous, to promise my beautiful son that his mother did not abandon him… for one last chance at a life I gave up to save Coral's own… yes it is worth it. For one minute with my family it would be worth it, for years… for years it is worth it a thousand times."

Lilly sat back down, a knot wriggling in her gut. She didn't know what to do. She didn't know what to say. She didn't even know what to think.

As Coral's grandmother opened her mouth to speak, a sudden banging sounded deafeningly loud on the front door to the shop.

"Who's that?" whispered Coral.

"I don't know," said her grandmother, a stern look settling over her face. She picked up a glass jar from the top of a bookcase then headed for the door. "Stay behind me child."

Chapter Fifteen

Brinly's eyes flickered open, the bright light of the warehouse making her eyes burn and trickle salty tears. "Hello?" she called out, her voice cracking as the dryness of her throat scoured her flesh.

As her vision began to swim into focus, she spotted a young man watching her curiously. "Hello," he said.

"Sam!" came a voice from the back of the room. "Get on with it!"

Sam looked round to the back of the room to a shadowy area that Brinly couldn't yet focus on. "I'm going, I'm going," he muttered, rolling his eyes as he turned back to Brinly.

"Help me?" she whispered, a pleading in her voice that she was ashamed of. "Please?"

"Can't," he said, Brinly detected a note of regret in his voice as his eyes flicked momentarily away from her own.

"Sam!" came the voice again.

"Alright, dad!" he groaned, then turned away and walked out of the warehouse, picking up a large clanking bag on his way.

"Sam!" Brinly called out, desperately trying to reach him, sensing something in the boy that she might be able to connect with, some hope that he could help her.

The door shut and the man's voice came again from the back of the room. "Don't strain yourself, Mer. Your vocal chords are worth good money."

As her vision cleared, Brinly saw a large man sitting on a chair. His clothes were shredded and a bloody mess was on the side of his arm as he carefully bandaged himself. "They'll stop you, you know," she said. "They're stronger than you."

He laughed, stopping his work on his arm and turning to her properly. "You still believe that?"

"Of course," she said.

"They've already tried, and failed twice," he said with a smirk. "Give up now, Mer. The less you fight the less it will hurt."

"They'll come for you," she said. She was chained and trapped, suspended in a watery coffin, and with no idea how she'd get out. But she would get out. They would come. "They will stop you."

₹

The banging came again as they tiptoed through the shop, past the counter and towards the door. The darkness outside was heavy now and the silver light of the moon crept through the grubby glass, silhouetting the old furniture and ornaments in creepy shadows. Lilly felt her heart banging and her palms sweating. If it was the Harvester come for vengeance she couldn't stop him and they would all die. It would have all been for nothing. She would die trying to save everyone, and they would all die because she would fail.

The banging came again, then a voice called out, "Hello? Hello in there? Lilly?"

"Who is it?" called Coral's grandmother as they stood before the closed door, the air heavy with tension, every hair on Lilly's arms standing on end.

"It's Bentley!" came the voice, deep and powerful. "Lilly! Lilly it's Bentley! Are you there?"

Everyone turned to stare at Lilly who stood in the centre of the tiny crowded shop and felt panicked. "I don't know a Bentley!" she said, looking around with wide eyes. "I swear!"

"Lilly, let me in!" came the voice more insistently. "I stopped him for you but he got away. He hurt my legs. I tried, Lilly, I tried. I'm so sorry."

"Oh my god!" cried Lilly, rushing past Coral's grandmother and quickly unlocking and opening the door.

"Lilly!" cried the enormous, black, Newfoundland dog that stood on the step outside. "It's me!"

He stood at half her height or more, his thick black fur fluffy and soft, his large brown eyes soft and kind. He held his front paw high in an awkward limp and was sagging on his left hip, struggling to maintain the weight of his own flesh.

"I'm so sorry," she whispered, hanging her head in shame. She'd forgotten. She'd created a life and it meant so little to her that she had been completely distracted by everything they were doing that she had forgotten it. But he hadn't forgotten her. He had been loyal to her to the point of being hurt, and then come to find her to apologise. "Come in, please come in."

"Thank you," he said, nodding his enormous head in gratitude then hobbling into the shop, struggling to balance on his two good legs as his back one dragged, barely offering any balance, and his front one he couldn't even put down.

"Erm…" came Coral's grandmother's voice from behind them as the dog shuffled into the room filling the last remaining inches of the shop that were free. "What?"

"This young man saved our lives on the beach," came Mi's voice from somewhere behind Coral's grandmother. Lilly wasn't sure where, the room was so full and Mi was so tiny, but she was pleased to hear her voice.

"I made him," said Lilly. "And he's hurt. Can we get him through where he can lie down?"

Everyone stepped back into the room and Bentley dragged his wounded body through before lying down in a heap on the floor by the cauldron. "I slowed him down," he said, looking up at the room of people, most with faces that looked completely astounded though he didn't seem to notice. "But he had a knife. I'm afraid he got away from me."

Lilly crouched at his side and stroked the thick black fur on his face, astounded by the size of his skull in comparison to her hand. She could have buried her whole arm in the fluff on his side.

"Lilly?" enquired Coral's grandmother. "Would you like to explain?"

"Can we heal him?" Lilly asked, ignoring the question. "I mean… I know… I know Dorothy is…" she paused, her eyes dropping.

"Perhaps not heal," said Mi, stepping forward, peering at the dog closely. "But I'm sure Opal will have something that can soothe him."

"Well I don't know," said Coral's grandmother, huffily. "Our stocks are low and these things are difficult to create. I'm not sure wasting a valuable potion on a dog is a good idea! Especially now Dorothy is no longer…"

"Wasting?" asked Lilly, standing up and turning on her furiously. "Wasting? If it wasn't for Bentley then Mi and I would not have made it away! The Harvester would have taken us down as well!"

"I realise that," muttered Coral's grandmother, holding her head high. "But still, it's just a dog. A good dog, of course, but a dog."

"And his life is worth less?" demanded Lilly, anger bubbling in her chest.

"Opal," said Mi, putting a gentle hand on the woman's arm. "Lilly created this dog to save my life, and her own. Without him The Harvester would win and we wouldn't be able to save either Maud or Sylvie, let alone stop him in the future. He is alive and any life deserves respect, even if it looks different from our own."

"I agree," said Coral.

Sylvie nodded her ginger face, eyeing the enormous dog out of the corners of her eyes. "As do I. Assuming the enormous thing doesn't decide to chase cats any time soon of course."

Coral's grandmother stared Lilly in the eyes for a moment then nodded and walked to a set of shelves at the back of the room, rummaged for a moment then returned with glass bottle containing a purple liquid. "This is Dulcification. It will not heal you nor will it stop the pain, but it will make it easier to cope with."

"Thank you," said Bentley gratefully, holding his head up. Coral's grandmother crouched down carefully then lowered herself onto her knees, tipping the glass bottle into Bentley's mouth as he slurped it down, his long tongue scooping out and swishing round his face to make sure he didn't miss any drop.

"How do you feel now?" Lilly asked him, stroking his head tenderly.

"Weak, but alright," acknowledged the dog.

"It'll take time to sink in," said Coral's grandmother. "And we have business to attend to."

"Come and lie near Saffron," suggested Lilly, helping the dog to his feet as best she could, though the solid weight of him was beyond her physical strength. He slowly hobbled his way to the corner of the room where Saffron still lay asleep, her skin pale and pallid with a clammy sheen as she seemed to suffer the lack of Dorothy's warmth.

"I will watch her for you," promised Bentley, looking up at Lilly earnestly.

Lilly watched him gingerly lie down on the floor in front of Saffron and then returned to where Coral and her grandmother, Maud, Mi and

Sylvie stood waiting. "Okay, ready to get him out?" she asked, nodding her head towards the shut closet door in the corner of the room.

"Ready," said Coral's grandmother with a severe look on his face. "And heaven help that boy if he gives us nothing."

The five women and cat approached the door, then Coral's grandmother stepped forward and turned the handle, pulling the door towards them.

Inside, Hogarth gazed out at them all with a look of terror on his face. His brown eyes were wide, his hair was a mess, and he had a bleeding gash to the side of his skull from where he had landed on a rock on the beach. Tape was wrapped several layers thick round his mouth, wrists and ankles and he looked, Lilly thought, like a classic kidnapping victim.

Lilly felt sick to her stomach. Now the immediate threat and the immediate fear had passed, the sight of this boy bound up like this, all his power stripped and totally vulnerable, did not sit right in her at all. She longed to free him, but knew she couldn't. For so many reasons. The threat he posed to them alone was enough to make sure she left him trapped. What was happening to Brinly right now? Whatever it was, he was partly to blame, and for that she could never forgive herself. He was in the right place, of that she was certain, but still, she wasn't happy to see him like that.

"Up," commanded Coral's grandmother. "Now."

Hogarth pushed himself up to his feet, leaning on the wall of the closet for support, a mop and broom falling against his head and onto the floor with a crash as he forced himself up. Awkwardly he hopped forwards, his body hunched as he tried to propel himself.

Behind her, Lilly saw Maud drag a chair over to the side of the cauldron. "Sit here, boy," she commanded.

They watched in silence, Sylvie's tail flicking, as Hogarth awkwardly manoeuvred himself towards the chair, then collapsed on it with an uncomfortable groan.

Much to Lilly's surprise, Mi pulled a small, silver blade from the side of her boot and approached Hogarth with it. Despite the cane and obviously frailty to the woman's body, there was a look in her eyes that made Lilly suspect that at one time she had been very adept with a weapon in those remarkably firm hands. Mi slid the knife under the tape, flat against Hogarth's cheek, then twisted it and pulled it out, slicing through the tape and leaving a red line on his skin which trickled blood.

"Lilly," Hogarth spluttered as Mi pulled the tape from around his face. "I don't know what's going on, but you've got to do something, you've got to let me go!"

Lilly turned away, her chest hurting too much to look at him. "Saffron's in a coma. I nearly died. Two women are dead. Mabli is dead and Brinly is captured. Why would I ever let you go?"

"Who?" asked Hogarth, his face riddled with panic. "People are dead? Who's Mabli? What's going on?"

Coral's grandmother issued a sharp strike across the boy's cheek and his head flung back with the impact. "Shut up, you lying rat," she spat.

Hogarth fell into silence, a red mark across his cheek and his eyes burning with tears. Lilly looked anxiously from Coral's grandmother to Hogarth. Then at Saffron's pale, broken body. The women of the coven stared at him intensely, none of them seemed to be struggling with this like Lilly was, but did that make them right and her wrong?

"Tell us how The Harvester fought resisted our spell," said Mi, pointing the knife close to his face.

"Who?" asked Hogarth, genuinely sounding bewildered.

Lilly started to get an unease in her gut. Was he the right guy? Was this an act or was he really completely ignorant to everything that was going on? Was this a total mistake and she was now to blame for an innocent boy being tortured?

"What were you doing down on the beach?" Lilly asked, stepping forward and putting herself between Mi's knife and Hogarth. She stared into his eyes, looking desperately for answers, any sign of honesty or deception she could cling to. He stared back at her, he looked afraid. "Why were you in the water?"

"I was looking for you," he said, looking away, embarrassed.

"But why?" she asked, cocking her head to the side.

"I... erm... I like you," he said, his eyes dropping. "Stuff seemed weird. You were being frog marched by these women. I guess I thought you might need help... I wanted to... help."

Coral pulled at Lilly's arm, "Lil," she hissed. "We saw him. We saw him in the water with the mermaid. Don't let him trick you."

"I know," Lilly said with a nervous nod, chewing on her lip and picking at her thumbnail. "It's just... It's just..."

"Lilly," Hogarth begged her. "Please!"

"I want to believe you!" Lilly insisted then turned to Coral's grandmother, imploring her. "Isn't there anything we can do to find out what's going on without hurting him? A potion? Anything? I know he's probably guilty, I really do, but we can't hurt him to find out or we're no better than the Harvester anyway!"

"Don't worry, we'll make him talk," said Coral's grandmother ominously, before rounding on Hogarth. "This is your last chance boy, tell us what we need to know or things are about to get a lot more unpleasant for you."

"I have nothing to tell!" Hogarth sobbed. "I swear!"

"Have it your way," snarled Coral's grandmother, pulling Hogarth up to his feet by his ear. "Back in the closet with you. You'll talk soon enough."

Chapter Sixteen

Lilly and Coral sat on the floor with Bentley, stroking his large, warm body and talking in hushed voices. Above them, still asleep on the chaise, Saffron lay sleeping; colour starting to come back to her cheeks and breathing sounding more natural and rhythmic. It was well into the early hours of the morning and the outside was dark and quiet, but Lilly knew that somewhere out there the Harvester was hard at work, no doubt furious at the abduction of his apprentice and plotting his vengeance for Bentley's attack. She hoped fervently that whatever deadline he was working too was far enough away that Brinly had a chance to be saved.

She wanted to sleep, knowing that what was ahead was going to require her to use both physical and mental energy if they had any hope of success, but she couldn't relax. Everything in her body felt tense and wired. She needed something to do. Sitting there watching the old women work, picturing Hogarth trapped in the closet, and having no outlet for the electricity that was surging through her body was driving her mad.

"We need to go down to speak to the Mer," Lilly whispered to Coral. "They need to know what's going on."

"Can I come with you?" Coral asked in a quiet voice.

"I will come too," said Bentley, looking up at them with his dark eyes full of concern. "I can protect you."

"You're still weak," said Lilly to the dog, shaking her head gently. "But thank you. You need to get well and look after Saffron for me. Me and Coral will be fine. Hogarth is trapped here and The Harvester will be too busy with Brinly to be down at the beach again already. We're safe."

"So I can come?" asked Coral eagerly.

"Yeah," said Lilly. "You're a part of this now and they might need to trust you. I don't know what's going to happen."

"Grandma," said Coral standing up, and approaching her grandmother who was hunched over her cauldron with a stern look on her face. She ignored her granddaughter. "Me and Lilly are going to go and talk to the mermaids."

Her face snapping round towards Coral, her grandmother looked at her with fascination as if she'd only just become aware of her presence. "Now?"

Lilly stood up, "We need to go now. Whilst it's still dark."

"Take Sylvie with you," said Coral's grandmother. "And ask them for some hair."

"What? No!" protested Lilly. "I don't want to overwhelm them with new people... animals... whatever. And I can't ask them for stuff!"

"You want the truth out of that boy?" asked Coral's grandmother, hands on her hips.

"Of course..." said Lilly, picking at her thumb nail.

"And quickly?"

"Yes..."

"Well if you want it fast, mermaid hair is the best option. I can substitute with arrow root but the process will take far longer and I don't know how much time we have until The Harvester has the strength back to come for us. Nor how long your friend Brinly has until he disposes of her."

"I'll get the hair," said Lilly with a painful sigh. She hated herself for it but Coral's grandmother was right, they didn't know how much time they had and however much it was, it wouldn't be a lot. And at least the potion would save Hogarth being put through anymore unnecessary pain. It needed to happen right now.

"If you need me," said Bentley, pushing himself to a sitting position. "I'll know."

Lilly thought back to when she and Saffron had both been on the brink of death just weeks earlier, and the animals she had previously created had sensed it and all shown up to save them. "I know," she said with a grateful nod. "Come on Coral, let's go."

ʒ

Sam pulled out his phone and sent a quick text to Coral. He had finished laying the potions around his father's workshop and was now tasked with monitoring the girl's progress. Just as his father was working hard and fast, they were certain Coral's gang of witches would be working equally hard.

"I fear they're not far off a suitable weapon," his father had said to him in a dark voice. "The Reader raises alarm bells. It could simply be they need the right words. They're obviously more prepared than we had anticipated."

Sam shuddered as he remembered how his father had appeared, broken and weak, raving about a huge black dog leaping out of nowhere and attacking him. At first he had thought his dad had lost the plot, gone mad from the attack he was under from Lilly, but as time went on and his father had calmed down and began to fix his wounds, the story hadn't changed. Things were happening beyond Sam's comprehension and he was afraid. He was scared of what would happen to him if the coven found out what he was doing, and he was scared of what would happen to Coral if his father decided she was too caught up in the attempts on his life. He was scared of what his father would do to him if somehow he failed. He was even scared of what would happen to the mermaid currently trapped inside. Try as he might he couldn't fully convince himself that what he was training to do was right, and Coral's insistence that it wasn't only made it harder to reconcile these doubts in his mind. But it was his duty, and his loyalty to his father that prevented him from fully breaking free of this life that he had been prepared for since infancy.

"We're going to the beach," came the reply from Coral. "We're meeting the mermaids."

"Can I come?" Sam texted back excitedly.

A few minutes passed then the reply came. "Lilly says yes. Meet us at the top in ten minutes."

Sam mentally high fived himself then, without telling his father where he was going, slipped out into the cold night air.

 R

"Ready?" asked Lilly to her two new friends.

"Yeah," enthused Coral with an excited look on her face.

"Let's do it!" said Sam, putting an arm around Coral and squeezing her tight.

Lilly remembered the impact meeting the mermaids had had on Saffron, how after weeks of seeming like she was drained of colour she had seemed to come alive. She wondered if she would have felt as excited by the idea of seeing the mermaids, like Coral and Sam, if she hadn't met them already by surprise. If she hadn't already found a shuddering chill creeping through her skin every time she looked into their eyes.

"I just hope they're looking out for us," said Lilly. "They might be in hiding since Brinly was taken."

She led them down onto the beach then they walked in silence across the sand and stones, their shoes scuffing beneath them and a cold breeze whipping through their hair. Ahead of them lay the ocean, its ink black water streaked with silvery white moonlight as the noise of endless miles of water shushed and echoed in the air.

"Are they there?" Coral whispered, her voice quiet and tense.

"Ashalia?" Lilly called out, stepping as close to the surf as she dared. "Hexanna?"

The sound of the water answered her. The three stood side by side staring out into the ocean, trying to spot anyone looking back.

"I can't see anyone," whispered Sam.

"It's Lilly," Lilly called out again. "Ashalia? Hexanna? Please, we need to talk to you!"

"Who are they?" came a voice as two eyes appeared out of the water, Ashalia's dark skin and hair barely visible against the water, but her bright white eyes watching intently, illuminated by the moon.

"This is Coral," said Lilly. "And this is Sam."

"Brinly's gone," came another voice as Hexanna appeared, her ghostly white face striking in contrast to her friend's.

"Oh my god," whispered Coral. "They're really here."

"We know," said Lilly, dropping her head. "I'm so sorry. We tried, we really tried."

"Where's Saffron?" asked Ashalia, looking across the beach and examining them.

"He hurt her," said Lilly, deciding not to go into details. "The Harvester hurt her, but she's okay. She's going to be okay."

"I'm sorry," said Hexanna. "But we still need to stop him, and we need to get Brinly back. She can't die like this. Not like this."

"We need your help," said Lilly. "We tried. We found a curse, a special curse. My power combined with a potion and with words read by a Reader were supposed to cut through whatever protection he has and stop him, but it didn't work. That's why he got Brinly. It should have worked but it didn't and we don't know why, and if we don't figure it out we won't be able to stop him."

"Your power?" asked Ashalia, frowning.

"Yes," said Lilly. "I'm so sorry, but is there anything else you can give us?"

"We might need to speak to the Ancients again," said Ashalia in a quiet voice, looking at Hexanna and chewing her lip. "What do you think?"

"I think Lord Bray might kill us if we go back," said Hexanna. "But I don't know if we have a choice."

"Ancients?" asked Sam. "What are Ancients?"

"Shush," whispered Ashalia hastily, casting a suspicious look over Sam. "We mustn't talk about this now. Especially not with him here. They'll kill us if the find out."

"We don't have much choice!" protested Hexanna. "We have to sort this out now! And they won't find out."

"But he can't be trusted," hissed Ashalia.

"Lilly trusts him," said Hexanna, eying Sam up and down. "And we need to trust Lilly."

Lilly didn't know what was going on, she didn't understand what they were talking about. She felt she ought to say something in Sam's defence, assure them he was a friend, but she was too frightened. She kept quiet, nervously watching the mermaid's having their whispered debate.

The two mermaids turned and stared at Sam, then moved silently and ghostlike through the water towards the shore. "Sam, is it?" asked Hexanna.

Sam hesitated and stepped back. Lilly didn't blame him. "Yes," he said, his breath fast.

"What do you know of the Mer, Sam?" asked Ashalia.

"I know… erm… you are… a species of… erm… Beings?" Sam stuttered, looking at Coral and Lilly desperately.

"Humans and Ancients regard us in similar ways," said Hexanna. "Like mongrels, neither one thing nor the other. Ancients are the origin of our species, they think of themselves as 'pure'. We are an adaptation of the Ancients, an evolution that occurred long before humans started to walk on the planet. But to the Ancients we are dragging the purity of the ocean through the mud of the land. Our blood too close to that of the humans, who they see as having even less value than us."

"I've never heard of them," said Coral in awe. "Has anybody?"

"No," said Ashalia. "And they want to keep it that way."

"They could end all of this if they wanted to," said Hexanna, tears rolling down her cheeks and splashing heavily into the water below her. "Easily. They could have stopped Brinly being taken. They could have stopped Mabli, Coler, Jadene and Attan being taken. They could have destroyed the Harvester and all who use his services. We wouldn't have had to come to you, nobody else would have had to be hurt. They could have stopped it all and they chose not to."

"Why?" asked Lilly.

"Because they don't care," said Ashalia, her voice full of pain. "Because they protect themselves and that's what matters."

"They sound powerful," said Sam, thoughtfully.

"Immeasurably," said Hexanna, staring at Sam with a look that made Lilly's skin crawl.

"We're going to keep trying," said Lilly, breaking the spell between Hexanna and Sam. "We captured the Harvester's apprentice. Coral's grandmother is making a potion that will make him tell us the truth. If we can find out what he's doing to block our magic, we might still be able to stop him."

"You captured him?" asked Sam, turning to Lilly in surprise.

"Yes," said Coral. "We caught him when Brinly was taken. He'll talk. My grandma will make him talk."

"But we need something," said Lilly, guilt in her gut. "To make the potion work more quickly."

"What?" asked Ashalia, swimming closer to Lilly and revealing her body and shimmering tail. Lilly tried to keep the chill that snagged in her blood from being revealed.

"Your hair," she said. "For the potion."

"Seriously?" asked Hexanna in disgust. "You're fighting to stop us being used as ingredients and then come to us for the same thing?"

"It's the best option we have," said Lilly, picking at her thumb and feeling wretched. "I'm so sorry. I don't know how long we've got, but the Harvester will be working fast and we need to beat him. At the minute we don't know how and getting answers from Hogarth could be our best option. I don't know what else to do."

Hexanna went to protest again, but Ashalia held up a hand to silence her. "You can have whatever you need. This is more important than my hair." Taking a hand up to her head, Ashalia took a clump of thick dark hair in her hand and ripped it from the side of her head. The ripping sound it made as it pulled from her scalp left Lilly feeling sick, but she stepped into the icy cold water and approached the mermaid to accept the offering. As their hands touched, the slick, oily skin of Ashalia brushed against her own dry skin, a sensation of ice creeping through her veins began crawling up her arm.

"Thank you," she stuttered, pulling her hand away quickly and hastily backing up out of the water, stumbling on rocks and hurrying back to Coral's side. "I, we, I'll do everything I can… we'll sort this…" she said, the horrible feeling still crawling further up and into the rest of her body, the place on her fingers where Ashalia had touched her felt clammy and wrong as if her fingers still lingered there.

"So will we," Hexanna promised, as the two mermaids swam back into the water then vanished below the surface.

Chapter Seventeen

"I won't come with you," said Sam, shuffling his feet awkwardly as they approached the shop and fixing an innocent look on his face. "I know it's a safe space and stuff."

"Yeah," said Coral, gratefully. "That's really good of you Sam. I'll talk to them though, okay? I'm sure it'll be fine. We need all the friends we can get at the minute, you know?"

"I understand," he said, pulling her in close for a hug. He felt her soft, warm body embrace him, her cheek against the side of his neck. She felt lovely. He pushed her back away from him again. "Text me, yeah?"

"See you later," said Lilly, waving.

Sam waved back to them both and, aware they were watching him leave, tried not to hurry with any degree of determination and kept his phone in his pocket until he was well out of sight of the shop.

The sun was coming up and grey light was tiptoeing down the road, so he stepped into a doorway and peered round to make sure nobody was following him. Listening carefully and waiting, nobody showed up so he pulled his phone out and quickly texted his father. He couldn't doubt Sam's abilities and worth with this information, information that could change everything for them. It could make them world famous. If it was true and nobody other than the Mer themselves knew of the Ancients' existence, then this would seal Sam's value in his father's eyes.

"I have big news," he text. "I'll be back soon."

"Oh my god!" gasped Lilly, spotting her friend sitting up on the sofa with Bentley's head resting gently on her lap as they returned to the back room of the little antiques shop. "Saffron!"

"Hey," Saffron replied, looking up at Lilly with heavy eyes. "I'm awake now."

Coral's grandmother, Maud and Mi sat on chairs nearby looking serious. Sylvie had retreated to the top of a bookcase, casting filthy looks towards the large dog. Lilly hurried over and sat beside Saffron. "How are you feeling?" she asked.

"I dunno," she said with a shrug. "They told me what happened. How they saved me and how a woman named Dorothy healed me, but how the Harvester then murdered her."

"Yeah," said Lilly, her eyes dropping. Saffron had been unconscious for so long, she'd missed so many things. There was so much to tell her, so many things to know. "But we're going to stop him. We'll figure out how, I promise."

Coral stepped forward. "I have the hair, Grandma," she said, holding up the tuft of Ashalia's rich blue hair that, now dry, seemed far coarser and thicker than human hair. There was skin and some blood tried onto the rooted ends. Lilly wondered how much it had hurt her to rip it out. Did she feel pain like a human?

"Excellent," said her grandmother, stepping forwards with her hands out covetously. "Give it to me!"

Coral handed the tuft over, and Lilly watched as her grandmother took it from her and examined it carefully. She could almost hear "My precious" coming from the old woman's mouth. Her eyes gleamed with delight. "This is a superb sample," she murmured, picking through the hair carefully. "And roots too. This is wonderful."

Lilly shuddered.

"How long will it take to get the potion ready now?" asked Maud.

"Oh, not long. An hour, perhaps less," said Coral's grandmother, taking the hair to a chopping block that rested on a side surface. She plucked three strands of the hair from the tuft then carefully placed the rest in a plastic tub, the sort Chinese food would be delivered in. Taking a large silver cleaver, she carefully and finely chopped the hair strands, leaving about an inch below the roots which she then carefully placed in the box alongside the original sample. Approaching the cauldron, the chopped hairs were then gently scraped from the wooden board into the mixture which hissed venomously. "Superb," the old woman muttered, her eyes flashing.

The room fell silent as they all watched Coral's grandmother stirring carefully, adjusting the flame below and occasionally sprinkling salts or herbs into the cauldron that simmered in the middle of the room, a strong smell drifting around the room that made Bentley sneeze with a booming harrumph. Lilly remained at Saffron's side. The two girls stroked Bentley's head. Coral sat alone watching, Lilly smiled up at her and she smiled back, though it didn't reach her eyes and Lilly wasn't sure it was genuine. She ruffled at Bentley's thick black fur and decided to wait it out, everyone was so tense and anxious. Until they had information from Hogarth there was nothing that could be done.

३

"What?" asked the Harvester, looking his son up and down with suspicion as Sam stepped into the building, feeling smug.

"I have information," he said, smiling. Impressing his father wasn't something he got to do very often in his life, or ever, despite varying degrees of effort. He was going to milk it.

"Which is?" asked the Harvester impatiently, turning back to the computer screen he'd been looking at.

Sam sidled over to the tank where the mermaid was contained. The table ready for the tail amputation was ready, but the Harvester had clearly been taking everything he could from her before the final cut. Her head was shaved and her tail had been scraped repeatedly. She had little red puncture marks up and down her arms where blood had been taken, her black skin faded to a dull granite. Her head hung low, she looked broken. The confidence in her future rescuing looked like it had been sucked out of her. "You might want to get this one here to tell you a bit about The Ancients."

"The Ancients?" asked the Harvester, turning around and peering at Sam out of his cold eyes. "What are you talking about?"

In the tank, the mermaid's head was rising and she peered at them out of glazed eyes, a look of fear and pain on her face. "How?" came her voice, crackling and hoarse, but full of confusion.

"Apparently nobody on land knows about them," said Sam casually, trying to contain his excitement and wandering away from the tank and back towards his father who was now staring at him. "They're pure bloods."

"Pure bloods?" the Harvester said, a trace of annoyance in his voice. "Explain."

"You can't," begged the mermaid. "Stop."

"Ancient Mer," said Sam, sitting down on the stainless steel table and picking up the large knife that was resting on it, twiddling it idly in his hands. "The Mer we know and use are like the bridge between the Ancients and the humans. The Ancients are the original species, they're powerful. They're hidden and protected and don't want anyone to know about them. Nobody knows about them. Except us."

The Harvester stood up and approached the tank. "Tell me, right now. Is this true?"

"Dad, the mermaids told me themselves!" protested Sam, irritated that his father would take this mermaid's word over his own.

The Mermaid looked away.

"Tell me, or I will make your death slow," said the Harvester. "Lie to me and I will make your death slow. Ignore me and I will make your death slow. Speak the truth and you will die fast. My potion is almost ready for the final ingredient. How long it takes me to acquire that ingredient is up to you."

She looked at him. "It's true," she said weakly. "But you can't Harvest from them. They're too strong."

"Their strength is in their anonymity," snarled the Harvester with pleasure. "Sam, we're about to do something incredible."

Sam grinned. He had success. Then he remembered something funny. "Dad, they think they've caught me."

"What?" asked the Harvester, turning on him.

"They caught some kid down at the beach last night," he said with a laugh, rolling his eyes, enjoying this sudden positive relationship he was experiencing with his father and feeling confident for the first time in ages. "Some idiot they think is your apprentice. They're making some potion to try and get information out of him about how to catch you. Poor dude's going to suffer before they kill him!"

"They've what?" demanded the Harvester, fury in his face. "And how long before they work out they've got the wrong person?"

"Uh, I dunno," he said, shrugging. "Does it matter?"

"You having this link to Lilly and her friends is the only useful thing you've got to contribute right now, Samuel," said his father with frustration. "How long will it take them to suspect you when they find out this boy is innocent?"

"I, erm," Sam hesitated.

"Get back there right now and fix this," he said. "I'll start working on a potion strong enough to pierce whatever shields these Ancients have. If they're as powerful as you say they are, we might never need to worry about the likes of Lilly Prospero and her cronies again."

Sam sighed and rubbed his temples. He was exhausted and now embarrassed and annoyed. "Yes, dad," he said glumly. "I'll need a distraction…"

"What kind of distraction?" asked his father, peering at him suspiciously.

"Something to get them out of the way so I can fix it with the kid they've got," he said.

The Harvester looked over at the mermaid who peered at him miserably, a look of dull resignation on her face. "Give me five minutes with this one," said the Harvester. "Then I'll give you one hell of a distraction."

Sam looked nervously at the mermaid, a familiar, uncomfortable and sick feeling starting to niggle in his gut that had stirred every so often his whole life. "Okay," he said. "I'll wait."

₞

"We can't go back," insisted Hexanna, her face riddled with fear. "Lord Bray will never agree to help us."

"What else can we do?" asked Ashalia, the side of her head raw and stinging where she had ripped her head out, but the soothing salt water worked it's healing properties and she knew the pain would soon ease. "We don't have a choice!"

"Lilly said they're going to figure it out," said Hexanna, the fight and anger seemingly drained from her. "We need to trust her.

"And how many more of us need to die?" asked Ashalia, shaking her head. "I'll give Lilly all the help she needs, believe me, but without Saffron…"

Hexanna nodded sadly. "I know," she said. "But the Ancients…"

"Oberus helped," Ashalia reassured her. "If Oberus was willing others might be willing too. We can give Lilly all the help in the world but we still need to help ourselves."

"What would Brinly say?" asked Hexanna.

"Right now?" Ashalia sighed. "If she's even alive I think she'd just beg us to save her life. If she's already dead… it doesn't matter."

"She can't be dead," wept Hexanna. "She just can't."

"If Lilly's plan fails she will be," insisted Ashalia.

Hexanna nodded and gulped, closing her eyes and setting her mouth in determination. "Right," she said, looking up at her friend. "Let's try. And let's hope they don't kill us for insolence."

"I'd rather die by their hands than by the Harvesters'," said Ashalia grimly.

"Yes," agreed Hexanna. "Me too."

ƺ

"It's ready," said Coral's grandmother, stepping back from the cauldron and looking triumphant through the wafting purple smoke. "Coral, fetch the boy."

"Yes grandma," said Coral with a sigh, standing up and walking towards the closet.

"Do you want help?" asked Lilly.

"No," snapped Coral, then pulled the door open. Hogarth had apparently been resting against it as he tumbled straight out onto the floor. "Get up," she commanded him.

Hogarth rolled over and looked up. At her side, Lilly heard Saffron gasp. "Hogarth," she whispered. "It's really him."

Hogarth looked over and spotted Saffron, his eyes widened and he cried out to her for help.

"Get him on the chair," instructed Coral's grandmother as she carefully ladled the potion into a large, round coffee mug. "And make him stop shouting."

Coral dragged Hogarth to his feet, manoeuvred him over to the chair, and sat him down. He went to call out again but she gave him a short, sharp smack across the cheek.

"Ow!" he howled, flinching away. "No, please. Saffron, please."

"How could you?" Saffron cried. "I nearly died because of you!"

"It wasn't me!" he insisted, pleading with her.

"Ignore him," snarled Coral.

Lily glanced at Saffron and saw a troubled look on her face, was she doubting this too? Hogarth looked genuine, but how could he be? Saffron glanced at her, worry in her green eyes. Lilly mirrored her expression then turned back towards Hogarth.

"Mr Hogarth," said Coral's grandmother quietly, approaching him with the hot mug of liquid. He looked up at her fearfully. "This is a potion called Perjuramercement."

"What?" he asked, gazing up at her, then round the room at the faces of the women watching him. "Potion? What?"

"It's also known as the Liar's Punishment," she said, holding the mug to him. "Drink it."

"No!" he cried, leaning back away from her, turning his face to the side and pushing his lips tightly together.

"Drink it," she said again. "Or we will make you drink it."

Sylvie leapt down from the top of the cupboard, carefully avoided getting too close to Bentley, and approached the boy. Lilly watched on, longing to stand up and stop what was happening. But she was too scared. The women were so strong, so determined, what could she do?

"Drink it," the cat said.

"What?!" cried Hogarth, staring at the cat in horror.

Sylvie stared back at him, her eyes narrow and unblinking. "Drink it," she repeated.

"How?" he cried, tears started running down his face. "That cat spoke! It spoke! The cat speaks! Did you know the cat speaks?"

Sylvie stepped forward and slashed her claws across his ankle. He howled and pulled his leg away quickly. "Drink it, now," she instructed him.

"Wait!" Lilly cried out, leaping to her feet. "Stop it!"

"Stop what?" demanded Coral's grandmother, glaring at Lilly.

"This isn't right!" Lilly protested. "Please!"

She stepped between them, turning her back to Hogarth as she confronted the women of the coven, panic surging in her body.

"What do you think you're doing, you foolish child?" demanded Coral's grandmother.

"We can't do this to him," Lilly insisted, looking back at Hogarth whose face was riddled with fear and gratitude. "It's just not right! We're the good guys!"

"Thank you," Hogarth wept behind her. "Thank you. I swear I haven't done anything. I swear it!"

"If that is true, drink it," snarled Sylvie. "It will prove your innocence."

"Or we will force you to," said Coral's grandmother coldly.

Ignoring them, Lilly turned to Hogarth. "I won't let them hurt you," she said to him quietly, crouching down and looking into his eyes. "I promise. But you have to help me. Please."

"How?" he asked, his voice trembling.

"If you say you're innocent, this potion will prove it," she said gently, pleading with him. "I don't know why you were there, and I don't know why you've been following me, but it all looks so suspicious. And somebody stabbed me, somebody who looked just like you."

"I don't understand," Hogarth wept, tears running down his cheeks.

"Ha!" barked Coral's grandmother. "Liar!"

"I want to believe you," said Lilly again, trying to keep his attention on her and not on the terrifying women that surrounded them. "I really do. But I can't just believe you and let you go when you could have killed so many people, when you could have tried to kill me and Saffron. I need to know. I need to protect us and I can't if I don't trust you. Do you understand?"

Hogarth hesitated, his eyes flashing around the room and the observing coven. "I understand."

"So please, Hogarth, please drink the potion," Lilly pleaded with him.

"Okay," he said, nodding with a pained look on his face. "I'll drink it."

Lilly took his hands in hers and felt so relieved she could cry, then stood and accepted the cup of potion from Coral's grandmother, who looked distinctly unimpressed, then turned back to Hogarth and handed him the cup. He took it from her nervously and inspected the peculiar looking contents. As he went to take a sip, a loud knock came on the door.

"Coral?" called a voice.

"Sam?" called Coral, jumping up.

Chapter Eighteen

Ashalia and Hexanna swam silently through the water towards the realm of the Ancients. Neither spoke. Ashalia was too scared in case they heard them coming and she assumed Hexanna felt the same. Lord Bray was terrifying. The Ancients in general were terrifying, in fact. Were they doing the right thing? Was there a wrong thing to do in this situation?

They swam below an arch and past faces full of disgust at their presence. Ashalia shuddered. Being loathed purely for the way you were born was something she could never get used to. Hexanna slipped a hand into hers and squeezed. Ashalia squeezed back gratefully.

"STOP!" came a booming voice.

"Oh crap," muttered Hexanna as they spun to see Lord Bray approaching them, his face ferocious.

"I told you not to return, yet you defy me?" he roared.

"Please," begged Ashalia, dropping Hexanna's hand and turning to him. "We are out of options. The girl who is supposed to save us, she's failed. The Harvester is getting stronger. Another Mer has been taken and soon another one will go too."

"Leave," commanded Lord Bray, brandishing his spear towards the open sea.

"You have to help us!" begged Hexanna. "Please! We have nobody left!"

"This is not my concern," he dismissed, glaring at them.

"And when will it become your concern?" asked Ashalia, anger boiling in her. "When he starts coming for your people?"

At her side, Hexanna gasped.

"What did you say?" asked Lord Bray, swimming closer to her, his eyes piercing her own. "Why would he come for my people?"

"I, uh," Ashalia felt herself start to shake. She looked at Hexanna who's already pale skin seemed to have turned to pure white.

Lord Bray turned from her and shouted, "Rosella! Come! You're needed!"

"Who? What?" asked Ashalia in a panic, looking around.

"I do not take the time to listen to lies," he said, looking back at her momentarily then turned away again.

"I, what?" asked Ashalia again.

"We should leave," whispered Hexanna, starting to swim back away from Lord Bray.

"Stay," he commanded, not looking back. "If you attempt to leave, you shall be stopped."

Ashalia looked in panic at Hexanna then turned and saw whom she presumed to be Rosella swimming towards them. Her scales were faded and grey, her skin mottled, her eyes pure white.

"Yes, my lord?" she asked.

"Sense from them," he commanded her.

Rosella turned towards them and Ashalia felt her skin crawl. She swam to them slowly, her tail seemed weak and her arms were thin. She held a hand out towards Ashalia's face, the long fingers claw like as they moved closer to her eyes. She tried to swim away but felt entranced, frozen in place, powerless to move.

"Oh dear," muttered Rosella, shaking her head as her fingers connected with Ashalia's face. "Oh dear."

"Well?" asked Lord Bray.

Rosella turned to him, her blind eyes somehow finding him precisely. "The realm has been broken," she said. "It's time."

"WHAT?" Roared Lord Bray, turning on the two mermaids and raising his spear.

"Go!" screamed Hexanna, grabbing Ashalia's hand and swimming straight upwards for the surface.

Behind them boiling water spun and rushed towards them, the burning heat chasing their tails behind as the bright sunlight above became more and more clear. Just as Lord Bray's vengeance began to burn the scales from their tails, Ashalia and Hexanna reached the surface of the water and dragged themselves onto rocks, the burst of boiling heat gushing from the sea and shooting high into the air in a foaming, gushing mass. It cascaded back into the water, splashing a volcanic spray of sea water across them.

"Okay," said Ashalia after a moment. "I'm pretty sure that was the wrong thing to do."

"You think?" cried Hexanna.

Ashalia looked at her awkwardly. "I'm sorry."

Hexanna shrugged and put an arm around her. "It's been a pleasure, my friend," she said sadly.

"It's not goodbye yet," said Ashalia, resting her head on Hexanna's shoulder.

"No," acknowledged Hexanna. "Not yet."

ᛈ

Sam stepped into the room and blanched when he saw Hogarth, "Is that the guy?" he asked, surprise in his voice. "He looks so normal!"

"Yeah," said Coral. "Erm, Grandma... can Sam stay?"

Coral's grandmother eyed him up and down, the cup of potion still held in her hand before a trembling Hogarth, then after a moment nodded slightly. "Yes, he can stay."

At Lilly's side she felt Bentley's huge chest rumble with a faint growl. "It's okay Ben," she whispered in his ear. "Sam's a friend."

The dog looked up at her with wide, anxious eyes but didn't say anything. Every few moments she felt the rumble against her leg though. She gently scratched his ear, partly for his reassurance and partly for her own. Something felt wrong. Why was Bentley so distressed? She looked over at Saffron who caught her eye and slightly shrugged her shoulders.

"If you're staying, stay out of the way," instructed Coral's grandmother, pointing at a chair against the wall near where Maud sat. "And don't interrupt."

Obediently, Sam sat. The women of the coven watched him in silence before turning back to Hogarth.

"Please," he begged, tears running down his face as the cup trembled in his hands. "I don't know what you think I am but my name is Dougal Hogarth. I work at a hotel. I'm seventeen years old. I have a hamster named Malcolm Reynolds."

"Drink this," commanded Coral's grandmother. "Now."

"Please, Hogarth," said Lilly gently.

Hogarth nodded silently and, with a final glance at Lilly with desperation and pleading in his eyes, sipped from the cup.

"All of it," instructed Sylvie at his feet, holding a clawed paw aloft.

Hogarth kept sipping, his face pained by the flavour Lilly assumed, though it could have just been the experience of drinking anything under conditions so close to torture.

"Now we wait," instructed Coral's grandmother, as Hogarth handed the emptied cup back to her. "In a few minutes, I'm going to ask you some questions. If you lie to me, you will regret it. This potion works by burning the lining of the stomach each time a lie is told. Lie to me once and it will hurt, lie again it will start to become agonising. I don't know how many lies you can physically survive telling, but then nobody has ever tested that."

"Oh god," whispered Hogarth, his head dropping and his shoulders starting to heave.

On the chair behind them, Sam started to shift. "You okay?" Coral whispered to him.

"It's just…" he hesitated, looking around at all the eyes suddenly fixed on him again. "Is this right?"

"What would you suggest?" asked Maud indignantly.

"I don't know," Sam admitted, his voice anxious. "But, what if it doesn't work? Will we even know?"

"Do you doubt me?" Coral's grandmother demanded, stepping towards him. Lilly was astounded by how imposing a woman of her age and stature could suddenly make herself appear.

"This boy," said Mi as she hobbled towards Sam and gestured at Hogarth with disgust, her cane taking a lot more strain now she showed signs of weakness and tiredness. "This boy is, however, indirectly, responsible for the deaths of not only the Mer we are fighting to save, but also our two fallen friends Dorothy and Iris. Two women who were true, honest and good. Women who are dead partly because of this boy."

"Then why not just kill him?" Sam asked. "I mean, he's a murderer, right? And you want to kill the Harvester, so why not him too?"

"Because even without him," said Lilly. "The Harvester will still keep going. And next time he might win. Iris and Dorothy are already dead, I nearly died last time, Saffron nearly died the time before. If we don't get answers from him what hope do we have of stopping him? What else can we do?"

Sam gulped and looked nervously at Coral. "All right, he gets it," she snapped. "Back off, okay?"

"So," said Coral's grandmother, returning to stand in front of the prisoner. "Mr Hogarth. What is your name?"

"Dougal James Mackenzie Hogarth," he said quietly but clearly, taking time over every word.

"And what were you doing on the beach last night?" she asked, folding her arms.

"I… I…" he looked at Lilly nervously. "I was following Lilly. I wanted to see what she was doing."

"Why?" asked Lilly.

"I like you," he said sadly. "I liked you. Now, not so much."

"Nothing's happening," whispered Coral, walking towards Hogarth and peering into his face. "Did the potion stop working?"

Outside, someone screamed. A long, piercing, blood curdling scream.

Everyone stood. Bentley leapt to his feet and rushed through the women that were standing, staring towards the door.

"Go," insisted Coral's grandmother. "Now."

Bentley ran and everyone followed, Lilly taking Saffron's hand and bracing herself for whatever battle was waiting them now. She didn't know if she could do anything, but she knew she stood a better chance than before now Saffron was back at her side.

ꝛ

"We need to find out what they're doing," Ashalia said, both Mer still too afraid to go back into the water for fear of Lord Bray catching them, but painfully aware that as daylight got brighter and brighter, and the humans descended from their homeland into the water for entertainment, that they were even more unsafe exposed on the rocks than in the depths of the ocean.

"Why?" asked Hexanna. "Haven't we learned our lesson?"

"That old woman, she said something," said Ashalia. "Don't you remember? Something about the realm being broken?"

"I remember," said Hexanna. "She said 'it is time', but so what?"

"Time for what?" asked Ashalia.

"I don't know!" wept Hexanna, putting her head in her hands. "Ash, why do you want to know? Why does it matter?"

"It's not going to be anything good, is it!" insisted Ashalia. "They know that humans are aware of their existence for the first time in history!"

"So?" asked Hexanna, shaking her head and looking completely exasperated.

"I'm scared of what they'll do," she said quietly.

"Do?" asked Hexanna. "To whom?"

"The people," said Ashalia, sadly. She knew it was insane, they had been persecuted by the humans for centuries, treated like second class Beings because of their species, and now she was actually expressing concern for their wellbeing. But it didn't matter, she felt it. "The humans."

"So the Ancients finally take out the Harvester for us," said Hexanna. "That's what we wanted! That's what we've been begging them to do!"

Ashalia shook her head. "I don't think they'll stop there," she said. "They don't want anyone knowing, not even people like Lilly. Like Saffron."

Hexanna hesitated, her face troubled as she chewed on her lip. Ashalia knew her friend wished the humans no harm, even if she cared nothing about their good fortune either. But she didn't know if she'd willingly risk herself in their defence.

"Fine," Hexanna grumbled after a minute. "We'll find out what we can. But if we get caught by Lord Bray again then it might not matter what the Harvester wants with us anymore anyway!"

"Thank, you. Let's go," said Ashalia with a grateful nod, surprised but relieved by her friend's kindness. She launched herself from the rock and back into the water, Hexanna following closely behind.

Chapter Nineteen

"What are you doing?" asked Hogarth, his voice faint and frightened.

"None of your concern," muttered Sam as he tipped a small blue glass vial up over the potion and allowed several drops to run out.

"LILLY!" Hogarth called out, but Sam reached over and slapped him hard across the cheek.

"Shut up!" he growled, and then quickly crouched down behind the tied up boy and loosened the restraints that held him to the chair.

"Why are you doing this?" Hogarth wept.

Sam stood up and fixed a confident look to his face. "Because I'm not going to let you ruin anything for me."

"Ruin what?" Hogarth wept.

"What I'm going to do to those girls…" sneered Sam.

"You did all this!" Hogarth suddenly cried out. "It's you they're looking for!"

Sam grinned again. He didn't feel confident but he knew this was what had to happen. Then he punched Hogarth square in the jaw.

Leaping to his feet, the restraints falling away, Hogarth launched himself at Sam.

ʒ

"Oh crap," muttered Coral under her breath.

Lilly looked in amazement and horror. The word "WITCH" had been splashed across the front of the shop in huge letters, written in the deep crimson of blood. Pools of it lay on the pavement along with congealed lumps of flesh and gore.

A middle aged woman was sitting on the bench opposite the shop, shaking and looking horrified. "What is that?" she howled, as Mi gently approached her and sat at her side.

"A cruel joke," Mi said gently, putting a reassuring arm around the woman's shoulders. "We'll clean it up in no time."

"It's horrible!" sobbed the woman. "The smell! So much blood!"

Bentley sniffed it. "It's mermaid," he said quietly. "I smelled it on the Harvester last night, and I smelled it in that potion you were making inside."

"Oh my god," whispered Lilly. "Brinly."

"Who did this?" asked Saffron. "Why?"

"The Harvester?" suggested Sylvie. "Who else?"

"But why?" asked Coral. "Why would he want to do this? What's the point?"

Lilly suddenly stood bolt upright. "It's a distraction," she said, looking around at them. "Why else?"

"A distraction from what?" asked Saffron.

Lilly looked around at the group. Women, girls and animals stood looking in horror at the gruesome mess that had been left across the building they considered their sanctuary. "Where's Sam?" she suddenly asked.

"Get back inside!" instructed Coral's grandmother, hurrying forwards and in through the door to the shop. Lilly kept pace, she had known something was wrong. Bentley had known something was wrong.

They pushed through the tiny shop and into the back room where they found Sam standing over Hogarth who lay sprawled on the floor, his arms and legs unbound, and a dagger lodged in his side. "He attacked me," Sam breathed, his hands shaking.

ζ

The two mermaids swam near to the realm of the Ancients, watching closely and trying not to be seen. Where usually they were seen lounging on rocks, discussing intellectual ideals with one another, there was nobody. Where they expected to see pompous looking military personnel swimming around wielding spears and looking important but almost entirely none functioning, now it was barren. They saw not a single Being on any rocks or any guard posts.

"Where are they?" whispered Ashalia, edging closer but keeping low to the plant and rocks of the ocean floor.

"Have they left?" asked Hexanna, poking her head up. "We can't find anything out if they're gone, can we!"

"Gone where?" asked Ashalia. "No, they're here. They're in a cave or something, planning. Something big is happening."

"Wait," whispered Hexanna, peering through the water. "I see someone!"

"Duck!" insisted Ashalia, reaching up and dragging at her friend's arm.

"No, I think…" Hexanna stopped and squinted, moving closer. "I think it's Oberus."

"Oberus?" asked Ashalia, raising herself up level to Hexanna. "It is, it's Oberus."

"What's he doing?"

The Ancient, his greying hair and frail body, was moving rapidly between rocks and plants, his tail thrashing silently but speedily as he whizzed stealthily through the water.

"He's leaving," said Hexanna. "Look, he's got a bag."

She was right, the Ancient carried a large brown, leather sack and moved like he didn't want to be seen. "We'll wait," whispered Ashalia. "He's headed right for us."

As the Ancient Mer appeared in front of them, Ashalia swam upwards and startled him. "Ashalia!" he gasped, his eyes widening as he looked around in surprise and panic. "What are you doing here?"

"We need to know what's going on," she said. "Where are they all?"

"Get out of my way," he insisted, swimming around her. "This is all your doing anyway, you foolish child."

Hexanna swam towards him hesitantly. "Please," she said quietly. "We just need to know what's going on. Are you planning to hurt those people?"

"I am planning no such thing," growled Oberus.

"Who is?" asked Ashalia.

Oberus went to argue, his eyes angry, then suddenly hesitated. He looked around again then beckoned to them. "I will not talk more here. Follow me, I will tell you what I can, and then I must insist you leave me alone."

The two nodded and swam after him. They swam on and on through the open water, past shoals of fish and over crabs that scuttled below. Soon they were so far from the realm of the Ancients that Ashalia felt completely lost. Where the shore was or even water she was familiar with she did not know, but she got the feeling Oberus needed the distance for everyone's safety, not just his own.

Eventually he stopped and carefully placed his large bag on a rock, sitting beside it and looking exhausted. They had moved at quite a speed, especially considering the age of the Ancient Mer, and it had obviously drained him of energy.

"Lord Bray has no sympathies with your kind," said Oberus after taking a moment to catch his breath. "And his view of the humans is pure disdain. Perhaps even hatred."

"We had noticed," muttered Hexanna.

"Do not take my words to imply I feel anything greater for the humans," said Oberus sternly, glaring at them through grey cloudy eyes. "However, I have no desire to be part of a massacre. Genocide sits uncomfortably in me, even when the victims of it are a violent and depraved species such as humanity."

"Massacre?" asked Ashalia, her eyes wide with horror. "Genocide? What is he planning?"

"Lord Bray will protect our people above all others," explained Oberus. "And the humans having knowledge of our existence is enough to lead him to war. The information must be contained above all else, and for that reason the humans will be annihilated."

"All humans?" asked Hexanna in shock.

"No," he said, shaking his head. "Just the humans in this vicinity. Perhaps forty thousand of them."

"Forty thousand people?" wailed Ashalia, grasping his hand. "Oberus! Please! You must help us!"

"Help you? I tried, child," he said, pulling his hand away from hers. "I gave you the information I was able, despite my people seeing you as a subspecies. I am not without a heart, however, stopping this is neither in my desire nor ability."

"Then why are you leaving?" asked Hexanna.

"Having no desire to stop it does not mean I have any wish to take part," said the old Mer, shaking his head sadly. "Time has come for me to move on and find somewhere else. Modern times are not suiting my constitution." He picked up his bag again. "Good bye."

"Wait," insisted Ashalia. "Please, before you go."

"What?" he asked, sounding tired. The pride and strength in his voice seemed to have dwindled. Ashalia wondered if he wasn't moving on to another realm, but perhaps moving on from this world entirely.

"When?" she asked him. "How?"

"Tonight," he said sadly. "They are gathering what they need to create enough energy to destroy all living things within range of their power. It shall not take long. Before midnight tonight, Whitstable and the surrounding areas will be destroyed."

ꝛ

"Where is my tail?" demanded the message from Iago Bane.

The Harvester rubbed his temples. He looked at the freshly harvested tail that lay severed on the cutting table. He could give it to Bane and be rid of the man, or, as he needed, he could use the tail and other parts of the mermaid in what was set to be the most complex and delicate potion he had ever created to crack through the protection surrounding these Ancients and Harvest the motherload of all power.

"Tomorrow," he replied. "And by way of an apology for the delay, I shall also deliver something more powerful than you have ever imagined."

"It's not good enough, I expect better," came the instant response.

"I can assure you, this will be worth the wait," replied the Harvester.

"If it isn't, I hope you are aware of the consequences."

The Harvester looked again at the tail. The Ancients must know that their secrecy had been broken. There was no way of knowing how long it would take them to build up additional defences or disappear altogether. The information he had managed to torture from the captured mermaid had been patchy, but he knew enough for now. He wouldn't have time to harvest a fresh mermaid to procure an additional tail to brew the potion needed and supply this one to Bane.

"I am aware," he replied. It would work. It had to work. "Tomorrow and all will be explained."

ㄹ

"What have you done?" demanded Coral's grandmother, stepping forward with fury.

Lilly rushed over and put her fingers on Hogarth's neck. She could feel a slight, very faint, pulse. Looking up at Sam she decided to keep quiet, and just held Hogarth's head on her lap, stroking the mop of brown hair from his clammy, pallid face.

"He attacked me!" insisted Sam again. "You all left because of the scream then he laughed."

"He laughed?" asked Maud, peering at the boy in Lilly's lap, then looking hard at Sam.

"Yeah," said Sam, his whole body trembling and his face white as a sheet. "He laughed and said you were stupid witches then the ties on his arms all fell off and he got up."

Coral's grandmother picked up the duct tape that had been wound around his wrists and ankles and now lay strewn across the carpeted floor. "The ties fell off?"

Sam nodded mutely then wobbled on his feet. Coral rushed forward and offered him support, leading him to one of the chairs.

"What happened?" she asked him in a soothing voice.

"He ran at me," said Sam, putting his hand over his eyes as if it hurt him to remember. "He ran at me and I could feel something in my chest starting to tighten and break, like something was being broken inside me, and I can't remember much else…" he paused and let Coral take his hand gently. "I had a knife. I keep it in my boot. I pulled it out and stabbed him then the pain in my chest went away. Then you all came back in."

"He was our only lead, you stupid boy!" roared Coral's grandmother, rage in her voice. "We have nothing else! Nothing! Lilly is supposed to be unstoppable against him and even she has failed! Now, because of you, we have no idea why and nothing to go on! You have ruined our chances!"

"Grandma!" protested Coral, standing between the boy and her grandmother. "It wasn't his fault! Would you rather he died so we could keep questioning Hogarth? The stupid potion wasn't working anyway!"

"Or was it?" asked Sylvie, her tail flicking. "The boy seemed petrified. I got no sense of a power he was keeping hidden from us."

"So what, you think the spell worked and Hogarth was innocent do you?" demanded Coral, glaring at the cat. "So he just attacked Sam for shits and giggles did he?"

"We don't know he attacked Sam," said Mi, peering at Sam through her glasses with dark, inquisitive eyes.

"Are you crazy?" Coral screeched. "You think Sam just murdered an innocent guy? For what? What the hell?"

Coral's grandmother straightened up and went to the cauldron. "We have enough potion here for another decent mug full. Perhaps Sam should be the one tied to the chair."

"You crazy old witch!" screamed Coral. "You are not torturing Sam! He's innocent! He's my friend! I'm sorry your plan hasn't worked and you've lost your only lead but you didn't want to save the mermaids anyway! You wanted them for your own uses so you're no better than the Harvester anyway!"

"Coral Friday!" roared her grandmother. "You will watch your tongue!"

"I'll take it!" said Sam, holding his hands up. "I'll take the potion. You can ask me anything you want, I swear."

"No, Sam," Coral insisted. "I'm not letting them treat you like you're some kind of criminal. You've done nothing wrong! You saw how they treated Hogarth!"

Coral's grandmother went over to the potion, stirred it slightly then took the spoon out and sniffed it. "You're happy to take this, are you?" she asked, raising her eyebrows.

"Of course!" Sam insisted earnestly. "I'll take anything you want."

"Maud, you're going to die," spat Coral, stepping between them. "Sylvie, you're going to stay a cat. Lilly, you can go back where you came from because the game is over. Come on Sam, we're going."

"It's okay, Coral!" Sam insisted, but Coral silenced him with a glare. Standing, he allowed Coral to take him by the hand.

"Coral!" snapped her grandmother. "I will find you! If you leave here, I will find you!"

"Not this time," snarled Coral, turning away.

Everyone stood back parting to allow the furious girl and the young man through in silence.

As they stepped out of the door, Mi called out, "Your leg looks better, Sam."

And then they were gone.

Chapter Twenty

For a moment nobody said a word, then in Lilly's lap Hogarth gave a spluttering cough, snapping Lilly's attention back. "Quick!" she insisted. "He's hurt. We need to get him to a hospital!"

"No," said Coral's grandmother, moving fast. "No hospitals. I'll treat him."

"We've no healer!" Lilly protested. "He needs proper care!"

"And what do you propose on telling the doctors?" asked Coral's grandmother, selecting potion bottles from a shelf. "We don't need him to survive necessarily, just be able to give us information should we need to interrogate him further. After that encounter with Sam he could have learned something. Sam spiked the Perjuramercement with an antidote so it's useless to us now, but Hogarth here has already been dosed, so it should last long enough."

"He does need to survive!" Lilly protested.

"He spiked it?" asked Saffron in shock, crouching down beside Lilly. "How?"

Coral's grandmother ignored Lilly and said to Saffron, "I can smell it in there. There's definitely some cilantro in here now, and it wasn't there before." She lowered herself carefully to her knees beside Hogarth's head. "Hold his head in position and I'll give him some Dulcification. Then I'm afraid we'll need to remove the blade and stitch him up."

"Can you do that?" asked Saffron.

"You have to save his life," Lilly insisted as she propped his head up to allow Coral's grandmother to start gently tipping the potion into his mouth.

The old woman sighed as she took a hold of the knife. "This is not something you need to see, dear," she said with an uncharacteristic gentleness to her voice. "If you'd rather step out."

"No," said Lilly grimly. "I'm staying."

"Me too," said Saffron, though her voice sounded more hollow and less certain of herself. She looked at Lilly with huge, green eyes so full of pain and questions that Lilly didn't know how to cure or answer.

"Very well," said Coral's grandmother. "Mi, if you could get wadding. Maud, I'll need the kit. I'm afraid there is no magical way of doing this."

Lilly watched in fascination as Coral's grandmother picked up the second bottle and took the top off. Inside she saw some kind of dark dusty sand, so black it was almost silver in the light.

"Ready," she Mi, holding some large, fluffy white pads in her frail hands.

"Ready," agreed Maud, a small box in hers.

With one last glance at Lilly and Saffron, Coral's grandmother carefully pulled the knife out from Hogarth's side, causing the boy to groan in unconscious agony, then as blood began to ooze out she tipped the black powder across it in one smooth movement. As soon as the powder landed on the wound it began to fizz, a pungent smoke billowing from it before Mi quickly applied the wadding to the spot and held it on tight. Lilly could still hear the strange fizzing from beneath it.

Holding the dagger aloft, Coral's grandmother inspected it carefully. "It is a short blade, he may recover from this, though there is no guarantee. So long as it isn't cursed, of course."

"Are you ready for the stitches?" asked Maud once the fizzing had stopped.

"Yes," agreed Mi, taking the gauze away.

Lilly looked and where had been an open wound was now a line of black, sludgy goop. Maud carefully wiped the goop away with an alcohol wipe then began stitching the wound very slowly and carefully. In her lap, Hogarth made a pained expression that made Lilly's heart hurt, but she took heart from the fact if he was feeling pain in any way; at least he wasn't dead yet.

"He'll be unconscious for a while now," said Coral's grandmother, inspecting the stitches and giving Maud an approving nod. "If he wakes up, we can ask him what we need to know. If not…"

"He will wake up!" Lilly insisted, her hands sweating and her head pounding.

"If he wakes up we can see what he knows," said Coral's grandmother slowly. "Until then he's best left where he is."

"How could Sam do this?" asked Saffron, her eyes wide. "Is he the one working with the Harvester?"

"Time will tell," said Coral's grandmother quietly, her voice oddly wistful. "Time will tell."

ℜ

"Thank you," said Sam as he and Coral arrived panting at the door to his flat. Neither had taken a chance to stop as they raced down the streets, passed confused shop keepers opening up in the early morning light, and now both were out of breath.

"What for?" asked Coral, watching as he pushed the key into the lock and let her inside. She stepped in, feeling calm wash over her. This small room with its bare wooden floors, its messy furniture and its small grimy window was safe. It was Sam.

"For sticking up for me," he said with a shrug, and kicked the door shut behind him. "I think your grandma was about to get real scary."

"She's a hypocrite," grumbled Coral. "Anyway, you're the most honest person I've ever met. I'd trust you with my life."

Sam nodded silently and went to kitchenette. "Water?" he offered her. "Tea?"

"You have tea?" she asked him with a coy smile, teasing him. She longed to flirt with him properly, test to see if he felt for her what she felt for him. But then she was younger, just sixteen. Did he see her as a child? A baby sister? Would he laugh in her face?

"Well, I've got tea bags," he said with a shrug. "No idea if the dust that's left in them could still be called tea it's so old." He pulled a cardboard PG Tips box out of the cupboard over the sink and sniffed it. "Could be tea."

"Water's fine," she said laughing and sitting down on the sofa by the window. He fetched a blue glass and a green mug from a cupboard by the fridge then ran both under the cold tap.

"Here," he said, handing her the mug as he sat down beside her. She accepted it but hated drinking water out of a mug, it just felt wrong somehow. Still, Sam probably felt the same way, which was why he'd kept the glass for himself.

"Coral," he said after a moment. "Do you want to save Maud and Sylvie?"

"Well, not particularly," she said with a grumble. "Bitter old cows. But, I mean, yeah I guess. But it can't be done now."

"What if it could?" he asked, and took a sip of water, looking out of the dirty window at the light that was trying to sneak past the smears.

"How?" she asked him, though her heart began to beat hard. Were they right?

"What if I knew a way we could still get the things we need," he said, sliding his thumbs nervously over the glass in his hands. "What if with them we could save more people, more innocent people. Not just Maud and Sylvie, but nice people. People like your friend Lilly."

"She's not my friend," grumbled Coral, remembering bitterly how as soon as Saffron had come to, Lilly had ditched her and forgotten she was even there. "But… what do you mean?"

"Would you want to?" he asked her, looking into her eyes, his face so close to her own. Coral felt her heart beating harder now for a different reason. His face so close to hers, the two of them alone, side by side. "Would you want to save people, other humans, if you could?"

"Yes," agreed Coral nervously, her hands sweating, her mouth feeling dry. "Yes I would."

"Do you trust me?" he asked her, his face moving even closer to hers, his soft brown eyes gazing at her earnestly, his breath close enough to taste.

"Of course," she whispered, setting her mug carefully on the table. "It's you isn't it… you're the one we were looking for…"

"Coral," he said breathily, one of his hands sliding onto her leg, gripping her thigh intently. "I need you. I need you to understand how complicated things are. How much more there is going on than you realise."

"You need me?" she asked, her voice going hoarse and her eyes glazing over.

"Will you help me?" he asked her, his nose touching hers. She felt herself trembling, her heart racing, her hands sweating.

She looked into his eyes, so close to her own that she could make out all the flecks of amber and yellow that decorated the brown of his iris. She could feel his breath on her skin. Nervously she licked her lips, her mouth feeling sandpaper dry.

"Yes," she said softly, then saw him close his eyes and move his face closer.

His lips touched hers and she felt her whole body melt into his. Finally. Finally he wanted her.

ɻ

"I need to get out of here," Saffron suddenly blurted out. "Lilly, please? Can we go?"

"Go where?" demanded Coral's grandmother. "It's not safe to be running off into town alone."

Saffron stood up and started fidgeting desperately, a look of panic on her face.

"They won't be alone," Bentley assured them as he stood, his head well up to Saffron's waist. "Wherever they go, I go."

Saffron looked on the verge of a panic attack and Lilly, whilst not keen on venturing out when they didn't know where the Harvester was nor what he could do to them, didn't want to push Saffron over the edge when she had already dealt with so much. "We won't go far," she promised. "And we will come back."

"Well," said Coral's grandmother. "For the time being we don't need you. We will clean up the mess on the front and do research and preparation in your absence, but without knowing when and where his next move will be we're rather stuck unfortunately."

"So we can go?" asked Lilly.

"Keep the dog with you at all times," instructed Coral's grandmother. "Get some air then come back."

"Deal," agreed Lilly, then nodded to Saffron and the three of them carefully stepped around Hogarth where he lay with his head on a cushion, and a soft blanket placed over him, left the stuffy little coven room, edged carefully through the cramped shop front, then stepped outside into the sunny morning.

Outside people were walking past and looking at the shop in horror and confusion, moving on quickly or stopping to gawp. The light was bright and clean, a light breeze drifted past them carrying the salt of the ocean waves.

"Are you okay?" Lilly asked as they walked away from the shop, Bentley loyally walking at Lilly's side against the kerb.

"No," said Saffron. "But are you? Hogarth was innocent, Lilly, and he's dying!"

Lilly gulped and felt her eyes sting. "I know. He genuinely just wanted to help us. He just wanted to help. But he might not die! She said he might survive!"

"And those women are dead too," said Saffron, her voice cracking. "And Coral's run off with that boy, and the mermaids are all dying, and we've failed and everything's ruined and I'm in so much pain and… and…"

"Hey," said Lilly gently, stopping and putting a hand on Saffron's arm.

"I can't do this anymore, Lilly!" Saffron sobbed. "This world, it's awful. People are awful!"

Aware that people were looking at them, Lilly pulled her into a hug. "Come on, Saff, let's go find somewhere to sit."

"I want to go to the beach," she said, pulling away and looking at Lilly with hope and desperation in her eyes. "Please?"

"Erm," Lilly hesitated. "Okay, but you know the mermaids won't be there? It's daylight."

"I know," Saffron insisted. "I just want to go. Please?"

"We'll go," agreed Lilly. "That okay with you Ben?"

"Of course," Bentley assured her.

Together they walked in silence through the town. Though it was a bright and sunny day it was still too early for most tourist traffic to make its way to the coast. They ended up walking towards the turning for the Harvester's warehouse and Lilly gripped Saffron's arm. She hadn't registered they were walking in that direction, too caught up in her thoughts about Hogarth and what they were going to do now they'd lost their only lead. Her mind had been totally distracted from her surroundings. Had Saffron lead them that way on purpose?

"We shouldn't be here," Lilly hissed.

"I want to go to Mermaid Cove," said Saffron. "And this is the only way I know."

"Saff," protested Lilly, pulling at her friend's arm. "Are you crazy? The Harvester!"

At her side, Bentley rumbled a low growl and stepped in front of them, his nose twitching.

"I'm going Lilly. He won't be there. He won't even see us." Saffron insisted, stepping forwards.

"How can you know that?" demanded Lilly, eyes wide and looking around in case he suddenly stepped out, knife in hand. "I can't save us! Don't you understand? They were wrong, the mermaids were wrong, Maud's vision was wrong. I can't save us. I can't stop him!"

"I'm going," insisted Saffron and wriggled away from Lilly's grasp.

Stepping around Bentley, Saffron headed purposefully down the path. She walked confidently by the track towards the warehouse, not even glancing to the side, and towards the Lobster Shack at the bottom of the street. Cursing herself, Lilly hastily followed her, darting past the track to her right with Bentley keeping pace at her side, and straight after Saffron who was heading over the road and onto the sand.

"Saffron!" Lilly called out. "Wait!"

Saffron looked back over her shoulder, her fiery red hair, though lanker and duller than normal, following her night in a coma, glowed effervescent in the bright morning sun. She waited until Lilly and Bentley had caught up to her, then turned and headed towards the water again.

Lilly followed, wondering when her friend would stop to talk. Worried that this stretch of beach would impact on her so heart wrenchingly again.

As Saffron approached the surf Lilly stopped, giving her some space to look out to sea and gather her thoughts. But Saffron didn't stop. She kept walking into the gently lapping tide.

"Saffron!" Lilly called again, hurrying forwards, but Saffron didn't answer. Soon she was waist deep in the water, then suddenly she launched herself forward and began to swim. "Saffron! Come back!"

Lilly rushed after her, pulling off her shoes and hoody as she went.

"Lilly! I'll go!" insisted Bentley, his huge black body streaking past her and splashing through the shallow water until he too was swimming, his head high over the surface and his enormous feet acting like paddles to rapidly propel him forwards.

Watching them with fear in her heart, Lilly decided there was nothing to do but follow, so she too threw herself into the sea.

Chapter Twenty-One

The water was cold. Not just cold, it was intensely, piercingly, bitterly cold. As she threw herself forward the sea water hit her in the chest and she felt her breath rip from her lungs.

"Fu…" she started to say before a wave of salty ice cold water flooded into her mouth and eyes. She spluttered, choking, blinking frantically and treading water as she thrashed around trying to clear her throat, blinking to get the salt from her eyes.

"Saffron!" came Bentley's deep voice, powerful against the suddenly loud crashing of the sea around Lilly's ears.

Lilly squinted forwards and saw the dog reach Saffron's side, the girl wrapping her pale arm around his firm neck. As she watched, the sun reflecting blindingly from the undulating surface of the sea, Lilly watched as two more heads appeared above the waves. Their faces moved towards Saffron, gliding through the water, one inky black and one porcelain white.

Lilly wanted to swim back to shore, her whole body coming over cold in a way totally different from the cold of the sea. Her veins ran cold. How did Saffron know they would be here? How did they know Saffron would be? Why were they here? What was going on? Something was wrong.

Ignoring her instinct, Lilly pushed forwards, forcing her freezing limbs to battle through the water until she eventually reached Saffron, Bentley and the Mer.

"Lilly," said Ashalia as she reached them. Lilly got the distinct feeling that a conversation had been stopped part way through. "We have bad news."

"What?"

"The Ancients," said Hexanna. "They're planning to attack."

"What?" asked Lilly again, confused. Her brain clouded by the chill in her body. She looked across at Saffron and saw her face looking serene, her movements gentle and flowing. She felt out of her depth in so many ways. "When? How? What?"

"Lord Bray, the leader of the Ancients, found out that we had told you of their existence," said Hexanna, her face dropping guiltily. "He's planning to mount an attack tonight, a pre-emptive attack to maintain their secrecy."

"What's going to happen?" Lilly asked. "What can they do? They're in the water, right?"

"Yes but they have powers beyond us, beyond you," said Ashalia tensely. "They are going to kill about forty thousand humans tonight, as well as other species and Beings you're not as involved with. It'll be a massacre."

"Sh…" Lilly started, then spluttered as water suddenly washed into her mouth again, the salt gagging her.

Bentley appeared at her side, nudging his head under her arm and hoisting her above the water, her weakness in the water obvious. Lilly coughed up water and looked around at Saffron, Ashalia and Hexanna, all of whom seemed unfazed by the waves, their bodies moving in time with the rise and fall of the water as if they were somehow connected to it, not battling against it like Lilly's body was.

Connected.

"Saffron," she said in excitement. "It's you, you're the one connected to the Mer!"

"What?" Saffron asked.

"It's obvious!" Lilly cried, feeling exasperated with herself as her head cleared in a sudden rush. "It's not me. Of course it's not me! It's all about you!"

"What is?" Saffron asked, looking at her with confusion.

"You're the one from the vision, you're the one they've been waiting for," Lilly insisted. "You're the one who can stop the Harvester!"

Saffron looked at her for a moment, her eyes wide and confused, then suddenly a look of understanding and acceptance washed over her. "Yes," she said. "Of course I am."

"Did you know?" Lilly asked the mermaids.

"We knew she was one of us," said Ashalia, shooting a pointed look at Saffron.

"Why didn't you say anything?" Lilly asked, confused. Lives could have been saved if Saffron had been the one to fight the Harvester! But how would Saffron fight? She had no physical power to be used, her only power enhanced Lilly's own, she had nothing with which to attack him. Nothing to defend herself with. How could Saffron possibly be the One when Lilly's own power was too weak to defeat him? "This doesn't make any sense!"

"We didn't know," said Hexanna, holding a long, thin arm out to Saffron, her long white fingers looking even paler than Saffron's own fair, freckled skin. "We suspected, but then you were hurt. You were unconscious and Lilly was the one to fight. Then everything failed."

"How can Saffron fight him?" demanded Lilly, grateful for Bentley's support as he furiously paddled his enormous feet below her, taking her weight with confidence. "She has no power!"

"I have power," said Saffron, glaring at Lilly. "I'm not as strong as you but I have it."

"He's so strong, Saffron!" Lilly insisted, terrified of what would happen to her friend if she went up against a monster like the Harvester. If Lilly couldn't take him down, who in the world could?

"Then I have to be stronger," said Saffron firmly, a gritted determination coming over her face.

Lilly went to protest but looking at Saffron realised she actually believed her. Plus, what other choice did they have at this point? "The Ancients are coming tonight?" Lilly asked, turning back to Ashalia and Hexanna.

"Yes," said Ashalia grimly.

"And forty thousand people?"

"Yes," said Hexanna. "And nothing we know of has the power to stop them."

Lilly's heart sank.

"Lilly does," said Bentley.

Lilly looked at Bentley who nodded slightly, his face dipping in and out of the water beside her. She looked at Saffron, Ashalia and Hexanna who watched her curiously.

Did she? Was she about to be another monumental failure? The lives she was already responsible for weighed on her. Not just previously, but now Iris, Dorothy, Brinly and Hogarth as well. They all died because she was arrogant enough to assume she was the one to save the day and failed, because she wasn't strong enough to stop one man, and now forty thousand more human lives depended on her? Forty thousand people would die if once again she was not the one who could save the day. And not against one man but against an army of Ancient and powerful Mer.

"Crap," she muttered under her breath.

3

"Why didn't you tell me?" Coral asked, cuddling up to Sam's bare chest.

"You were so angry at what was happening, I didn't think you'd understand," he said quietly, stroking her thick dark curls. "It's such a complicated subject."

Coral boosted herself up on her elbow, pulling the blue patterned duvet over herself crossly. "I'm not stupid, you know?"

"I know," he said calmly, smiling at her. "But it's a lot to get your head around. Taking lives to save lives."

"So is that what you're doing?" Coral asked, resting back down. "Saving lives?"

"Partly," he said. "But it's impossible to exist just for the sake of charity, you know?"

"So making money *and* saving lives?"

"I've struggled with it myself," he said. "It's bigger than whether a mermaid dies every now and then. I don't like that anymore than you, I really don't, and so many times I've thought about leaving or even betraying him."

"Why didn't you?"

"Because of the real people who are benefitting so much," he said. "Did you know one mermaid's body could literally save hundreds of lives? Cure hundreds of illnesses?"

"No," said Coral.

"Well it could," he said earnestly. "The magical community has succumbed to diseases that had been practically erased in the time of the Harvester. Innocent people, children. Mermaid parts are some of the most potent Being products there are, and easier to come by than say Dragons or Jinn. And there's kids out there, Coral, kids who are blind or dying and stuff. Kids who could be saved if the law was changed."

"But what about the mermaids?" Coral asked anxiously. "Why don't they get saved?"

"Because sometimes you have to pick your side," Sam said gently. "Sometimes you have to say who you want to save more, your friend or a stranger."

"I just…"

"If you could go back and save the life of your mother, would you?"

"Of course!" Coral insisted, the familiar overwhelming sadness threatening to surge from her eyes as thoughts of her mother swam in her brain. "Of course I would."

"Even if it meant using the blood of a mermaid, or the hair, or kidney or heart?" asked Sam gently, gazing into her eye intensely. "Would you sacrifice a stranger that isn't even your species, to save the life of your own mother?"

Coral gulped, sickness churning in her stomach. "My mum would have hated it… She was totally against using Beings in anyway…" she said, screwing up her face and feeling wretched. "But if I had the chance to be with my mother again? Yes, I would. I would do anything."

"That's what people are facing every day," he said, taking her hand in his and looking deeply into her eyes. "Only they used to have that option to take. Now, without my father's work, nobody would have that choice."

"I understand," said Coral, and gently laid her head back on Sam's chest.

"I knew you would," he said slowly, kissing the top of her head then resting back down. "That's why I want you to meet him."

Coral fixed a confident and certain look on her face whilst inside her nerves were smashing through her at the idea. "I'd love to."

ϡ

The shop front was now clean, no evidence of poor Brinly's blood was left anywhere on the front nor on the ground in front. Lilly idly felt herself wonder if that was the work of a fast and efficient clean up job, or whether it was the consequence of magic. Her body now completely drained, she pushed open the door and the three of them traipsed into the tiny shop, leaving a trail of water and sand behind them.

"What happened to you?" asked Coral's grandmother.

"We, erm," Lilly hesitated. She looked at them all. They were soaking, dripping, and sand was stuck across their skin, clothes and hair. Bentley, whilst having shaken liberally on the beach spraying them heavily with water in the process, was still soaking, his thick black fur matted with wet sand. "We went for a bit of a swim."

"I see that!" exclaimed Coral's grandmother.

"Come on," said Mi. "We'd best get you cleaned up. Some nice hot water will do you the world of good."

As much as she longed to put her stiff, freezing cold and filthy body beneath a hot shower, Lilly shook her head. "Wait," she said. "There's stuff we need to tell you first. And it's important."

Coral's grandmother cocked her head to the side, but gestured the three in. They carefully stepped around Hogarth who looked peaceful, Lilly was grateful to see, though still very weak and vulnerable. His breathing was ragged and faint, but it was there. He was holding on.

"We spoke to the Mer," said Saffron. "They were there, at the beach. Ashalia and Hexanna."

"I see," said Coral's grandmother. "And were they able to give you any more help?"

"Sort of," said Lilly, looking nervously at Saffron. "But we have some bad news first."

She started to explain about the Ancients, what they were and how they maintained their secrecy. Their shocked faces transitioned to fear and anger when she explained about their plan. About the forty thousand human lives they planned to eradicate that very night to protect their secret. Then she remembered it wasn't just humans and that other Beings would be killed too. She began to feel like a hypocritical imperialist and picked awkwardly at her thumb nail.

"What can we do?" demanded Maud. "We have come so far! We can't all die now!"

"I don't know," said Lilly sadly. "They said nothing is strong enough to stop them."

"Can you try for a vision, Maud?" suggested Sylvie.

"My head," said Maud miserably, a look of shame befalling her. "I don't know if I can."

The cat jumped onto the chair at Maud's side and put a gentle paw on her hand. "I understand," she said.

"What else have you got?" Coral's grandmother asked after a moment, her voice heavy.

"It's about the Harvester," said Lilly, the guilt suddenly becoming too much to bare. Their friends were dead because of her. "It's not me. It's Saffron."

"What?" asked Coral's grandmother. "What's Saffron?"

"The one," said Lilly. "The one who can stop him. It's not me."

"But how?" demanded Coral's grandmother. "What power do you have? Aren't you an Enhancer? Why is it you? We've been working with the wrong person this entire time?"

"Iris and Dorothy…" said Mi quietly, her head dropping and a tear sliding from her eye. "Perhaps they would be here…"

"Stop," commanded Coral's grandmother, raising a hand. "Perhaps a lot of things would be different if many circumstances had been changed. We deal with the now. The then can wait until the now is sorted."

Lilly looked at her gratefully. Hearing the women grieve for her error was not an idea she relished.

"Very well," agreed Mi, leaning forward on her cane. "Then now we need to figure out how to move forward, because unless you plan on relocating in the next twelve hours, then the now isn't going to bring us much to think about because we'll all be dead!"

"I think I have a plan…" said Saffron hesitantly. "I think I know what we can do."

"You do?" asked Lilly in surprise.

"Yes…" admitted Saffron, looking at her guiltily. "But it won't be easy."

"Let's do it," said Coral's grandmother. "Whatever it is, it's the best we've got."

Chapter Twenty-Two

Nervously, Coral followed Sam towards the warehouse. Every time she turned around she expected to see Lilly with her hands raised ready to kill her, or her grandmother's face loaded with the kind of rage she reserved for the most heinous of betrayals, but nobody around even looked at her let alone responded with any horror. She moved anonymously through the town that suddenly felt alien to her. Was she doing the right thing? Would they understand her choices? Would she ever be forgiven?

"He might not be happy that you're here," said Sam anxiously. "I know that last time he saw you it wasn't great…"

"No," agreed Coral, thinking back to when she has astral-projected out to where Sam had been injured as the Harvester advanced on them with menace and malevolence in his eyes. "But it was different then… I didn't understand."

Sam nodded, trouble on his face. "I hope he sees that," he said anxiously.

The look on his face made Coral even more nervous. She wiped her moist hands on her jeans and tried to clear the scratching, clawing gunge that was clagging up her throat. Could she do this? Was it worth it? It had to be… nothing else mattered more. This one small choice could give her what she had always wanted. It had to be worth it. It just had to be.

Their feet crunched over the rough ground as they approached the warehouse, the hot mid-morning sunlight that had been so brightly illuminating them on their walk from Sam's flat seemed somehow duller. Coral glanced up and saw a fluffy cloud had drifted across it, casting the entire area in a faded shadow.

"Dad?" called Sam, pushing the door open.

Coral followed him inside, the terror that she had felt the first time they'd entered this building seemed no less now she was being invited in.

"Samuel?" came a voice from inside the huge room, the empty tank glinting menacingly, the smells a mixture of sea water, blood, and something mysterious she couldn't put her finger on that reminded her of when her grandma was hard at work. "What have you got for me?"

Coral looked around for him, and spotted him just as he looked up and saw her. He stood over what she assumed was Brinly's tail, the bottom fin severed lay on a set of scales at the side of the metallic work table, and she had no idea where the rest of Brinly's body was. He held in his hand a peculiar implement that looked a little like an eyelash curler, and there were deep tracks up the tail in various spots where the scales were being ripped out.

"Dad... this is Coral Friday," said Sam nervously.

The Harvester stood straight and placed the eyelash curler down on the table with a clink. "What is she doing here?"

"She's here to help," said Sam. "Her grandmother was about to attack me and she protected me. She's going to help us."

The Harvester walked slowly towards Coral, his large body imposing and strong, his eyes carrying no less venom than last time he looked at her. She felt herself start to shake and tried to look away but couldn't. She wondered if the mermaids felt this way as he approached them, knowing what he was going to do to them, and seeing that murder playing out in the brown of his irises.

"Coral Friday," he said, his voice low and almost melodic. Like he was singing her name without actually singing it. She felt the hairs on the back of her neck standing on end. "Why have you become a turncoat?"

"A, erm, a what?" asked Coral.

"Why have you left the safety of your grandmother's home and coven, turned against a quest you were so passionately committed to, and joined up with the man you perceived so recently as your enemy?" he said. "Is my son really so appealing that you would leave everything you care about and believe in just to be at his side?"

"Sam is all I have," said Coral quietly, her eyes finally flicking away from the Harvester and looking at the boy who stood at her side, suddenly looking so much younger and more vulnerable than she had ever seen him look. "I haven't left everything I care about to be at his side, and I haven't left safety, I've left people who see me as a hopeless child with no real value other than messenger. People who resent me for things that I have never asked them to do for me, and treat me like I'm dirt because they've suffered from doing things they never asked my opinion on. I've not left everything I care about to be with Sam. Sam is everything I care about."

"Are you aware of our plans?" he asked her, glancing at Sam who shuffled on the spot. "Has Sam told you everything or do I still maintain some secrecy?"

"Erm," Coral hesitated. Should she tell him what she knew or act ignorant to protect Sam? She opted for honesty. Sometimes lies are essential, but lies are best covered with layers of truth. "I know you're planning on attacking the Ancients, and I know you're protected from Lilly's powers because of a potion that deflects magic. I know they can't stop you."

The Harvester crossed his arms and nodded, a peculiar smile creeping over his face. "Interesting," he said. "Sam, a word."

Coral watched as Sam silently followed his father to the other side of the room. What would happen she didn't know, but she knew she was in the right place.

ꝫ

"We need to get into the water," said Saffron, an air of confidence to her as she laid out the plan. "If we're going to stop the Ancients we can't do it from land. They won't come ashore and their powers are strong enough to reach us from the ocean. If we are going to stop them, we'll need to do it on their territory."

"How?" asked Lilly, bewildered. She had struggled in the sea just being a few metres from shore and treading water. Asking her to go out to sea to battle Ancient and powerful Mer seemed beyond a stretch.

"There's a spell," said Saffron, her green eyes flicking momentarily to Lilly with guilt on her face. "To become a mermaid."

"To what?" demanded Lilly, her mind flashing back to their first night in the hotel, how Saffron's face had lit up at the sight of that spell on the fake magic site. "That's not possible! That was fake!"

"No, she's right in a way," said Coral's grandmother sagely. "It doesn't exactly make you into a mermaid, but we can get you in the water."

"The Subaqueous," muttered Mi quietly, hobbling towards the bookshelves and running her finger along the books whilst whispering quietly under her breath. "It's not an easy one, and I've never seen it performed."

"What?" demanded Lilly, panic in her chest as she looked around at the women's thoughtful faces in horror. "You actually want us to go into the water? As in *into?* As in *under?*"

"The Subaqueous," said Coral's grandmother confidently, ignoring Lilly's frantic questioning and opening a cupboard. "Liverwort is essential, but do we have any in?"

"Hang on, hang on," demanded Lilly. "This is nuts. What exactly are we expecting to happen here?"

"You don't become a mermaid," explained Coral's grandmother, pulling a glass jar with some green stems in from the cupboard and holding them up to the light, then taking the top off and giving the plant a sniff. "That is magic beyond our abilities, though I'm sure it is possible for some. However, The Subaqueous will grant you, for a time, the ability to breathe and speak under the water just as easily as you do above it, just like the Mer. You won't change by appearance or grow a tail, you'll need to swim like you do now, but for a time you will be, for all intents and purposes, a Mer."

"Do we have what we need?" asked Mi, handing Coral's grandmother a dusty old book.

Peering at the list, the old woman nodded. "We do, but it's a very delicate process. Very fragile. And it won't last long."

"How long?" asked Lilly.

"No more than an hour," said Coral's grandmother, beginning to finely chop a stem of the Liverwort, sniffing the entire time. "Maud, the scales?"

"An hour?" asked Lilly in consternation. "I have an hour? To find the Ancients and either convince them not to kill us all or fight the entire army alone?"

"You won't be alone," said Saffron. "I'll be with you."

"But you need to fight the Harvester!" protested Lilly, her mind spinning. "What if you get killed? We'll still need someone to stop him! How are we going to do this?"

"We don't have a choice," said Saffron, matter-of-factly. "I'll help you stop the Ancients, then we'll get back and go and find the Harvester, then we will figure that out. But if we don't do this, there's no point putting energy into working out how to stop the Harvester because we'll all be dead anyway!"

"But, but," Lilly protested wildly, but the plan was already underway. It was happening. She was going under the water. And the most horrible thing was she couldn't see any other option.

Saffron grinned at her. She looked alive.

Lilly felt like death.

"Before we do though," said Coral's grandmother, looking around the room for a moment. "We have a problem."

"What?" asked Lilly, wondering how much worse it could possibly get.

"We are two down," she said. "For a potion this fragile, for work this important, we need a complete coven to give us the strength we need."

Lilly's eyes dropped again and she picked anxiously at her thumb nail. "I'm so sorry," she said quietly. Yet another reason to hate herself for the deaths of Iris and Dorothy.

"Sit with us, girls," said Mi, smiling at them gently, a reassuring look in her eyes.

Maud, Mi, Coral's grandmother and Sylvie the cat carefully positioned themselves on the floor in a circle, leaving a space between Mi and Coral's grandmother. "Join us," said Coral's grandmother.

Nervously, Lilly and Saffron approached the circle of powerful women and lowered themselves to the floor.

"Take my hand," said Mi to Saffron.

Saffron obeyed, and at her side, Coral's grandmother took Lilly's hand. Lilly held her palm out to Saffron who smiled then took it. As Saffron's soft, cool skin landed in Lilly's hand, she felt a rush of heat and energy through her, a surge of confidence blasted into her brain and her heart began to beat harder and faster. She closed her eyes, feeling the power taking over her body and believed, in that very moment, she was unstoppable. The Ancients would succumb, the Harvester would be killed, and nothing could possibly get in her way. She would win. They would win. Nothing could go wrong.

Coral's grandmother pulled her hand from Lilly's and the power rush stopped as soon as it had begun, but left a lingering sensation of courage and determination in its wake.

Lilly opened her eyes and looked around the room. By the smiles on their faces she assumed they felt the same way as she did.

ろ

"Coral," said the Harvester, approaching her again. "Tell me everything you know."

"About what?"

"Your grandmother's coven," he said. "Why they're doing what they're doing, what their weaknesses are. How they plan to stop me."

"They can't stop you," said Coral emphatically, taking this as a sign she was being trusted. "But their plan was that Lilly's power, and her connection to the Mer, combined with an old reading from Mi and a potion from my grandmother would be enough to overpower you."

"But why do they want to?" he asked, leaning in. "I happen to know that one Opal Friday has on a number of occasions attempted to arrange the purchasing of products from me. Why try and stop me, if they have need of the products I supply?"

"They want the products because Maud, the Seer, she has cancer," said Coral. "She is struggling to get visions and they want to do something that could cure it. And so that Sylvie, she's a shape shifter, can transfigure out of cat form. She was cursed. They've both not got long left without the mermaid parts to go in a potion for my grandmother."

"I see," said the Harvester, nodding, listening with genuine interest to her speak. Coral felt her confidence grow. She was rarely listened to with such intensity.

"They used to be this really powerful coven," said Coral. "They used to buy mermaid bits and other stuff, dragons and pixies and stuff I guess, and they were pretty strong and... I guess relevant? But now they're not. They can't get the stuff they need to be all powerful and their stocks are running low and it pisses them off."

"So why try to remove me?" he asked, approaching Coral and gesturing to a seat at his desk. She sat and he pulled up another chair, putting his elbows on his knees and staring at her with fascination. "Surely we are on the same side. Had they been able to offer me suitable compensation we'd have, I'm sure, formed an alliance. Lives would have been saved and their power could have been increased. We want the same things, after all."

"Removing you puts the Mer in their debt," said Coral, shifting on her seat, wondering what Sam was doing and looking around. He was watching quietly from beside the severed tail. She shuddered. "Lilly has a connection to the Mer, with the Mer indebted to them and Lilly already having their trust and the ability to talk to them..."

"They remove the middle man," said the Harvester, leaning back. "Clever girls."

Coral scowled. Women. Then she shook it off and smiled up at him. "So can I do anything to help you?"

"Yes," said the Harvester. "If you're willing to join us there will be many benefits I can grant you. But there will also be many risks. If we are to conquer the Ancients and harvest them for their power and resources, it will not be easy."

"I understand," agreed Coral, nodding earnestly.

"Very well," agreed the Harvester, smiling. Pleased at her compliancy, Coral assumed. "Let's get to work. We have much to finish before we set out, and only a few hours in which to do it."

Chapter Twenty-Three

Making the Subaqueous was an intense process and nobody dared speak. Nobody dared move. Lilly wasn't even sure she was supposed to be breathing because it certainly didn't sound like anyone else was.

Coral's grandmother kept checking the temperature with a long, thin, glass thermometer, never letting it get too hot and turning down the heat when the mercury rose, turning the flame higher if it dropped, though each movement on the temperature was a fraction Lilly had struggled to see for the first few alterations.

"Soon," she said after what felt like several hours, but Lilly knew in reality it was not even two.

"Are you ready?" asked Sylvie, looking at the two girls, her tail twitching.

"Yes," said Lilly, confidently. The power of the coven's unity was still in her veins, still powering her heart. "We can do it."

"Changing your form, even if it is purely your internal biology not your physical appearance, is intoxicating," said Sylvie, a note of warning in her voice. "It can consume your mind, make you question your true identity and what it means to be you. Be aware of that at all times. Hold in your mind a confidence about who, and what, you are."

"I'm sure we'll be fine," said Lilly. "It's only for an hour and we know who we are."

"Just remember," Sylvie said. "Changing into a species with qualities such as the Mer will get to you. It's not like you're becoming something pointless like a rat or, say, a dog."

"Hey!" growled Bentley, standing up and looking at her defiantly.

"Down boy," said the cat, her claws creeping out and a sly look in her eyes.

"Sylvie," said Coral's grandmother, her tone sharp but quiet. "Behave. The potion is ready."

Lilly's confidence began to wane. What she was about to take on suddenly weighing her down again.

"Let's go," said Saffron, an eagerness in her voice.

Lilly carefully checked Hogarth's pulse and made sure he was tucked in. Coral's grandmother assured her that he would remain unconscious for some time yet, assuming he'd ever wake up. After she was satisfied he was warm and safe, she agreed to go.

For the second time in the past twenty-four hours, though with notable differences in their numbers, the collective from the coven's shop moved herd like out of the door, down the road, and towards the sea.

३

The Harvester stood over his cauldron, piles of open text books around him, some so old the pages were mottled yellow and brown, some so new they smelled shiny.

"The blueschist," he said, holding out a hand.

Coral frantically checked the labels on the tubs that surrounded her and found a fine blue powder, which she handed to him. He took it and carefully measured out three spoons on a small silver scoop, sprinkling it gently into the cauldron.

The smell was horrific. She looked at Sam, hoping to share a moment of amusement over the horrific odour that was attacking their nostrils, but he didn't return her gaze. He looked tense, angry. She watched him, trying to catch his eye, trying to ascertain what was happening with him, but he seemed to pointedly look anywhere but at her.

"Now the liquorice," said the Harvester, right hand out again as the left continued to carefully stir.

Coral handed him the sticky black goop and watched him carefully spoon it out. The smell worsened, the air seeming to thicken with it until she could taste it in her mouth like a thick syrup sticking to the back of her tongue. She coughed and gagged, her stomach churning and acid burning its way up her gullet in protest.

After a few moments the Harvester stood back and admired his work. "This will simmer now for an hour," he announced. "And then we shall be ready."

The late afternoon sun was high and hot when they reached the beach. Crowds of families littered the sand, some starting to pack up to head back to their hotels and houses for dinner, others making the most of the sun before it started to sink. The air smelled salty and fresh from the ocean, and of BBQ and sweat from the land.

Lilly looked out towards the water and saw the deep aquamarine water surging back and forth, crested with white as the waves broke against the shore. She shuddered. She was dreading this.

At her side, Saffron looked like her feelings inside were the exact opposite of dread. The light breeze washed through her hair, rippling it gently like a waterfall of wafting tangelo coloured waves. Her face beamed out towards the water, luminescent in the yellow light. Joy, excitement and life radiated from her.

"This way," said Coral's grandmother quietly. "We need to be well away from people to do this. We will find a quiet spot."

They walked down the coast, waiting for the crowds to thin until they found a quiet area away from the bustle of restaurants and hotels where just a man with a dog and stick played. Bentley stayed close to Lilly's side, ignoring the barks of the little terrier that seemed fascinated by the horse sized creature that smelled of his species. The crowd of stony faced women and their animal accompaniments seemed to give the man an uncomfortable stir and he summonsed the barking terrier and hastily headed through the surf towards the more populated area.

"Oh jeez," Lilly whispered as they walked towards the beach.

"You're going to need to breathe under the water," said Coral's grandmother, handing each of them a glass vial. "If you don't breathe in you will pass out as if you had never taken the Subaqueous. But that will mean fighting every natural instinct you have. Your whole brain will be telling you not to breathe, that you'll drown if you breathe, and that will be nearly impossible to ignore. But you absolutely must ignore it, you must force yourself to breathe in or this entire thing will have been for nothing and the Ancients will destroy us all. Do you understand?"

"Yes," said Lilly, she meant it with everything she had though didn't feel any certainty that she could do what she knew she had to do.

"We'll do it," insisted Saffron, confidence and certainty emanating from her.

"Let's go," said Coral's grandmother.

"Lilly, please be safe," begged Bentley, gazing at her with huge brown eyes full of devotion. "If anything goes wrong, I will be here. I won't leave this beach until you're back."

Lilly bent down and kissed him gently on the top of his large black head. "Thank you, Bentley," she whispered to him.

The coven and their dog walked towards the water. Lilly took off her sandals and cardigan, but left her shorts and t-shirt in place. Saffron followed suit. Stepping into the water Lilly felt the same icy shock to her skin, the water biting her flesh despite the warmth of the sun heating it throughout the day.

"Ready?" Saffron asked her, holding the glass vial up like a champagne flute.

Lilly looked at her, then to the watching faces on the sand, then back to Saffron. "Ready," she said, and clinked her glass vial against Saffron's own.

Together they downed the potion inside. It felt cold. It felt cold like the water round her feet. She felt it creeping like an ice cube down her throat and filling her stomach with ice. She grimaced and saw Saffron pull the same face.

"Go, quickly," said Coral's grandmother insistently. "You have an hour."

Lilly and Saffron turned and walked into the water. Lilly felt herself shivering in horror, the water stretched in front of her like a terrifying ocean of unknown. The surface she could see, but it wasn't the surface she'd be exploring. It was whatever was below. Whatever was waiting in the darkness of the deep.

As the water came up to their waists, Saffron looked at her with a wide eyed grin and launched herself forwards in an elegant dive, disappearing below the surface in a swoop. Lilly looked back to shore and saw everyone staring. She had to. She had to do it. Saffron wasn't reappearing, the potion must be working. She had to go in. As she prepared to jump she felt herself take a deep breath, wondered if it would make any difference, then dived.

The cold of the water bit into the sides of her head giving her an instant headache. She swam below the surface trying to force herself to breathe, or at least to open her eyes. It was horrible. She couldn't see, she couldn't tell where she was, and she was starting to panic.

Hands gripped her, cold hands wrapping onto her arms. She opened her mouth in a silent scream and tried to pull away, thrashing frantically in horror. Who or what had just taken hold of her? Was it an Ancient?

"Lilly!" she heard. "Lilly it's me!"

It sounded like Saffron. She sounded strange, she didn't know how to describe her friends voice other than wet, but it was clear and it was definitely Saffron.

"Lilly!" came Saffron's voice again. "Open your eyes! You need to breathe!"

Terrified in a way she had never known, Lilly flickered her eyes nervously, expecting the pain of the salt water to slice into her eyeballs. Bizarrely she felt nothing. It was as if she was opening her eyes on land. She couldn't even feel the water.

She opened them fully and saw Saffron in front of her, a huge smile across her face as her red hair fanned around her.

"It's okay, Lil," she promised her, nodding happily. "But you have to breathe. Just breathe in. Do it now or you'll pass out."

Lilly knew she was right. She was feeling her head start to fog over and panic rising in her chest. She had to breathe. But everything inside her begged her not to, begged her not to breathe and inhale in sea water that would flood her lungs and drown her in moments. But she had to. Saffron was breathing, so easily, she watched as her chest rose and fell.

"Now!" Saffron insisted, panic starting to show on her face as Lilly felt darkness beginning to creep in around her eyes.

Lilly opened her mouth and breathed in.

"Oh my god," she gasped. The water somehow seemed to feel like air in her lungs. With huge relief she gulped in the water, though somehow it was going no further than her mouth, the oxygen of the water seeming to break free and wash down her throat leaving the water behind.

"This is wonderful!" Saffron cried, spinning in the water so her hair spun like an orange whirlpool about her face. "I've never felt anything so incredible."

Lilly looked up and saw sunlight breaking gently through the water, glowing like yellow pools on the surface. Around her the water seemed almost green but somehow clear. She could see far, though the further away she looked the less she could make out and things seemed to fly around slowly, dark shadows that she couldn't decipher, creatures or Beings she didn't know, and it made her feel dizzy.

"We need to find the Ancients," said Lilly. "We don't have long."

"Ashalia and Hexanna are near," said Saffron, turning slowly in the water.

"How do you know?" Lilly asked her, looking around in confusion.

"I don't know how I know," Saffron admitted. "I just know."

"Saffron," came a voice behind them.

Lilly startled as Ashalia suddenly swam into view. "You're here," she said, smiling warmly at Saffron. "You look beautiful."

Saffron's face lit up even more and she allowed Ashalia to embrace her. The mermaid's long, thin arms wrapping tightly around her, Saffron's long red hair flowing like a veil about the two of them.

"Where's Hexanna?" Saffron asked.

"She's watching," said Ashalia. "We think they're preparing to make their move. The water is starting to move really violently; some big power is definitely being used."

"Show us," said Saffron confidently.

"This way," said Ashalia, turning and flapping her tail to propel herself forwards. Saffron followed, her legs kicking furiously as she kept up with relative ease. Behind them, struggling to move at their speed, Lilly swam as hard as she could, but they kept moving beyond her easy range of vision, stopping to wait for her for a few minutes with urgent looks on their faces, deep in conversation, then swimming on again as she began to keep up.

A huge eel creature suddenly swam up from below her, swerved in front of her and swam away. Lilly discovered she was unable to scream underwater, but she could thrash in a hysterical panicked way and end up nearly somersaulting from shock.

Looking around in fear, Lilly pushed forward, desperate to get into the company of Ashalia and Saffron, but scared of what she'd find when they reached the realm of the Ancients. Terrified of what she was expected to face. Terrified of failure... again.

The two stopped ahead of her and allowed her to catch right up. "We're nearly there," said Ashalia quietly. "From here we need to go quietly. We'll dive down low to the floor and keep to the reeds. Hexanna is waiting for us."

Lilly looked down. The sunlight seemed to not reach down there. It just got darker and darker, the deep teal of the water fading to black.

"Let's go," said Saffron, and together the two descended.

More scared of staying there alone than following them to the murky depths, Lilly followed quickly.

Through the water they moved, lower and lower. Lilly couldn't tell how far they were from the shore but it felt like they were going a long way down. As they reached the blackness and the ocean floor, Lilly saw the light was managing to reach here and though it was gloomy, it was still perfectly easy to see. She didn't know if that was reality or the effects of the spell though. A shoal of tiny silver fish whizzed past them, swirling and swishing as one.

"Quick," came a voice as Hexanna darted up from the reeds. "Down here."

The three followed the porcelain skinned mermaid down into the shelter of the plants. Lilly hated how they felt on her skin, like slimy fingers tickling and stroking her without her consent.

"Any news?" asked Ashalia.

"There are more patrols, and the water keeps rushing violently away," she said. "It won't be long."

"We only have an hour," said Lilly. "Well… however long is left since we took the potion."

"Then we need to move right now," said Hexanna. "The longer we leave them to brew this power, the more potent it will become and we can't risk them unleashing it. Not if you want your people to survive."

"Ready?" Saffron asked Lilly.

Lilly popped her head up from the reeds, looking towards the realm of the Ancients. It stood, surrounded by large standing stones, with a swirling mass of water moving within them. It looked intimidating and oppressive, like great power was contained within it, ready to be unleashed on the unsuspecting humanity that waited on land.

Could she stop it? There was only one way to find out. "Ready," she confirmed.

Chapter Twenty-Four

"STOP!" came the roar of a sentry, spear aloft, as Saffron and Lilly swam towards the realm of the Ancients.

The water was now a thick whirlpool behind him, swirling grey climbing higher and higher above them, a rushing wide mass of energy pummelling past them with a rushing, gushing, menacing sound.

"We need to speak to Lord Bray!" Lilly demanded with more confidence than she felt.

"What are you?" demanded the sentry, swimming towards them.

Lilly felt her skin crawl. The way the Mer looked was unnerving enough, but this scales-covered Ancient with his piercing green eyes and wild, serpentine hair like thick tendrils of seaweed, was something beyond that. Something more primal. He almost looked like he was made of the ocean rather than existing within it.

"Humans," said Lilly.

"You are abominations!" he roared, brandishing his spear at them with disgust in his eyes. "You do not belong here! I shall not let you intrude on the sanctity of this area!"

"You have to!" demanded Lilly, looking up as the maelstrom headed towards the surface, carrying within it something powerful enough to destroy forty thousand of her people. She needed him to move. He had to let them pass, but there just wasn't time! "If you don't, I'll have to kill you and go anyway!"

"Try it, you pathetic halfling," he snarled, holding his spear towards her as the tip began to glow like liquid metal. "How you exist in our territory I do not know, but I shall destroy you if you attempt to go any further."

Lilly sighed and glanced at Saffron. She didn't want to do it, she didn't want to be responsible for any more deaths for the rest of her life. But that included the deaths of the people above and if she didn't prevent that when she was able, she knew she'd be partly to blame. "Move now," demanded Lilly. "This is your last chance! Please! I don't want to have to hurt you!"

The sentry emitted a war cry of fury and rage and launched himself at her. Lilly took Saffron's hand and carefully blasted him with a power that sent him reeling back, his face hanging slack and his spear drifting free of his hand.

"Is he dead?" asked Saffron, watching the Ancient as he hung limply in the water before them.

"I hope not," admitted Lilly. She had aimed to knock him out, though wasn't certain she had accomplished it. "But we don't have time to wait around and see so let's go."

Silently, Saffron followed Lilly forward towards the whirlpool that raged before them, a huge, wide funnel that was creeping higher and higher towards the surface.

Lilly didn't know how long they had left, but she knew it wasn't long, breathing was starting to feel unnatural.

"What do we do?" Saffron asked as they passed through the standing stones and were confronted with the swirling mass of rushing water before them.

"Whatever we can," said Lilly.

Then she kicked forward and swam into the churning water.

ʒ

On the shore, Coral's grandmother noticed a strange bubbling starting to appear on the surface of the water, about a mile out to sea. The sky overhead darkened as huge, grey storm clouds crept across the sun.

"It's happening," she said grimly.

Then her phone beeped. Pulling it out of her pocket she looked at the message and then gasped.

"Is everything okay?" asked Mi.

"No," she said, looking upwards as huge, fat raindrops began to fall, her face clouding over like the sky above. "And it's about to get a lot worse."

ع

The water hit her like she was being body-slammed by an iron bar. It crashed into her side, dragging her with the rushing mass of water. The strain to breathe became more intense and she felt herself being tossed and turned, flung about and pelted by stones and debris. She couldn't open her eyes. She couldn't hear anything beyond the rushing screaming of the water around her. She didn't know which way was back into the open water and which way was forward, but she knew she had to swim in any direction or she would certainly die right there.

Kicking and clawing through the water she forced herself in the direction she hoped was forward and tumbled out into a shocking stillness and eerie silence.

Opening her eyes, she looked around. She was surrounded in a wide circle by the wall of violent whirlpool but could hear nothing except an unnatural and deathly silence. A hundred faces stared at her from where they floated in the water, surrounding a tall rock, their eerie faces and large eyes locked onto her own. On top of the rock was a large, powerful Ancient with his arms aloft and a fiendish spear clasped in his right hand. Lilly couldn't tell what he was doing, but his concentration was entirely focussed above him, the water that spun around them in a bizarre and ominous silence seemed to be controlled by him, and nothing mattered more.

Nobody made a sound, nobody seemed to even be breathing. She could hear her blood pumping through her veins. Everyone looked intense and serious, and her intrusion was as unwelcome as it was startling. Like walking in on a church service in progress and being stared at by the entire congregation.

Saffron suddenly tumbled out of the water a few metres away from where Lilly silently treaded water, trying to work out what her next move should be. In outraged panic, Saffron began screaming swear words prolifically, breaking the intense and sombre silence that Lilly felt trapped within, as she battled with the tangled mane of hair that had mummified around her head and arms.

"What the hell?" Saffron demanded as her face emerged, staring around at the silent Ancients.

"Lord Bray!" Lilly shouted, Saffron's obscenities snapping her out of the fearful daze in which she found herself.

Above her the Ancient leader ignored her. The faces of the surrounding audience watched Lilly and Saffron in fearful silence. Confused, perhaps, how two human shaped creatures could have not only discovered them but were able to survive in their world.

"Don't come any closer," called a russet headed Ancient, his scales the colour of driftwood and his eyes like coal. "You don't belong here."

"I'm going to stop you," said Lilly as ferociously as she could muster. "You can't kill all those people."

"Nothing can stop Lord Bray," the Ancient declared. "Not now."

"Leave here!" barked another.

"You don't belong here!" came another voice.

Lilly ignored them and began to swim upwards, Saffron at her side. Soon they were eye level with Lord Bray who glinted like a suit of armour, his face displaying the power he harnessed inside. Whatever magics they had working for them were strong, and they were all directed through that one Ancient Mer and his solid, muscular arms that pointed towards the surface of the ocean.

"Lord Bray!" Lilly shouted. "Stop! Now!"

"You have no power over me, and nothing can stop me!" declared Lord Bray, glancing momentarily at them with scorn on his face. "And if you try, my people will destroy you."

Lilly knew there was no knocking this one out. If he survived this then he would try again, and next time she might not be there to stop him. If he didn't die right now, forty thousand lives would be the price of that mercy. She glanced at Saffron and took her hand.

"Stop!" came a voice from below as an Ancient began swimming towards her, brandishing a sword.

"Please!" Lilly shouted at him. "Nobody else needs to die today!"

Lord Bray let out a hearty laugh as he watched his soldier swimming up with furious loyalty on his face. As their attacker reached level with them, his sword over his head ready to swing down, Lilly felt herself panic, held out her hands and shouted "Die!"

Instantly the sword dropped from his hands, the heavy blade sinking fast through the water. The Ancient, his rust coloured hair and glistening brown scales, hung in the water, his once coal black eyes now greyed over with death.

Below them the watching Ancients shrunk back away from the two girls, fear in their eyes as they watched the strong and powerful soldier fall through the water like a piece of old rope, his life taken so easily by two human, teenage girls with no weaponry.

"Lord Bray!" Lilly shouted again. "Stop what you're doing!"

The Ancient on top of the rock looked down at them, his arms still raised high and the water still rushing around him like a vortex.

"Get out!" he roared in a furious rage.

Lilly felt her heart get heavy. She knew she'd have to do it. For one thing the water was starting to clag in her mouth, she wouldn't physically have the time to talk him around. "If you don't stop I will kill you."

Lord Bray looked at the numbers of his people that had died by their hand, then back up to Lilly's face. "You have power, child, I am not blind to that," he said in his booming voice. "But I am stronger than any of my people!"

"I won't let you do it!" Lilly shouted at him, meeting his gaze with as much determination and ferocity as she could master. "I won't let you kill all those people!"

For a moment she thought Lord Bray was going to attack her, his face turning thunderous as he glared at the two girls, his arms high as the whirlpool crept higher and higher. But then he began to laugh, his laugh echoed through the water around them.

"You pathetic creature," he roared, still laughing. "There is nothing a Halfling like you can do to stop me. Our power is magnificent. Our power is unstoppable."

Above them Lilly saw the swirling current meet the surface, the water starting to churn violently above them like a shark attack and the energy seemed to rush about them. It was happening. Time was up. Either he would die, or thousands of her own people would.

"Lilly," Saffron whispered at her side, panic on her face as she gripped Lilly's hand tightly. "I can't breathe!"

Saffron's face was pale and terrified and Lilly felt herself begin to choke. The spell was ending. They were not going to survive down there for much longer.

"Help," Saffron cried, spluttering in the water in panic.

Lilly held out her hand, held Saffron's own tightly in the other, and sent a powerful jet of death blasting towards Lord Bray. He let out a roar of anger, and lowered his arms to launch a counter attack. But then Lilly's power hit him and he fell. His strong body collapsed, crumpled, and fell backwards into the water behind him, lifeless and limp.

The rushing water began to disperse. The surface above stopped churning, the whirlpool slowed and cascaded, falling into the ocean around it as sticks, stones and debris that had been churned up in the rushing water began to drift to the ocean floor. Lord Bray's body fell too, his powerful form now limp and powerless. The lower he got, the more the vortex of water slowed, until eventually the ocean fell still again, and Lord Bray's body landed on the sand below with a gentle thump, surrounded by his horrified followers.

Ancient faces looked up at them. Faces full of terror and awe. Their leader had been killed and by humans no less, and now they were left with no plan of attack and no powerful commander to focus on. They looked lost and remarkably vulnerable for a race that held such power and history.

Saffron started scrabbling at Lilly's arm. Lilly realised she had started holding her breath and her eyes were starting to hurt. The surface of the water felt like miles away so she started to kick. Together they swam as fast as they could for the surface, fear taking hold as the spell wore off.

The water ahead looked darker and the closer they got the rougher it looked. Just as she felt she was starting to lose control, her head beginning to fog over and her chest beginning to scream, they broke the surface.

Lilly gasped and heard Saffron at her side sucking in the air desperately. The sky overhead was dark like night, and huge raindrops battered down on them. Lilly breathed in the air and looked around frantically. Where was shore? The rain was so heavy and thick and the water so choppy it was hard to tell.

"Did we win?" asked Saffron. "Have we saved everyone?"

"Yeah," said Lilly, her voice loud to combat the sound of the waves and the rain, but her whole body drained of energy. "We won. But now we need to find land!"

At their side, Ashalia and Hexanna appeared.

"You were amazing," said Ashalia. "But those Ancients are in a panic! They've never seen power like you!"

Her voice was nearly lost to the increasing wind and rain that thrashed the water.

"You just need to stop the Harvester now!" declared Hexanna, practically shouting to be heard.

"We'll find him," promised Lilly, treading water as best she could whilst wiping the rain from her eyes, her hair plastered to her face and a horrible taste of saltwater contaminating her mouth. "He'll be out there somewhere. Saffron can do it. We'll do it. But now we need to get to land!"

"This way," said Ashalia.

The water was rough and battered at their sides, crashing into their faces and forcing them down below the surface then fighting them as they dragged their way back up. Even Saffron struggled, the Mer regularly gave up fighting the weather on the surface, and swimming below where the water was calmer, popping up in front of them occasionally to keep them on course.

ᚱ

"Don't move," commanded the Harvester as Sam stood between him and the coven, a large knife in his hand.

Coral watched from behind him, a sick feeling in her stomach.

The Harvester stepped towards the water with a large pot containing the potion he had created to paralyse and drag the Ancients to the surface. She desperately wanted to ask her grandmother whether they had a plan, whether they expected to be able to fight the Harvester, but she dared not move.

Watching silently, Coral saw the Harvester tipping the pot so a thick, oily black solution that crept like tar or treacle slid into the sea as if it knew where it was going, a sinister deliberation in the creeping way the substance moved. Despite being a relatively small amount, as soon as it connected with the salty water, the potion began to spread and expand, sloshing about on the waves as it crept forwards into the deeper water, a slimy thick black skin crawling towards the Ancients it was designed to hunt, moving with it's bizarre and horrifying intention and desire. She knew it would reach the surface above their realm then sink like a suffocating, molasses blanket that would cling to them, drown them in their own sanctity, and force their bodies to the surface to be gathered like leaves from a swimming pool.

Coral's skin crawled. The Harvester laughed a victorious roar of satisfaction.

"You're a monster!" shouted Mi, her body shaking with rage.

"I'm a businessman!" the Harvest retorted with a roar. "You want to save the lives of this old woman! This cat! The lives of Beings you see worthy! You'll sacrifice animals and UnBeings all day without hesitation for causes you deem to be deserving!"

"People who need saving!" said Coral's grandmother with disgust on her face. "You! You kill for profit! For vengeance! You seek to murder innocent girls just because they get in your way!"

"Why my clients seek their products is none of my business," said the Harvester. "But I can assure you, they believe their needs are as admirable as you do. I may be a monster, but you, madam, are a hypocrite."

Coral's grandmother looked Coral directly in the eye and Coral felt ice chill through her veins. Could she do this? Was she strong enough? Was it worth it?

"Dad!" Sam suddenly shouted, pointing out to sea. "Someone's coming!"

Chapter Twenty-Five

Lilly felt weak. Exhausted. Forcing her body to fight the waves that threatened to drag her back to the depths was debilitating. It took everything she had. At her side, Saffron was fairing little better, she looked cold and scared and drained of all energy. But still they swam on.

"Something's coming," came Hexanna's voice as she appeared by their side. "Look! In the water!"

Lilly forced her eyes to focus further ahead and saw a darkness rushing towards them. It looked like an oil spill she had seen on the news, the sticky stuff that ravaged the oceans and coated sea birds and fish in a disgusting substance that ended their lives.

"What is it?" Lilly asked.

"It's coming straight for us!" cried Saffron.

Sure enough, slow as their progress to shore was, the sticky oil was moving three times as fast towards them. Lilly tried to scream in horror as it reached them but was too cold and too weak, all she managed was a strangled gargle as the slime slid over her, crawling over her skin like cold, greasy hands, slipping and sliding, leaving behind a trail of discomfort and violation.

Ashalia and Hexanna began to thrash wildly, gasping for air as the sticky blackness coated them, clinging to them in a way it didn't cling to Lilly and Saffron. It gripped them, sliding up over their faces and weaving its ghastly tentacles of slime into their hair.

"What do we do?" cried Saffron.

"Help them!" cried Lilly, splashing through the slime to reach their two friends.

Lilly grabbed Ashalia and Lilly grabbed Hexanna. Carefully as she could, she treaded water with leaden legs whilst she tried to wipe the oil from Ashalia's eyes and mouth and nose, pushing the slime aside to try and reach clean water from below the surface, splashing her face desperately, but the slime clung on.

"It won't come off!" Lilly cried out, frustrated and scared. "If they go under the water covered in this they'll drown!"

"We need to get out of this!" cried Saffron. "Get to shore!"

"Can you swim?" Lilly asked Ashalia, frantically wiping more goo from her face as it purposefully recoated her.

"Maybe," spluttered Ashalia. She tried to move her arms but the slime pinned her down, wrapping around her body. "My tail can move, but…" she tried to speak more but the oil slid into her mouth making her choke as she frantically spat the disgusting substance out with little success.

"We've got to help them," Lilly cried. "Don't speak, we'll get you to shore!"

Lilly put an arm around Ashalia's waist and frantically began to kick through the water. Safe below the surface where movement was still possible, Ashalia's tail pushed them forward whilst Lilly kicked and pulled her. If she had thought it was hard work before, if she had thought she was drained of everything, Lilly was discovering new depths of exhaustion and new abilities, summonsing energy from nowhere. Do or die, she thought to herself. Get to shore or it's all over.

"Lilly!" Saffron gasped as she pulled Hexanna along in the same way. "Look."

"What?" asked Lilly, pushing her head up and away from the thick oily water. "Who is that?"

On the shore they could see a crowd of people, more than they had left behind them.

"It's him!" cried Saffron. "There's Coral! It's the Harvester! He's got them all trapped!"

"We've got nothing ready!" said Lilly. "How are you going to fight him?"

"We'll just have to try!" Saffron insisted.

"Now?" wept Lilly, barely able to get to shore let alone fight a foe of such magnitude.

"Now!" agreed Saffron.

ঽ

"They're coming," said Sam, laughing. "They must know they don't stand a chance! We've nearly destroyed them every time, what hope do they have when they're unprepared and tired?"

"Why aren't they swimming away?" asked Coral, looking out to sea, observing the two girls swimming awkwardly through the stormy waters, struggling to drag two people covered in the black tar potion with them.

"They're trying to save the mermaids," said the Harvester, his voice a mixture of amusement and also admiration thought Coral. "They must know they can't fight me, not without all their potions and things at the ready, but they know the mermaids will die if they're left."

"But they'll die if they come!" said Coral.

"They're sacrificing themselves," said Sam. "Stupid little girls."

"It's brave," said Coral, glaring at him.

Sam went to argue but the Harvester held up a hand to his son. "Coral is right. They don't stand a chance but they're facing me head on with that knowledge. I admire that."

Sam's eyes flashed bitterly and he looked away from them and back at the coven. He brandished the knife at the watching women with resentful and painful fury. The women, dog and cat all remained rooted to the spot, watching the girl and the mermaids struggle towards them.

ꝛ

Whilst the focus was on the girls as they swam ever closer, Opal Friday slipped a glass vial out of her coat pocket and pushed it up her sleeve. Mi caught her eye and pulled a tightly folded sheet of paper from her handbag. Bentley, with Sylvie at his side, nodded his head ever so slightly at them then looked away again. With a momentary glance towards her granddaughter, Opal looked back out to sea and waited.

ꝛ

Lilly's feet struck ground and she splashed awkwardly with Ashalia at her side, the black slime gripping to every inch of the mermaid that Lilly dragged up through the water.

Ahead of them, standing on the beach with a cold smile stretched across his face stood the Harvester with a long sharp knife glinting in his right hand, Coral stood to his right and Sam wielding a knife at the coven who watched wide eyed in the gloom.

Lilly glanced towards Saffron who was struggling with Hexanna in the same way. The two mermaids, their eyes now sealed shut by oil, their ears clogged and their mouth barely able to suck in air lay still, the fight gone, completely reliant on Lilly and Saffron as they lay limply in their arms.

"Hello, Lilly," said the Harvester, smiling more as she struggled, soaking and exhausted, to drag Ashalia out of the black slime.

She had nothing. She could do nothing at all. If he came at her with that knife she would die. Even if she had been rested and at full strength, she was physically incapable of defending herself from the attack of a grown man, especially one as strong as the Harvester. With her power useless against him, she was helpless. And Saffron, however much she was destined to fight him and win, could do nothing without the potion and words to enable that power to come to the fore. They were two teenage girls, exhausted and half drowned, and two poisoned and near death mermaids, lying in the surf at the feet of a monster, with nothing they could do to stop him.

"What are you doing?" Lilly asked him, gazing up at him as the tar covered water lapped around her, and just wanting answers before she died.

He looked at her curiously. "What am I doing?"

"Yes," she said, carefully lowering Ashalia onto the sand, letting the slime coated water wash back and forth over her as the rain splashed down. "What are you doing? What is this slime? Why are you holding my friends hostage? They can't hurt you, let them go. What's the point?" He went to speak but she interrupted him, pushing herself to her feet and slowly walking, stumbling, towards him, so much fear replaced with a dull acceptance and a desire for understanding. "Coral, why? Why are you there? Is Sam really worth this? Your grandma and her friends are at knife point, the mermaids you wanted to save are nearly dead, why are you doing this?"

"Nobody else needs me," said Coral, glancing momentarily at her grandmother. "Nobody else respects me."

The Harvester held up a hand to silence her. "Lilly Prospero," he said with a growl in his voice. "Because of you I am able to bring those Ancients to the surface, harvest their power, change the world."

Sam watched her intently. Behind him Sylvie started to move.

"They're innocent!" Lilly protested, wiping rain from her eyes as the water ran like tears down her cheeks. "Why do you want to hurt them?"

"Is that not where you have been?" he asked her, pointing the silver blade through the rain toward her. "Have you not murdered those who tried to get in your way?"

Lilly was taken aback, how did he know? "Yes," she said. "I have."

"Don't look surprised," he said with a cackle. "Your good friend Coral here told me. You should know by now, the smart and ambitious will always come to those who can help them succeed."

Coral? But Coral had already left when they found out about the Ancients plan to attack. She hadn't told Coral anything. She glanced towards Coral's grandma and saw a funny smile creeping on the old lady's lips. Sylvie was now snaking low against the sand towards the water, something shiny held in her jaw. Certain the Harvester should not see whatever was happening with the creeping cat, Lilly moved closer towards him.

"I didn't kill them for pleasure, believe me," said Lilly. She thought of how the Ancient's body had sunk in the water, the life ripped from him by her will. "I was saving lives."

"Taking lives to save lives," said the Harvester, stepping towards her, now just an arm's length away. He could kill her that very second with ease, and in doing so Saffron, Bentley, and all the other lives that only existed because of her would end simultaneously. But he was choosing not to. He was choosing to talk to her instead. Did he respect her opinions? Did he want to earn her approval? "What difference is there, Lilly Prospero, between you murdering Beings to save human lives, and me doing it?"

"I didn't do it for money," said Lilly, holding his gaze despite the wind that whipped the raindrops hard against her face.

"I do it for passion!" he declared, his arms wide and his face proud. "I do it for love of my species, the same as you! The potion will find them, it will bind them and force them to the surface. They feel superior but they

are not and in proving it I can save hundreds, thousands, of human lives!
Much like you did this very afternoon."

"I didn't want to kill!" Lilly cried. "I never want to kill! I killed because
I had to. Because if I hadn't they would have killed me, Saffron and forty
thousand people on land, yourself included!"

The Harvester looked up to the sky, his eyes staring straight up and
away from Lilly, so she allowed herself a moment to glance behind her.
Sylvie was nearing Saffron now, moving very slowly through the gloomy
light, black slime was sliding like oozing mucus up to the cat's neck,
masking her nearly completely from view. Lilly looked back at the
Harvester as he lowered his face back to hers.

"Your power is magnificent, Lilly Prospero," he said with a smile.
"Nearly as impressive as my own. It could be even greater if you
embraced the infinite possibilities that lie in your hands. But you are
weak because you refuse to acknowledge nature for all its beauty. You
refuse to see the truth, the survival of the strongest. Humans are by
nature strongest, those with power are stronger still, and those with
power like ours top the league. Join me, Lilly Prospero, work with me.
We would be rich and strong and leaders of the world! With the power
contained in the bodies of the Ancients at our disposal, nothing could stop
us!"

"No!" Lilly said, feeling disgusted. "I would never work with someone
like you!"

The Harvester nodded and sighed. "I expected as much," he said with
dull acceptance, holding the knife up and examining it carefully before
staring at her, a cold malevolence bursting from his eyes. "But then I'm
afraid I cannot risk you interfering anymore, it's becoming a nuisance. So
I'm going to have to kill you."

Lilly stepped back in genuine fear as the Harvester went to charge towards her, his knife ready, when behind her she heard Saffron shout, "NOW!"

Chapter Twenty-Six

Mi began to Read. She held a torn out sheet of paper in her frail hands and read in a clear voice, the language Lilly recognised from the last time they faced this man. Saffron walked with a smooth confidence from the water, straight at the Harvester, who held out his knife to her in shock but to no avail. An energy was emanating from Saffron in a golden light that radiated from her skin with pure heat; the knife in the Harvester's hand simply melted away.

"WHAT?" he cried, staring at Saffron in horror and outrage. "Sam! Shut that woman up!"

Sam ran at Mi, his knife held high as Bentley prepared to leap, but Coral got there first. She ran from the Harvester and jumped on him from behind, gripping onto him limpet like and wrestling him to the ground whilst he cried out and thrashed with the knife in his hand, swiping behind him. Despite the furore, Mi's voice carried on uninterrupted and strong, reading the strange squiggling symbols to work the potion inside Saffron.

The Harvester swung for Saffron, his enormous fist so strong and ugly aiming straight for her face, but as he touched the heat around her he howled in agony and dragged his arm away from her.

"What is this?" he shouted, stumbling backwards from her.

"The end," said Saffron, her voice loud and deep, almost not Saffron's voice at all.

Lilly noticed it had stopped raining. The light was brighter not just because of Saffron's golden glow, but because the clouds overhead were themselves thinning.

"NO!" he shouted. "You can't stop me!"

"Yes, I can," said Saffron, walking towards him. "Lilly, take my hand"

Despite the way the heat from Saffron had hurt the Harvester, Lilly trusted Saffron that she was safe to obey. She approached her friend and took Saffron's hand in the way she had done hundreds of times before, and instantly felt a surge of the power enhancement blasting through her body.

Saffron held out a hand towards the man, whose face had been shredded of confidence and poise, fear and helplessness now riddled across his features, and together the two girls walked towards him.

"Stop," he shouted. "Stop! Or I'll kill them all! The old women, the animals, the girl; all of them will die because of you!"

"No," said Saffron in her peculiar voice. "All of them will live because of me."

Then a blast of energy burst from Saffron's hand, pelting into the Harvester like a mallet and knocking him from his feet. He screamed as the heat hit him, washed over him, a golden energy left burning over his body as Lilly and Saffron stepped back to watch, the light around them fading.

It moved like liquid, like the water his victims had found such safety in but were ripped away from so viciously. The golden light ebbed and flowed as below it he writhed and screamed. Lilly felt sick, horrified, but couldn't look away. The light grew brighter, hotter, until they had to step further away to avoid being burned themselves. Then, in one violent bright white burst of energy that illuminated the entire beach like a firework, the light vanished. All that was left of their fearsome nemesis was a pile of ash and a few fragments of bone.

"It's over," whispered Lilly as silence fell.

"Dad!" screamed Sam, rushing towards the pile of ash on the ground. He landed on his knees, his face broken. "You killed him! You killed my father!"

"Lilly!" called Bentley. "Come quick!"

Lilly looked over at the dog and saw him lying on the ground beside Coral, who's body had been slashed deeply across the chest, arms and belly. She and Saffron ran over, leaving Sam crouched on the ground by his father's remains.

"Sam did it," said Coral's grandmother who had fallen to her knees at her granddaughter's side, tears washing over the dark crinkles of her skin and landing heavily on the wet sand as she stroked Coral's thick dark curls so tenderly, her heart visible breaking. "Coral stopped him from attacking Mi so he killed her. He killed my baby."

"No he hasn't," came a voice from behind them. "Not just yet anyway."

Looking round everyone was startled to see Coral standing there, her translucent visage faint as the sun broke free from the clouds that were quickly dispersing above, but still clear.

"Coral?" wept her grandmother. "Is that you?"

"Of course it's me, Grandma!" laughed the girl sadly. "How many of your grandchildren can astral project?"

"You're not dead?" asked Lilly.

"Nearly," said Coral, looking down at her feet. "My body's useless now but my mind's not gone yet. But I don't have long."

"I'm so sorry," her grandmother sobbed. "I should have protected you better!"

"You've protected me since I was a baby!" insisted Coral. "It was my choice to insist on getting out there, not yours. You respected me enough to make the choice and I knew what I was getting into! I knew the risk!"

"But baby girl!" protested her grandma.

"But nothing, Grandma," said Coral gently. "I don't regret it. And if I could go back I would do it again. If I hadn't gone I could never have warned you what was coming, you'd never have been able to send Bentley and Sylvie for the potion, and that evil old bastard would have killed you all, and who knows who else!"

"I don't care," wept her grandma. "Coral please, you can't leave me! I can't watch another of my daughter's die! I lost your mother, I can't lose you too. Please, Coral," she begged, her hands clasped together and her face crumpling as tears flooded from her eyes. "Please, my baby girl. Please don't go. Please. This world needs you. I need you. Please. Oh please, baby, please."

"I'm going to be with my mum, Grandma," said Coral gently, kneeling in front of her grandma. Though there was no physical aspect to Coral's form, she gently placed a translucent hand on her grandma's face. "All I ever wanted was to be part of something important, to make you and my mum proud. And I've done it. I've actually done it. And now I'm finally going to be with my mummy."

"But it's too soon," sobbed her grandmother, looking into Coral's big brown eyes that Lilly noticed were nearly identical to her own. "You're only sixteen years old, Coral!"

"And I have you to thank for those sixteen years, Grandma," said the girl, full of earnest sadness. At their side Coral's body coughed, and a trickle of blood escaped from her lips. "And I hope in sixteen more we'll be together again; you, me and mum."

"Oh baby girl," sobbed her grandmother. "I'll find you. I promise I'll find you."

"I know you will," said Coral with a smile. "You always do."

"I love you," said her grandma, putting a hand to her face so it lay on the same spot as Coral's own. "I've always loved you."

"I love you too, Grandma," said the girl softly, her image fading away as they gazed at each other. "Goodbye."

"Goodbye my darling," wept Opal Friday as her granddaughter vanished, and her body went still.

Lilly felt tears running down her cheeks and watched as Opal's coven came to her side, arms wrapping around her as the old woman broke her heart over the body of her granddaughter.

"I'm so sorry," Lilly heard from behind them and spun around.

"You!" she roared as Sam started backing away.

"Please," he sobbed, his face pale and tears running down his cheeks. "I didn't mean to! I swear I didn't mean to!"

"You killed her!" Lilly shouted. "You killed her to protect that monster!"

"He was my dad!" Sam cried. "I didn't want to hurt Coral. I swear. I would never want to hurt her! She was all I had! I just... she jumped on me... and... my dad he... if you hadn't... I had no choice, I had to... I'm so sorry, I'm so sorry!"

"It's not good enough," said Opal, her voice harsh.

"Nothing ever was for you, was it?" spat Sam indignantly. "You and my dad were peas in a bloody pod! You do this to people! If you hadn't treated her like this it would never have happened! This is all your fault!"

Then he began to run, heading as fast as he could across the sand and up towards the road.

"Stop!" Lilly screamed and went to make chase.

"Lilly!" called out Opal from behind her. "Wait!"

"But he's getting away! He killed Coral! And Dorothy and Iris! And he tried to kill us!" Lilly cried.

"There will be no more deaths on this beach," said the old woman, pushing herself carefully to her feet and standing proudly. "Not today. I shall let the authorities deal with this death and young Samuel will be caught and punished appropriately. The Commission may stay out of many issues, but I have a feeling that this one will not be left adrift."

Lilly nodded and stepped back towards them. "Did you know that Coral was faking?" she asked.

"Oh, I certainly anticipated as much," she said, a proud look on her face as she carefully wiped tears from her cheeks. "She contacted me as soon as she knew his plan. She's impetuous like her mother, always following a misplaced instinct or other and trying to vanish into the night, but she had a solid heart and a good mind. She wouldn't let a pretty boy distract her for long."

Saffron put her hand up awkwardly, as if she was in a classroom. "Erm, can I say something?"

"Of course," said Opal.

"I think the mermaids want to talk to us," she said, looking out to sea.

They all turned to look. The water was now clear, glinting beautifully in the evening sun that fell across the clean blue waves. The curse had died with the Harvester and the sticky black slime had dispersed into nothingness. But what struck Lilly was not the absence of the oily tar that had poisoned the water, but fifty or so faces that now poked out just above the surface, with Ashalia and Hexanna closest to them.

"We want to thank you," said Hexanna, swimming closer and speaking loudly enough that everyone on the beach could hear. "For everything you've done."

"How?" asked Lilly.

"We saw the girl die," said Hexanna. "We are sorry. We see how much you've sacrificed for us. We are in your debt."

"Your witches," said Ashalia, gesturing towards the watching coven. "They need things we can offer, right?"

Opal stepped forward. "Desperately," she said, her hands pleading. "We've saved your lives, now you could save lives of two people who mean the world to me."

"What do you need?"

"The curse that has trapped Sylvie in the body of a cat," said Opal, gesturing towards Sylvie. "We need blood scales, enough to make an antidote for a powerful and long lasting spell."

"Done," agreed Ashalia, turning to an Ancient behind them. "May I use your knife?" He pulled a golden dagger from a sheath and handed it to Ashalia. His face looked hurt, as if Ashalia's offer was going to hurt him and not her. "Do you have a vessel?"

Saffron handed Opal the glass vial she had drunk the potion from that stopped the Harvester. Quickly, Opal rinsed it in the sea water and dried it on her top, then cautiously approached the mermaid with her dagger.

Ashalia swam towards her with her hand outstretched, then held it over the vial that Opal held out and, using the dagger, sliced a large cut across the palm of her ink black hand. Thick, red blood began pouring into the glass tube until it was full, then without comment or complaint, Ashalia sat carefully on the shoreline and scraped the blade up the side of her tail, a bloody, pulpy mass of deep blue, gleaming scales fell in a heap into her hand. Opal quickly reached into her handbag and pulled out a silk handkerchief and gratefully accepted the offering that Ashalia presented her with.

Turning, pain on her face but still making on complaint, Ashalia swam back into the water to join her friend.

"You said two lives," said Hexanna. "What is it you need from me?"

"Maud has cancer," said Opal, gesturing to Maud who shifted nervously on her sensibly shoed feet. "We need hair, flesh and… bone."

"Bone," said Hexanna with a wince. "Of course."

"You don't have to!" cried Lilly, horrified at what she was about to witness.

"I am indebted to you with my life and the lives of all of my people," said Hexanna with a proud look on her face. "And I will not let debt go unpaid."

Opal hurriedly gathered up her handbag and pulled a small plastic packet of tissues out, the kind Lilly's own mother always had stashed in pockets and bags for sneezing emergencies. Hexanna accepted the dagger from Ashalia then swam towards them and took it to her hair. She sliced a mass of locks of her short but thick green hair away from her head, and dropped them into Opal's hand, who then carefully coiled them up and wrapped them in a second handkerchief.

"Do you want me to do it for you?" asked Ashalia, putting a gentle hand on her friend's shoulder as Hexanna then held the knife to her finger.

"No," said Hexanna, gritting her teeth and shaking her head. "I can do it."

She sliced, one hard cut straight through her pointer finger on her left hand. It dropped into Opal's hand as Hexanna unleashed a horrifying, blood chilling scream and flung herself into the water, her mutilated hand held close to her chest, the salt water washing away the pouring blood.

"Oh my god," sobbed Saffron, looking away in horror.

"Thank you," said Opal earnestly. "I cannot save my beautiful granddaughter but I can save my friends. You don't know what that means to me!"

"Saffron," called Ashalia, ignoring the old woman's thanks.

Saffron walked towards the water, her face glazed over with a weird calm. "Yes?"

"It was really you who saved us," said Hexanna. "All of us."

"Even us," said a male voice. Lilly looked round and saw an Ancient swim towards them, his dark green beard and hair long and flowing into the water around him. "Despite Lord Bray's murder, despite the attack on our sanctuary, we saw what you did. We acknowledge that whilst your power has caused those in our number to die, we would all have perished had you not intervened."

"We didn't want to attack," said Saffron humbly as she stepped back into the water she had only recently escaped. "We were saving our people."

The Ancient bowed his head. "War is a cruel dance," he acknowledged. "We respect you as victor in ours."

"We have a way to make it right for you," said Ashalia, holding a long fingered hand out to Saffron, who approached her, wading through the gently lapping waves then taking her hand. "Sterlion says he can arrange it for you."

Lilly moved closer, trying to figure out what they were discussing.

"Really?" asked Saffron, no longer walking but gracefully treading water at the mermaid's side. "I could become one?"

Ashalia placed her hands on either side of Saffron's face so gently and tenderly that Lilly felt guilty for intruding. "Really," she said, her voice full of affection. "Your sadness can end."

"Saffron!" Lilly called to her, stepping into the water and shuddering as the coldness once again bit her skin. How could Saffron be so comfortable in this temperature?

"Lilly," Saffron said, turning to her, her green eyes full of tears, but tears of joy. A smile stretched across her face and something in her looked at peace. It was as if the glow from the potion had returned, but in a soft and peaceful way. "I can finally be happy!"

"What are you talking about?" Lilly asked, her heart going cold. She felt sick.

"You don't know what it's been like," she said, her voice cracking as she shook her head. "You can't! You belong! You're where you are meant to be! I'm nothing, I'm a Halfling. A mongrel. I'm not part of your world or the mortal world. I'm not even fully alive! I don't belong here anymore."

"What's going on Saffron?" Lilly cried, terrified she knew. She realised she had always known. She'd known since they had first met the Mer that first night on the beach. "You're coming home, right?"

"No," said Saffron, her green eyes glinting beautifully in the light. She looked so natural and calm in the water. She looked like she belonged.

"Please?" Lilly begged. "Saffron, you're my best friend. You're my family."

Ashalia swam between them. "She's coming with us," she said, a slight edge to her voice that made Lilly's skin crawl. "She belongs with us."

Saffron began to swim away towards the waiting Ancients, flanked by Ashalia and Hexanna. Lilly didn't try and follow. She knew it was pointless. Even if she could persuade Saffron to come back, her body was so weakened by the lack of sleep, the fights, and the emotional toll of the day that she didn't believe she would be able to get to her in time.

Stumbling back up to beach to where the coven stood watching, protectively standing around Coral's body, Lilly allowed Opal to embrace her in a tight hug as they watched Saffron swim away.

"I'm sorry," said Mi, her voice gentle as her hand found Lilly's own and gripped it tightly. "We are all losing those we love in this battle."

"But she's choosing to go," Lilly suddenly broke down, sobbing. "I don't know what to do! How am I going to do this without her? How am I going to tell my parents? Or hers? What's going to happen? She's just disappearing!"

Next to her Bentley suddenly started to growl, a deep growl like thunder rolling in the hills. "She needs help," he said, his hackles rising.

"No she doesn't," said Lilly miserably, looking out to sea. She could see Saffron's red hair through the Ancients that now surrounded her, performing some sort of spell she assumed, granting her wish.

"No," said the large black dog, standing up and walking towards the water. "Something's wrong."

"How do you know?" asked Lilly, squinting to see.

"It's my duty to know," he said, then suddenly rushed into the water.

Chapter Twenty-Seven

"Bentley!" Lilly called out to him, but the dog didn't stop. He landed heavily in the water with a splash and began a frantic doggy paddle that swept him forward at an impressive speed.

"What's he seen?" asked Opal, clutching her now full handbag protectively to her side.

"I don't know, but they have weapons," said Lilly anxiously, chewing on her lip and picking her thumb nail. "And if he gets in their way they might kill him. They don't respect humans let alone dogs!"

ን

"Your power will serve us well," declared the Ancient. "You shall bring about our glory."

"What?" Saffron asked, spinning around and looking at the faces that stared at her. "I don't want to bring about glory, I don't have power, I just want to be free!"

"In your death you shall be reborn," declared the Ancient. "To live with us, to be anointed, to never need to move again. Treated as the Being of Power you are!"

"Death?" Saffron cried. "No! I don't want to die!"

"To convert fully you must die by the words of the Mer-Stone," declared the Ancient, as the surrounding audience whispered excitedly amongst themselves. "This is a rare gift, and one not granted to many. You are honoured by the change, and we are honoured to receive your power as you join our number. You shall truly be one of us."

Saffron tried to swim away, frantically moving towards the crowd that surrounded her, but hands pushed her back, forcing her towards the Ancient who held out a powerful arm to her, ready to drag her below the surface.

She was surrounded. She desperately looked for Ashalia and Hexanna but they were lost amongst the faces that seemed to spin around her the more frantic she became.

"Help!" she cried out. "Someone! Help me! Lilly! Help!"

ॽ

Lilly watched in horror as Bentley reached the crowd of Ancients and a fight broke out. Bentley barked a commanding bark and several roars erupted. Lilly watched nervously, the fight too far away to be clear but she could see Mer splashing around in the water with Bentley swimming frantically between them all, Saffron staying in the middle of the chaos, her red hair swishing around as she frantically spun about in the melee.

Lilly tried to call Bentley again. As much as she hated giving up on Saffron, she needed to respect her wishes and was scared for Bentley's life.

Then she heard Saffron scream.

Lilly rushed into the water, the chill not bothering her at all, and jumped forward to swim.

"Lilly!" she heard someone shout from behind her but ignored it.

"Saffron!" she cried out, frantically trying to swim to the crowd and prepared in her heart to do whatever needed doing. She found strength from somewhere and propelled herself forward, the movement of the water, the current and the cold merely a nuisance now, not a hindrance.

As the water bobbed ahead of her, blocking her view then letting her see again, she noticed the crowd of Mer thinning. Slowly fewer and fewer were there and, as she neared them, they dropped away entirely, descending back into the depths and leaving just Saffron and Bentley behind.

"We're coming!" Bentley barked as he swam towards Lilly with Saffron's pale arms wrapped around his tree trunk thick neck, her long red hair flowing into the water as her face rested against his head.

"Is she okay?" Lilly gasped anxiously.

Bentley panted and nodded, so Lilly turned to swim at his side, the familiar lethargy beginning to take hold now her friend was safe again.

Together the three swam back to shore and Lilly helped Bentley drag Saffron onto the beach where they lay her down in the sand.

"Saffron?" Lilly whispered gently, smoothing hair from Saffron's pale, freckled cheek. "Are you okay?"

For a moment Saffron did nothing but breathe slowly and deeply, staring at nothing in particular, then she looked up at Lilly. "I was wrong," she said quietly.

"Wrong about what?"

"Not belonging," Saffron said, glancing down again. "Not having a real life." She pushed herself to sit up and pulled her knees up to her chest, wrapping her arms around them and gazing out to sea. "I thought in the water I was free. That finally I found the place I was meant to be because nobody saw me as anything but Saffron. I wasn't expected to be anything special, nor anything pointless. I was just alive."

"I…" Lilly started to say but Saffron shook her head.

"Please let me explain," she said. "I'm connected to the Mer because, like me, they're not fully one nor the other. They're not fully Mer like the pure blooded Ancients, but they're not human. I'm not fully magical, but I'm not without power either. We're halflings. A bridge between two worlds. They told me they can feel it too, and they could tell I was lost. We're different from all other Beings." She paused again but Lilly stayed silent, listening. "But I'm not meant to be with them. I'm not free in the water. It's no different from up here. They're prejudiced against everyone different from them, they're fighting and judging and using one another. They don't see me as Saffron, they see me as some sort of powerful, special creature they can convert into one of their own and use in their own magics as a link to the world *they* want power over! They didn't want to reward me, they wanted to use me! It's no different down there than it is up here, except up here I have you."

Lilly smiled and slipped a hand into Saffron's. "You definitely do," she promised.

"And together we're unstoppable," said Saffron with a sad smile. "Assuming we're not brutally murdered by your mother for disappearing and all…"

"Crap," Lilly muttered. She hadn't even checked her phone. Too much had been going on to even think about phoning her mother.

"Erm," Opal interrupted, stepping forwards. "I might be able to help there."

ʒ

Lilly watched in confusion as Coral's body was silently evaporated into thin air. She looked around for answers but saw nothing and nobody who could be responsible.

"The Commission," said Opal quietly. "They're going to examine her."

"Nobody's reacting," said Saffron in confusion, looking around at the beach that had gradually repopulated since the magically induced storm had been brought to an end, the last of the evening sun shining down on some dinner time family picnics and romantic couples walking in the surf arm in arm.

"The Commission," said Mi, giving Saffron a meaningful look.

The Coven came together in a circle around where Coral's body had fallen and carefully sat on the sand. Holding out hands and paws, under the watchful eye of Bentley, the six of them placed their hands together and allowed the energy to flood through them. Only this time it wasn't the surge of confidence and power that Lilly had felt previously, it was quite different. It was emotion, sadness, heartbreak and hope. It was an overwhelming mix of emotions as all of them felt one another's pain in a huge hit of shared experiences.

Lilly began to cry, and looking up she realised not a face in the circle was dry.

"We've lost so many," said Opal. "My beautiful daughter and hers, our friends and lovers, our families. We've lost ladies of strength and power, dignity and grace. Ladies who have changed the world in life and left it emptier in death."

"If you could all join me in writing the names of those we have lost in the sand," said Mi. "We can say our goodbyes."

Lilly watched nervously as names were written and overwritten and overwritten around the circle, fingers and paws tracing out names in the sand and faces crying at the memories that flooded in with each name that appeared.

Carefully Lilly wrote "Keren" in the sand in front of her. The name of her birth mother. A woman so encompassed with her desire for power above all else that she had sought to murder hundreds of innocent people just to enhance her own strength, until Lilly had ultimately killed her. But, none the less, the woman who had given Lilly life. Then she wrote "Mabli" then "Brinly", the lives she had tried to save but failed. Then "Dorothy" and "Iris", and finally "Coral", the women she had admired, respected and cared about who had been murdered by someone they believed they could trust. Someone who was still out there, free, with their blood on his hands.

"One day we shall meet again," said Opal when everyone had finished. Then she closed her eyes and began to sob.

ζ

"Mrs Prospero," said Opal, holding out a hand and smiling gently. "It's so lovely to meet you. And yourself, Mr Prospero."

"Lilly," said her mum in a tone that made Lilly's hands sweat, the relief and gratitude she had heard on the phone apparently having vanished. She distractedly shook Opal's hand, but stood with tense shoulders and a look of granite on her normally soft face. "What's going on?"

"This is Opal Friday, mum," said Lilly sheepishly. "She's the grandmother of my friend Coral."

"Is Coral who you girls were staying with when you ran off?"

"I'm sorry for the interruption," said Opal, taking Lilly's mum's hand again, holding it tenderly between her own two leathery ones, a look of deep and true sadness on her face that gave Lilly's mother a moment of pause. "But before you say anything more, you need to know that my Coral died today."

"What?" exclaimed Lilly's mum, the hardness falling from her face instantly. "What happened?"

"Please, may we sit down for tea?" asked Opal, gesturing to the table in the Tea and Times where Lilly and Saffron had first sat with Coral.

Lilly's parents sat side by side on the chairs, whilst Lilly and Saffron sat opposite them on the bench, either side of Opal. Lilly's mum reached out and took both of their hands, squeezing tightly.

"I raised Coral from a very little girl," said Opal, pouring tea into china cups and, Lilly noticed, dripped something extra in with the cups she then handed to her parents. Lilly's mum released her grip on their hands and Lilly watched as both her parents took a sip on the spiked tea. "Her mother was the victim of a violent and abusive husband. I did my best but the poor lamb was terribly sickly. She met your girls, your lovely, kind girls, on the beach and immediately befriended them. It was her last chance to get to the beach. She knew it and I knew it. And, because of Lilly and Saffron, she finally made some friends."

"Oh girls," cried Lilly's mum, her pupils widening. "How tragic."

"They stayed with me and Coral," said Opal, wiping away a tear before sipping on the tea that she had placed in front of herself, watching over the top of her cup as Lilly's mother and father followed suit. Lilly watched anxiously, unsure what was happening and feeling decidedly uneasy about the entire thing, but not daring to speak. "Until then, Coral's only friend had been Bentley, her dog. But because of your girls she ended her life with real friends at her side, friends who respected her enough to not draw attention or drama to her death, but just stay peacefully with her. I cannot explain the comfort they have brought me in these final hours."

"I am so, so sorry for your loss," said Lilly's mum, her voice now slightly distant, wiping tears off her cheeks then taking another sip of tea.

"We are very proud of you girls," said Lilly's dad as he seemed to lose a little bit of focus and took a sip on the tea. "Though I still wish you had spoken to us, it makes sense that you wanted your privacy."

"Of course it does," said Lilly's mum, sniffing and wiping at her eyes carefully with a napkin, before sipping on her own drink.

Lilly stayed silent, her parents' expressions beginning to give her the creeps. How she wished this story was true. That the events of the last few days had never taken place, and that Coral's death had been a peaceful slip into eternity rather than a violent and painful butchering.

"Coral had a request, which I am hoping you will grant," said Opal. "Her dog, Bentley. He's young and fit, too much for a weak old woman like me. She wanted your girls to take him."

"Of course," said Lilly's mum, a vague and glazed smile drifting over her face.

"We love animals," agreed Lilly's dad, the same vacancy settling over his own expressions.

Lilly glanced at Saffron who looked both relieved and perturbed. Lilly, herself, felt decidedly creeped out. She had witnessed her mother being, for want of a better word, brainwashed before in the pursuit of magical gain and it still sat poorly in her gut.

"And I realise you had planned to stay a while longer," Opal went on, her voice slowly becoming less emotional and more instructive by tone. "But for all concerned you would be better taking your girls home now."

"Now?" asked Lilly's mum.

"Yes," said Opal. "Tonight. Pack up and go home tonight. No good can come of your girls remaining here now."

"We'll go tonight," agreed Lilly's mum.

"And be proud of them," Opal finished. "They have accomplished great things."

"We are," said Lilly's mum emphatically, smiling dopily.

"The girls shall come with me now to collect Bentley and say goodbye," said Opal. "You return to your hotel and collect yours and their belongings. They shall join you in half an hour."

"We'll go and pack now," agreed Lilly's dad.

With a tension in her belly that wouldn't shift, Lilly watched her parents stand and walk out of the café, heading back to the hotel.

"Your friends donated significantly more than we needed," said Opal with a smile, her voice normal again now Lilly's parents had left. "I was able to use the last of my Coaxation on them. I can replenish my stocks of so many of my more useful products with ease now."

"Will they be okay?" Lilly asked anxiously.

"Of course," said Opal smiling reassuringly, and taking another sip of tea. "A slight headache and some halitosis I'm sure, but no long term damage."

Lilly was about to say something else when the door of the café opened again and this time the women of the coven walked in, accompanied by a tall, slim and proud looking woman with thick brown curls streaked with grey and an elegant suit whom Lilly didn't recognise, and, she was stunned to see, Dougal Hogarth.

"Sylvie!" exclaimed Opal, standing to her feet with her arms out. "You look incredible!"

"Hogarth?" Lilly gasped, getting up and walking towards him.

He looked at his feet then up at her, not saying anything. Lilly didn't know what to say, or what to do. But he was awake and he was alive, two things she wasn't sure she'd ever see.

"It worked! Your potion worked!" said Sylvie, joy on her face as she held out her arms to her friend. Opal went to her and embraced her. "Not long after you left. I started to feel different and then I just started to grow! I haven't felt the sensation of changing form in so many years!"

"Wow," gasped Saffron. "You're the cat!"

"My name is Sylvie Jane," said Sylvie haughtily, then stopped and smiled kindly at them. "Thank you girls. I am going to finally hold my son, and meet my grandchildren, because of what you have done."

"Young Dougal here woke up about fifteen minutes ago," said Mi, putting a hand on his shoulder. He flinched at her touch and then looked embarrassed.

"Can I talk to you?" he asked Lilly in a timid voice, looking around at the watching women out of the corners of his eyes.

"Of course," agreed Lilly, and together they stepped outside into the street. "I'm so glad you're okay," she began to say, but he stopped her.

"I get it, okay?" he said quietly. "Something big went down. That guy, that Sam guy, he hurt you and he killed people and you thought it was me."

"Yeah," Lilly started again but he held up a hand.

"Please, let me finish," he begged her, looking into her eyes. "I know I could have been in a way worse state if you hadn't stepped in. And I know you have... something... in you that you can do stuff. All of those women can do stuff. Stuff I don't understand. Stuff I don't *want* to understand."

Lilly gulped. She felt awful. "I'm so sorry."

"Your world is so massive," he said. "You've got animals that talk and mermaids and magic and murder. Stuff that I only see in the movies. And you see it every day. You deal with it every day. And I get why it's made you do the things you do. I admire you, Lilly Prospero. I've heard enough talk from those women to know just how impressive you are."

"Impressive?" Lilly asked, her breath tight in her chest.

"And I won't tell anyone," he promised her earnestly. "For as long as I live, nobody will know. I liked you Lilly, I wanted to help you because I liked you. I liked you because you're beautiful and feisty and smart."

Lilly felt her heart pounding. "You do?"

"I did," he said. "Now... now I'm sorry, I can't. I can't be in that world. It's not for me. I'm just a guy who likes to drink a couple of beers and watch Netflix. I'm not designed for this world you live in."

"I understand," said Lilly, wiping tears from the corners of her eyes. "Thank you, though. For being cool."

Hogarth laughed. "I'm not cool, Lilly Prospero," he said. "I'm going to go home and feed my hamster and call in sick for work, and try to forget about the beautiful grey eyed witch who nearly got me killed."

"Bye Dougal," said Lilly.

"Bye Lilly," said Hogarth, then turned and walked away without looking back.

Lilly watched him walk away, forcing herself to get a grip. She wasn't going to cry over a guy she hardly knew, whom she had hardly spoken to. Well, she was. But not on the street like that. It could wait until she got home.

Taking a deep breath, she stepped back inside Tea and Times and was greeted with a huge hug from Saffron.

"Are you okay?" Saffron asked her.

"No," admitted Lilly with a shrug. "But I will be soon."

"You girls go home and live your lives now," commanded Opal. "And remember my girl. My wonderful Coral."

Opal stepped forward and pulled them both into a hug, and soon the rest of the coven women joined them, relief and gratitude flooding through them. The happiness was palpable. Lilly suddenly felt better about the whole thing. No, it wasn't perfect and mistakes were made, but good had come from it and of that there was no doubt.

The drive away from Whitstable was so similar and yet so different from their arrival journey just days earlier.

Bentley took up the entire boot of the car, and the sound of his contented snores shook the windows. Lilly and Saffron had their legs crunched up uncomfortably and their arms pinned to their sides because of the displaced luggage which was now occupying the back of the car with them.

Lilly's parents were different too, far hazier in their communications and regularly missing turnings.

But the biggest change was Saffron. Lilly watched her as she gazed out the window then turned to smile at Lilly. A real smile. A smile that included her eyes. A smile that said she was finally grateful to be alive, and definitely ready to start their next adventure.

The End

Read More
Siren Stories: The Ultimate Bibliography

***Lilly Prospero And The Magic Rabbit** (The Lilly Prospero Series Book 1)*
By J.J. Barnes

Lilly Prospero And The Magic Rabbit is a young adult urban fantasy exploring the corrupting effects of absolute power on a teenage girl. When the unpopular and lonely Lilly Prospero is given a talking pet rabbit, her life begins to change. She is thrust into a world of magic, mystery, and danger, and has to get control of a power she doesn't understand fast to make the difference between life and death. The first in a new series by J.J. Barnes, Lilly Prospero And The Magic Rabbit is a tale full of excitement, sorrow and mystery, as Lilly Prospero shows just how strong a girl can be.

Available in Paperback and for Kindle.

Alana: A Ghost Story
By Jonathan McKinney

Alana is a ghost, trapped in the New York Film Academy dorms, where she died. She has friends, fellow ghosts, with whom she haunts the students living there, passing her time watching whatever TV shows and movies the students watch.

But she is restless. She wants to move on. And when a medium moves into the dorms, Alana gets a nasty shock, which turns her mundane afterlife upside down.

Alana is a light yet moving short story about a miraculous love that travels many years and many miles to save a lost, trapped and hopeless soul.

Available in Paperback and for Kindle.

Emily the Master Enchantress: The First Schildmaids Novel (The Schildmaids Saga Book 1)
By Jonathan McKinney

Hidden, veiled behind the compressed wealth of New York City, is a dank underbelly of exploitation and slavery, which most people never see, or sense, or suffer. A cruel, expanding world.

And when Emily Hayes-Brennan, a proficient enchantress with a good heart and a tendency to overshare, is recruited to the world renowned crime fighters, the Schildmaids, she will find that that cruel world threatens to expand around her, and everyone she cares about.

She will be confronted by conflicts of fate and choice, as she seeks to find her place in the world.

Available in Paperback and for Kindle.

After the Mad Dog in the Fog: An Erotic Schildmaids Novelette
By Jonathan McKinney and J.J. Barnes

Emily Hayes-Brennan wants to get through a simple night out in her home city of New York, introducing her new boyfriend Teo to her friends, so she can get him home and have sex with him for the very first time. But when an obnoxious admirer and old flame shows up, she begins to fear that her plans are going awry.

After the Mad Dog in the Fog is a wild and energetic novelette about love and desire, and about the free joy that comes from prioritising the one you love before all others.

Available in Paperback and for Kindle.

Lilly Prospero And The Mermaid's Curse (The Lilly Prospero Series Book 2)
By J.J. Barnes

Lilly Prospero And The Mermaid's Curse is a young adult, urban fantasy following Lilly Prospero and her friend Saffron Jones on a magical adventure to Whitstable.

Whilst on a family holiday, Lilly and Saffron meet mermaids under attack from a mysterious and violent stranger, work with a powerful coven of witches, and fight to save not only the lives of the mermaids, but their own lives as well.

Available in Paperback and for Kindle.

The Inadequacy of Alice Anders: A Schildmaids Short Story
By Jonathan McKinney

Alice Anders can summon vision of the future, which guide her heroic friends through heroic acts. Sometimes she'll see vulnerable people in danger; sometimes she'll see her superhero friends in places where they can help those who can't help themselves.

But, for the last three and a half weeks, she's not been able to summon a single vision—and given that she started working for the superhero team of her dreams, the Schildmaids, exactly three and a half weeks ago, she's becoming anxious about her worth. And to figure out why her power has gone away, she'll have to push herself, and face some hard truths.

The Inadequacy of Alice Anders is a light and bittersweet short story about the pain of loss, and about facing that pain when it threatens to hold you down and hold you back.

Available in Paperback and for Kindle.

The Fundamental Miri Mnene: The Second Schildmaids Novel (The Schildmaids Saga Book 2)
By Jonathan McKinney

Miri Mnene is the Syncerus, a warrior, and the strongest of the Schildmaids, the New York team of legendary crime fighters. But she was not always the Syncerus. Once, she was the Xuét□ N□nrén Shashou, the final student of the man-hating, man-killing Guan-yin Cheh.

And when she is sent to South Dakota to investigate a mystical brothel, which has been kidnapping women, kidnapping girls, and forcing them to work, she is confronted by the darkness that lives within her when her past and present collide.

The Fundamental Miri Mnene is a powerful novel about the lengths to which you should go, the lengths to which you must go, in order to see justice in the world.

Available in Paperback and for Kindle.

The Relief of Aurelia Kite: A Schildmaids Novella

By Jonathan McKinney

Aurelia Kite is a young New Yorker at Christmas, trapped in an abusive relationship, dreaming of escape. And when her controlling boyfriend Trafford takes on a new job, her path crosses with two highly serious female crime fighters, causing her to make a big decision about what she will and will not tolerate.

The Relief of Aurelia Kite is a harsh novella with a soft centre, about hope in the face of toxic romance, and about the salvation that can be found just by talking to a sympathetic stranger.

Available in Paperback and for Kindle.

Not Even Stars: The Third Schildmaids Novel

By Jonathan McKinney

Teo Roqué is journeying through Europe with Emily Hayes-Brennan, the woman he loves, when ancient hostilities give way to a war between powerful, clandestine organisations. A war which puts the young couple's lives in danger, as well as all those they care about.

And as a new threat emerges, fanning the conflict's flames, Teo and Emily must work together to end the war before it leads to a disaster much, much worse than they'd imagined.

Not Even Stars is an incredibly intense novel about all-consuming love, about awe-inspiring heroism, and about the cost of making the right choice when the fate of the world hangs in the balance.

Available in Paperback and for Kindle.

The Mystery of Ms. Riley: a Schildmaids Novella
By Jonathan McKinney

Alice Anders and Rakesha McKenzie are members of the Schildmaids, the legendary New York crime fighters. And when Alice sees visions of Nina Riley, a young New Yorker carrying a deep, hidden pain, the two heroes fight to determine what has caused that pain, and how to save Ms. Riley from a prison she cannot even see.

The Mystery of Ms. Riley is a harsh yet hopeful story about self-doubt, about ordinary, everyday oppression, and about the kind of love that defies the testimonies of everyone around you.

Available in Paperback and for Kindle.

Unholy Water: A Halloween Novel
By Jonathan McKinney

In the misty Lancashire town of Ecclesburn, kids go missing. But no one talks about it. Everyone knows why, but they don't talk about it. The grown ups smear garlic and holy water over their necks and wrists while walking the dog after dark, but they never say the V word.

And when one of the local pubs is taken over by a group of undead monsters, and a trio of vampire hunters is called to clear them out, a terrible series of events begins to play out, which will change the way Ecclesburnians live forever.

Unholy Water is a dark and bloodthirsty novel about desire in wild excess, about whether you should defy your circumstances or adapt to them, and about the kind of inflexible determination that can save or destroy those that matter most.

Available in Paperback and for Kindle.

Emerald Wren and the Coven of Seven

By J.J. Barnes

As a child, Emerald's grandfather gives her a magic lamp with the promise that she can change the world. As an adult Emerald is working hard as a waitress by day, and as part of a crime fighting coven by night.

And when they get news of a man working his way across the country, burning women to death in his wake, Emerald's coven of seven must take on the biggest challenge of their lives, and risk everything to save the people they love.

Available in Paperback and for Kindle.

Printed in Great Britain
by Amazon